Praise for

CAROLYN DAVIDSON

and her novels

"Carolyn Davidson creates such vivid images, you'd think she was using paints instead of words."
—Bestselling author Pamela Morsi

"Davidson wonderfully captures gentleness in the midst of heart-wrenching challenges."
—*Publishers Weekly*

"Like Dorothy Garlock, Davidson does not stint on the gritty side of romance, but keeps the tender, heart-tugging aspects of her story in the forefront. This novel is filled with compassion and understanding for characters facing hardship and hatred and still finding joy in love and life."
—*Romantic Times BOOKreviews* on
Oklahoma Sweetheart

"This deftly written novel about loss and recovery is a skillful handling of the traditional Western, with the added elements of family conflict and a moving love story."
—*Romantic Times BOOKreviews* on
A Marriage by Chance

CAROLYN DAVIDSON

Haven

HQN™

ISBN-13: 978-0-373-77179-0
ISBN-10: 0-373-77179-7

HAVEN

This story was harvested from the busy, brewing mind of Rachel, one of my grandchildren. She came to me and asked, "Grandma, what if a woman named Susannah was running from the law and ended up in a hospital in Colorado tending to a wounded lawman?" And so was born this book, thanks to my beloved Rachel. To her I dedicate the completed work, with all my love.

And as always, to Mr. Ed, who loves me.

Haven

CHAPTER ONE

Ottawa Falls, Colorado, Spring 1878

AARON MCBAIN. HIS NAME was Aaron McBain, and he was lying in a narrow bed, surrounded by a bevy of cots, similar to his own. Perhaps not so many, he decided, maybe three other men occupied this room, one cot containing a familiar figure, that of an elderly man who frequented the bench in front of the Mercantile.

A man he'd notice while making his rounds. His mind dwelled on that thought. Rounds of the town, a twice daily task as part of his job. He was Sheriff McBain, his memory reminded him—a lawman. His gun...he knew its size and shape, knew the leather holster that tied to his thigh, and the feel of bullets in his hand as he loaded the cartridge.

The sound of footsteps approaching caught his attention and the figure of a woman, uniformed in white, filled his vision.

"I'm your nurse, Sheriff McBain," she said softly, reaching one hand to press gentle fingers against his forehead. "Your skin is cool, and that's a good sign." She smiled, a dimple appearing in her right cheek, catching his eye and blurring his thoughts. She resembled the angels in his old Sunday-school lessons.

But no angel ever stroked his forehead so nicely before, and unless he'd gone to heaven, it was unlikely this was an ethereal being come to visit. But it was lovely to dream, to coast along easily, the vision before him whispering his name.

"Sheriff McBain? Are you with me?" At his nod, she smiled, lifting her hand from his skin, leaving only the warmth of long, slender fingers behind.

"I'm happy to see you finally awake, and on your way to recovery," she murmured.

"Recovery from what?" His tones were rasping, the sound impatient—his mind blank.

"You were shot by a man attempting to rob the bank, Sheriff. You've had an infection, causing a high temperature and giving us quite a scare." Her smile faltered. "Do you remember being shot?"

Aaron searched through the fog in his head, found the image of a grizzled man, pistol in hand, and nodded his head. "Yeah, I remember," he said. "At least I think I do."

"I'm going to call the doctor in," his nurse said, her gaze sweeping from him, across the large room, where an open door seemed to lead into a corridor. "Just lie quietly, Sheriff, and I'll fetch Dr. Grissom."

Since there seemed no alternative to her plan, he merely nodded and closed his eyes.

Within minutes, a young man, dressed in a white coat, stethoscope hanging from his neck, lifted Aaron's hand, ostensibly to check his pulse. "You seem to be doing much better, McBain."

"I need to go home. How long have I been here, and, for that matter, how long am I going to be kept here?" Aaron asked impatiently. "Who's taken over at the office? Do I still have a job waiting for me?"

"So far as I know, they haven't found a new lawman, sir," Dr. Grissom answered. "You're quite a hero over at the National Bank. And after just a week in the hospital, I doubt the town council is about to take your position from you."

The mist that had gathered in his mind lightened, even as the doctor spoke, and Aaron saw a mental picture of the town he served. One long street, business establishments on both sides, and beyond the town proper were houses and fields. Ottawa Falls General Hospital was at one end of the main street. "When can I leave here?" he asked more impatiently this time. "I've got a bed at home that's a hell of a lot more comfortable than this miserable cot."

"Just give us another day or so, allow us to be certain of your condition, and we'll see about turning you loose," the doctor said, a smile that appeared to approve of his patient's condition appearing on his face. "In the meantime, we'd like you to try eating your dinner. Your nurse will bring you a tray and help you with it."

"I think I remember how to use a fork," Aaron said sharply.

"You've been a sick man, Sheriff, and we're only trying to get you on your feet as soon as possible."

Aaron felt a bit embarrassed, as if he'd been scolded and put in his place. And so he had, he decided, and by an expert, no matter how youthful the medical man appeared. Nodding his agreement, he allowed himself one last word of dispute as he watched the young doctor leave his side. "I want out of here, today. Tomorrow at the latest."

The young man glanced back with a dark look that vied with the amused grin he wore and walked through the doorway, disappearing into the hallway.

Dinner. The thought of food was not appealing, but if eating whatever appeared on his tray was the solution to being discharged from this place, he would do as he was told. For long moments, he watched the doorway, aware of the other occupants in this room, of moans and murmurs from men he assumed were patients in this place.

"I've brought your dinner, Sheriff." The same woman appeared beside his cot and he watched as she placed a tray on the table beside him. "I'll help you sit up a bit," she offered, and bent to him, lifting him from his pillow, deftly shifting him into a better position to eat.

Aaron filled his lungs with the soft scent she carried, a blend of soap and fragrance of some sort. Whatever the woman had used to bathe in, he'd like to borrow a bottle of it, to remind him of her.

"I think you'll need another pillow to lift you a little higher," his nurse said cheerfully and turned to a rack near the door. Taking two plump pillows from a supply there, she returned to his bed, offering him her hand and with his cooperation fitting the pillows behind him. He held her long, slender fingers in his, glancing down at the narrow wrist, then noted the closely clipped length of her nails.

His shoulder felt the impact of his movement, a sharp pain piercing the area just above his collarbone, and a soft groan from his lips brought instant attention. "Do you need something to help with the pain?" his angel of mercy asked, her brow furrowing as she bent toward him.

"No," he muttered. "Just the food will do. It's my understanding that if I eat well and appear to be healed up, I'll be allowed to leave."

She pulled a chair beside the bed and lifted a bowl to rest against his lap. "Not exactly," she said, lifting a spoon full of food to his lips.

"Yes, exactly," he muttered. "I'm leaving here, tomorrow at the latest." And then he eyed the unappetizing broth she stirred. "What's that? It looks like dirty dishwater."

"Chicken soup," she answered, returning the spoon to the bowl, perhaps in hopes of finding some bit of vegetable or meat in the liquid.

"Doesn't smell like the soup my mother used to make," he told her.

She laughed softly. "It probably doesn't taste much like it, either, but let's give it a try."

He opened his mouth, accepting the bland liquid she offered, and his gaze swept up to meet hers as his nose wrinkled, disdaining the offering. "Don't they have anything more substantial in the kitchen here?"

She considered him a moment. "Let me check with the doctor. I'd think you could handle a soft dinner."

In a few minutes she returned, a fresh tray in her hands. She deposited it again on the table and sat down, her smile a welcome sight. "Let's try this," she said, lifting a fork to his lips. It contained a gluey mass that had been cooked and mashed almost beyond recognition, and he accepted it from her hand and then moved it about in his mouth, wishing it tasted like something other than paste.

"That is supposed to be a potato, isn't it?" he asked dryly.

"Hmm, I think so. Mashed potatoes, the menu said. But it doesn't look to be very tasty," she whispered. "The cook is not gifted, sir. Why don't we try the meat loaf?" So saying, she again filled the fork, offering its contents with a smile that tempted him much more than did the gray, unappetizing bit of meat he was given.

"Is that better?" she asked, casting a dubious look in his direction.

"No. I'm sure I'd find more appetizing food at the hotel restaurant." In fact, if memory served him, the fried chicken offered by Hayden Hitchcock's establishment was top-notch.

"I'm certain you would," the nurse said. "But for now, this is all we have to offer."

"I'll eat it, if it'll get me out of here," he told her, awaiting the next bit of nourishment, valiantly chewing and swallowing the bits and pieces of food she gave him over the next few minutes. And then he shook his head. "I've had enough."

"All right, Sheriff," she said quickly. Lifting the tray and rising easily, she left his side, and for a moment he wished for her return, felt the need to fill his senses with her faint, flowery scent, the sight of wide gray eyes and dark hair twisted up beneath the white starched cap she wore.

Not your type. As if the words had been spoken aloud, they rang in his mind. And what was his type? he wondered. A lady from one of the finer homes in town, virtue intact, reputation spotless? Certainly not the slender nurse who carried out her duties with a smile, even though she likely was not happy in her work. She didn't seem to fit the mold, he decided. Nurses were notorious for having dark pasts, reputations that prevented their working at a decent job. For what woman would choose to work in a position where she might be required to lay hands on a man, even though her touch might bring healing and comfort?

Nursing was not an occupation chosen freely, of that he was certain. Most of the women in the profession were at the bottom of the barrel, professionally speaking. They accepted the job no decent woman would apply for.

Still, this female had struck him in those few minutes as a lady, as a woman who deserved his respect. And Aaron McBain had been taught to treat ladies decently. His mother had been vigorous in her methods, making her son toe the mark when it came to being polite and respectful of all adults. And mostly of women.

So he must make amends. "Ma'am?" His voice reached her apparently, for she appeared in the doorway within seconds.

"Yes, Sheriff? Do you need something?"

He nodded and watched as she walked toward his cot. Her white apron hung almost to the floor, the dark dress beneath it uninspiring, but for the curves it contained. For even the starched fabric could not conceal the figure of the woman, the narrowing of her waist, the flare of rounded hips and the long length of her legs.

"What's your name?" he asked quietly.

She flushed beneath his look of inquiry, her cheeks stained pink by a rush of blood. "I'm Nurse Whitfield," she said. "Anna Whitfield."

He noted the slight tremor of her flesh as her fingers clasped at her waist, and wondered at the trembling she could not hide. "Do I know you?" His brow furrowed as he attempted to place her from somewhere in his past.

She shook her head, an abrupt movement. "No, I think not. I've never had the occasion to be in your office, and I doubt we travel in the same social circles."

Still, there remained a sense of familiarity about her, some niggling memory of seeing her, a faint whispering knowledge that pricked his mind, as if asking entry.

"It makes no difference," he said. "I just wanted to know your name, put name and face together, and so recognize you once I'm out of here and back at home."

"Will there be someone to care for you?" she asked.

"I won't need any help. I should be feeling much better by tomorrow."

"Perhaps." Her low reply was noncommittal, and he wondered for a moment if she could be persuaded to visit him at home, perhaps tend to his bandages and allow him to pay her for her services. Surely having a nurse visit him would be above reproach, he thought. He'd ask the doctor about the procedure, somehow make the proper arrangements for home care.

"Do you live nearby?" he asked.

She nodded, reluctantly, he thought. "Yes, I have a room with a family just to the western side of town. Mr. Owens works in the post office, and his wife occasionally takes in boarders."

"You're not married." It was a statement, not a query, and she shook her head in silent reply. "How do you get back and forth to work?"

"I walk most days," she told him. "And I have an application in to live in the nurse's quarters here at the hospital. Space is limited there, but I'm hoping for an opening in a few weeks."

"Have you lived here long?" The thought that this woman had been nearby, without his knowing of her existence, bothered Aaron. Surely he must have seen her in the Emporium, perhaps at the bank, or simply walking down the sidewalk.

"A while," she answered.

The vague reply troubled him, but he plunged on. "Have you been asked to visit homes, to continue their care when a patient leaves the hospital?" And if she did...

Her nod was brief, her explanation no more forthcoming. "I've been offered work of that sort, yes. But my hours here keep me from accepting outside nursing jobs."

"What if the pay were enough to compensate for your salary here?"

"You mean..." She seemed startled, taken aback by his words. "Are you offering me a position in your home?"

"For the length of my recuperation," he said quickly. "I'll pay you more than the going wage for nursing. Could you get back your position here if you left?"

"I don't know." She seemed to consider the notion for a moment. "I've heard of other nurses who took outside assignments, cut their hours

short, and came back to work here when their
patients no longer needed care." She smiled briefly
and shook her head. "I've just never considered it
as applying to me."

"Consider it." His word was formal, almost an
order, yet the smile he offered was one he hoped
would gain him her help. He wanted to go home,
away from this room of cots, where others slept in
close proximity and he had no privacy.

"Nurse." The strident tones of another patient
interrupted, and Aaron felt somehow deserted
when Nurse Whitfield turned away to respond. She
had not far to go, for the man who required her help
was but one bed removed from his own. As she bent
over the stricken patient, Aaron watched intently.
There was nothing familiar in her movements, no
memory of seeing her in his past, only the nagging
thought that somewhere, sometime, he had known
of her, had caught a glimpse of that face.

ANNA STOOD JUST OUTSIDE the hospital room where
the tall, dark-haired lawman lay, considering his
request. He was strong and fit normally; the
setback of a bullet wound would only be short-
term. The thought of seeing the man known as
Sheriff McBain on a daily basis was appealing, in
one way. Acknowledging the fact, she looked a
little further into the idea. Attaching herself to a

lawman was not a smart idea. Allowing the man access to her could only cause trouble. And trouble was what she had left behind. The possibility that she was the object of a search by the police could not be discounted.

Anna Whitfield was a new person, a woman without a past, holding down a position that smacked of ill repute. And yet, she had chosen to apply at the hospital in Ottawa Falls upon her arrival three months ago, knowing that though the position was far removed from anything she had done in her past, it would likely be available to her, since nurses were in short supply.

But now, she was considering the care of a man who could, conceivably, shatter her life into shards of misery. He'd said she looked familiar. Yet, if she'd met Aaron McBain in person, she would not have forgotten that face, or the width of shoulders and chest he bore. And the chances of him finding out her identity might be small.

He stood tall, she estimated, well over six feet if she was any judge. The bed he resided in at the moment was too short for him to lie in with comfort, his feet almost hanging over the end, his wide shoulders challenging the narrow width of the hospital cot. Even now, he obviously resented the restrictions imposed by the hospital atmosphere. The man wanted to go home.

Aaron McBain was a man who would leave a lasting impression, she was certain. A man to be respected, perhaps an opponent to be feared, given knowledge of her past.

No matter. If he could pay her wages, she would visit his home daily, tend to his wound and care for his needs. And then it might be time to travel farther west, find a new town to settle in. The urgency to move along had been preying on her mind over the past week or so anyway. The chance of anyone ever recognizing her, here in the wilds of the frontier, were small, but the fear of being found out, of making a mistake that might lead to—the possibilities were too dreadful to be considered.

She closed her eyes, wishing, not for the first time, that she'd never heard of the brute she'd married. The senator from Philadelphia, who had tarnished her life by the dirt of her association with him, whose memory made her wish yet again that her marriage had never taken place. A quivering sigh, drawn up from her depths, brought her back to her current status, to the decision she knew was already a reality in her mind.

She would accept the sheriff's offer, should he decide to make one, and when the job was finished, she would leave Ottawa Falls for another place where she would not be known. She would once again be Anna Whitfield, a far cry from the woman who had lived, on occasion, in close proximity to the White House, who even now was no doubt a fugitive from the police.

CHAPTER TWO

AFTER MAKING THE NECESSARY arrangements, Aaron was discharged that afternoon and sent home in the company of Nurse Whitfield. Equipped with several rolls of bandages, a tin of salve and orders to take his pain medication as prescribed, he rode in a buggy from the livery stable. His nurse would see to his care, settling him in and being sure he had a meal for this evening. Beginning tomorrow, she would arrive promptly at nine every morning and stay with him over the next week or so throughout the day, until such time as the doctor deemed him well enough to care for himself.

The ride took more of Aaron's strength than he would have believed, and though the trip was short, less than half a mile, he was ready to seek his comfortable chair in the parlor once he made his way into the house, a task accomplished by the aid of his nurse.

His home was a small place, with but a single bedroom in the rear of the house, a parlor at the front and a long kitchen to one side. A pantry stood, nearly empty, at the end of the kitchen, his needs usually being met by the restaurant at the hotel or at the single café in town. His few food-stuffs were on the kitchen cabinet, a convenient arrangement for him, but one he knew would bring lifted brows from any woman who attempted to put together a meal there.

Nurse Whitfield apparently had no such qualms. She settled him in his chair, pulling a light quilt over his lap and lifting his feet to a footstool before she headed into the next room to prepare him something to eat.

He heard the sound of a fire being built in the cookstove, hoping there was wood in the box. Apparently she had no problems, for soon a sound of humming drifted into the parlor, and next the scent of bacon frying filled his nostrils. In a moment, she peered around the corner of the doorway.

"I thought potato soup might go down well," she said, wiping her hands on an apron she'd apparently brought with her. "I found a piece of bacon in your icebox and you have some potatoes and onions in a storage bin."

"Not much else in there, is there?" His eyes were having difficulty staying open, the smell of food being cooked seeming to soothe him and lull him into rest.

"No, not much," she agreed, "but we'll make do

with what you have. I'll stop at the Emporium tomorrow before I come by in the morning and pick up a few things for you."

"Money's in my desk," he muttered, waving a hand at the large piece of furniture sitting in front of the window. "Middle drawer, in a wallet."

"You're a trusting soul," she said, smiling. "Especially for a lawman. I thought such men as you were more careful."

His eyes opened fully and he pinned her with a sharp look. "I haven't told anyone else where I keep my extra cash. Do I need to doubt your honesty?"

She flushed at his words. "I'm probably as honest as most, Sheriff. I doubt there's much robbery going on in town, so your money is no doubt safe from thieves. At least I haven't heard of anyone locking their doors."

He nodded. "Pretty peaceful, hereabouts." His eyes closed again and her footsteps returned to the kitchen.

It was a comfort, he thought, just dozing and waiting for a pretty woman to bring him his supper. There'd been no woman in his life, at least not on this basis. No one to cook for him, to cover him with a lap robe as had Anna Whitfield. He stretched his feet out, relishing the feel of comfort. He could get used to such treatment, he decided, hovering on the edge of dozing off again.

"Sheriff." He heard her speak and forced his eyes open. She stood before him, a bowl of soup balanced on a pie plate. "You don't have a tray," she said, "so we're making do with what's available."

She had pulled a chair close by and now she settled on it, awaiting his awakening it seemed. He watched as she reached to place the pie plate on his lap. "Can you handle it alone?" she asked. "I'll be glad to lend a hand, if you like."

He shook his head, holding his thighs steady for the slight weight of the soup. "I'll be fine." He bent to lift the spoon and stirred the thick mixture. "Sure looks better than what they offered in the hospital."

"I have a good eye and I learned the basics of cooking when I was young," she said. "I'd have added a bit of carrot if you'd had any to be found."

"There's some in a garden out back," he told her. "Probably got a few young ones about ready to pick. I should have told you."

She looked surprised. "You planted a garden? You have time to work in your yard?"

He nodded. "Helps me to relax, puttering around after I get home. Not that I spend much time here, what with all day at my office and then going back to check out the stores at night after dark. But I've always enjoyed watching things grow. So I put in a few rows of carrots and beans, and my neighbor brought me a couple of nice tomato plants."

She shook her head, allowing a smile to appear as she looked at him again. "I can't imagine our illustrious sheriff digging in the dirt. It doesn't go with your image," she told him.

"I'm not sure I have an image to uphold. I'm a pretty ordinary citizen in Ottawa Falls. It just happens I'm also the law around here. Folks pretty much mind their own business and everyone seems to get along."

For three years he'd been in Ottawa Falls, a small town northwest of Denver, keeping the peace; not a difficult position to be in. The folks were stable, neighborly and proud of their town. All of the town council apparently had been properly scandalized by the bank robbery that had earned their sheriff a bullet in his shoulder.

He lifted the spoon to his mouth again.

"You're a good cook, Nurse Whitfield."

She shifted uncomfortably. "Perhaps you could call me Anna. If you like."

Her words pleased him. "So long as you're going to be part of my household for a bit, that sounds like a good idea." The soup was disappearing quickly, and his spoon soon scraped the bottom of the bowl. "Is there more?" he asked.

"Later on, I think, Sheriff. You've put away a good amount. If you're still hungry in an hour or so, I'll dish up some more."

"One thing," he said, as she rose to take his dish from him. "If I'm to call you Anna, I think you could leave off with my title, don't you?"

"I don't know your first name," she said, standing before him, her eyes seeking his. The soft gray color reminded him of a mourning dove's breast, and he swallowed the thought, deeming it foolish.

"It's Aaron. But most of my acquaintances call me McBain."

"What about your friends?" she asked. "What do they call you?"

He shifted uncomfortably. "Friends aren't something I've managed to collect much. I know most everyone in town, but—" His words dwindled to a halt and she laughed softly.

"I don't suppose making friends with a lawman is too long-lasting. They either move on to another place or..."

"Or they get shot and someone else comes in to take their place."

"I wasn't going to say that," Anna murmured.

"It's the truth though."

She turned to the kitchen, and he leaned back in the chair, relishing the comfort of his own surroundings. Outdoors the sun had slipped to the western horizon, and twilight had begun to blur the trees in his yard. Anna would be leaving soon to go home, and the thought of her walking across town on her own was not an appealing one. He found his natural instincts to protect coming to the surface.

"Anna." He called her name without forethought and heard her footsteps crossing the kitchen floor before she appeared in the doorway.

"Do you need something?" A dish towel hung over her shoulder, her apron had several spots marring its pristine surface, and he thought for a moment how comfortable she was to have in his house.

"I just wondered about you walking home alone in the dark," he began.

"It's going to be even darker before I can leave," she said, waving a hand in his direction. "So don't start worrying yet. You aren't even tucked in for the night, Aaron. And I have to change your dressing before I go."

He frowned at that. "It'll be full dark by then, Anna. What are the chances of you staying here overnight?"

"Here?" She looked taken aback, and her eyes blinked before she gained her equilibrium. "I don't know if that's a good idea. Mrs. Owens will wonder what has happened to me."

"We can send her a note with my neighbor boy. Young Jim, next door, has been known to carry messages on occasion."

"She knows where I am," Anna said slowly. "And it probably wouldn't be any surprise to hear that you need someone with you during the night." Her face cleared, the indecision a thing of the past. "All right. That will work, I think. How do I get hold of this boy, Jim?"

He grinned. "That's not complicated. Just walk across to the back door, the other side of my hedge and you'll find the young man. He may even be out in the yard. His mother has chickens and he feeds them at night."

"I'll check and see." Without another word, Anna left the room and in moments he heard the kitchen door open and close. Before many minutes had passed, she came back in the house, accompanied by Jim, his eyes wide as he beheld the figure in his chair, covered up like an invalid.

"I heard you came home, Sheriff," the boy said. "I'm sure glad you got somebody to take care of you. Your nurse said you wanted me to carry a message to the Owen place."

"Miss Whitfield will write a note for you, Jim," Aaron said. "She'll be staying here tonight, and if there should be any emergency, I'll have her run across and get you."

The boy puffed up with pride at the task assigned him. "I'd sure be proud to help you any way I can, sir." Jim turned then to look fully at Anna, who was signing the note. "You just let me know if you need me for anything, ma'am. I'll come a'runnin'," he said as he took the note she handed him.

The back door closed behind the lad and Anna faced the night ahead, having committed herself to sharing this house with the sheriff. She could not change her mind. Indeed, she had no desire to do that. But deep within her was the knowledge that should she be found out, should the town know that she'd spent the night in his house, she would have ruined her chance of ever being employed again in Ottawa Falls. And the fact was that since the neighbors next door knew of her plans, the whole town would be informed within a day or so.

As if he sensed her thoughts, Aaron spoke, his voice low, his words suiting her mood. "I know you'll be putting yourself on the line by staying here, Anna, but I can't see any way out of it. If I could handle things by myself, I'd do it, lickety-split. But just getting from here to my bed is gonna take about all the vinegar I've got tonight. I sure as hell won't be making any advances of any kind toward you."

"I'm aware of that, Sheriff," she said quickly,

unwilling to let him assume the mantle of being a bad guy. "I'm familiar with the mores of society, but I feel I should have some bit of freedom in this town. Not to mention the fact that nursing requires close proximity to the patient, and I'm here solely as your nurse. Let the gossips do their best. I had no job before I got to Ottawa Falls and if I have to move on, I'll find another."

"Well, I'll increase your wages to compensate for staying here tonight. You won't lose any pay by tending me and my house." Aaron cleared his throat and shot her a look of frustration. "I'd hoped we were friends of a sort, Anna. And if that's so, then I'm responsible for what happens to you, more specifically your good name in this town. I'll be sure it's known about that you're staying with me in lieu of my remaining in the hospital. And, as I said, I'll make it worth your while." He shifted the lap robe and folded it with clumsy gestures, and in seconds she took it from him, redoing the process and placing it neatly on the back of the sofa.

"I'll help you into the bedroom now," she said, "and then I'll find an extra sheet and quilt or blanket and make my bed out here. Should you need me, you only have to call out and I'll hear you." As she spoke, she helped him rise from the chair, taking his weight upon her shoulder, draping his arm around her neck, and with her other arm she supported him, her left hand firm upon his back.

"I'll need help getting my shirt off," he said, almost apologetically. "Doggone shoulder just won't take any strain yet."

"I know," she murmured soothingly, making slow but steady progress toward the bedroom. He faltered once, caught his breath and continued, his big frame trembling. The effort to walk involved his whole body, he found, including his arms and legs, and seemingly all the muscles and bones he possessed. The urge to curse his own weakness tempted him almost beyond measure, but he gritted his teeth and flattened his lips, aware of the sweat that poured from his forehead into his eyes.

"I'll wash you a bit once we get your shirt off," Anna told him, steering him around the corner into his bedroom. She'd been there before him, he realized, noting the sheet and quilt pulled back, the pillows fluffed and waiting. And there across the sheet was his nightshirt, a garment that had been washed, but never used. It was not his custom to dress at night, finding the freedom of his body between the sheets was more to his liking without clothing to pinch or bind.

"You can toss that nightshirt in the corner," he

grumbled, shooting the garment a look of pure disgust.

"You ought to have something on in bed," she told him. "The doctor will be stopping by tomorrow morning, and he'll be upset with me if you're without clothing."

"You mean if I'm naked?" he asked, his sarcasm well in place.

She glanced up at him, meeting his gaze, and he thought he saw the glimmer of a smile twitch at the corner of her mouth, but she smoothed the lines of her face and nodded, her features assuming a stern visage.

"I won't be able to stay if I'm not doing a good job," she warned him. "The doctor will find someone else to take my place."

"I don't want anyone else." As edicts went, this one was definite, and his jaw was hard, his eyes narrowed as he shot her another look of defiance. "You'll do just fine, Anna. That young white-coated refugee from some high-class medical school has nothing to say about my nurse not doing her job to his satisfaction."

She flushed a bit, settling him on the edge of the mattress, and he reached for her hands, holding her before him. "Don't get all snooty now, Anna. I'll put the nightshirt on, if I have to, but I'll need help, and I hate to embarrass you."

"You won't embarrass me. I've bathed men at the hospital. I'm pretty aware of what's under those clothes you're wearing." Her fingers were busy with the buttons of his shirt and he allowed it without protest, not willing to cause her any more fuss than he already had. She rolled down the sleeves he'd not wanted buttoned and then slid the garment from his shoulders.

"Don't pull or try to help," she said. "This is easy enough to do if you'll just hold still and let me work it off your arms." In moments, the garment lay on the bed behind him, only the hem still tucked into his trousers. "I'm going to dress your wound now," she said, "before you lie down."

Fetching the required equipment, she stood before him and in moments had removed the dressing and wiped the area clean with a damp cloth. The salve was strong smelling, and he wrinkled his nose as she coated a folded bandage with it and then pressed it against the wound. Soon she had wrapped the area and pronounced the job finished.

"Let's get you out of your clothing now," she said, kneeling before him, lowering her head and working at the laces on his shoes.

It was almost more than he could handle, he thought. A beautiful woman in his bedroom, kneeling before him, and he was as weak as the proverbial kitten. He watched as she pulled his low shoes from place, then removed his stockings. She'd have had a dickens of a time with boots, he thought idly, watching as her slender fingers set aside his footwear and then moved to the fly front of his trousers.

"Do you think you can stand up long enough for me to finish getting your trousers off?" Her brow furrowed in a frown as she stood and offered him her hand.

"I can do the pants thing," he told her, a bit brusquely perhaps, but then his mind was having difficulty sticking with the simple matter of his disrobing. If the woman only knew how ready he was to pull her down on the bed with him, she'd run and hide. And should she undress him any further, she'd be in for the surprise of her life. Aaron McBain was a needy man and having a lovely woman in such close proximity was having the expected effect on his physical structure.

As if she knew his thoughts, she frowned and then pursed her lips as she murmured words obviously intended to soothe his fretting. "I'm a nurse, Sheriff McBain," she reminded him. "I'm used to working with patients who happen also to be men. Undoing your trousers isn't going to embarrass me beyond measure."

He couldn't help the grin that quirked his lips

upward. "Yes, ma'am, I know all that. But I'm just old-fashioned enough to feel a little embarrassed myself when I think about a lady undressing me, especially a lady with no ulterior motive in mind."

She shot him a look that bordered on anger. "I'm not sure what you meant by that remark, but I wouldn't want to cause you any trouble of any kind, sir. Get yourself out of those trousers and into bed in five minutes, or I'll do it for you." Turning her back, she squared her shoulders and marched to the open door, walking around the corner and into the parlor.

"Five minutes." The words were muttered beneath his breath as he undid the fly front of his pants and slid them down, kicking them aside, but retaining the drawers he wore. "I'll be damned if I'm about to wear a nightshirt to please some persnickety female," he growled, absurdly pleased to find the comfort of the mattress beneath him as he sat down. Lying prone was a matter of easing his aching shoulder to the bed and then attempting to lift his legs to the surface of the mattress. It didn't work. Well, it might have, if he were willing to put that much strain on his wound, but somehow sleeping with his feet on the floor didn't pose a problem right now.

Apparently it did to his nurse, however, for in about four minutes, she sailed back into his bedroom and uttered a sigh, laden with tolerance, as she bent to lift his legs to the bed.

"You don't have the brains you were born with, Sheriff," she said, standing erect once more as she pulled the sheet over his body. "I assume you've decided not to put on your nightshirt." And then without waiting for a reply, she picked up the rejected garment and refolded it before she carried it to the dresser that held his clothing.

"At least keep the sheet up over you, so you don't take a chill," she told him. "I'll get you some water and one of the pills the doctor prescribed."

"I don't need any damn pill, Nurse Whitfield. Once I get settled in this bed and things are quiet, I'll be just fine."

She closed her eyelids for a long moment, and he was stricken. What if he'd gone too far, hurt her feelings? And then she opened those wide gray eyes and he felt as if he were about three years old and in danger of a harsh scolding from his mother.

"Go to sleep, McBain. I'll be on the sofa if you need me."

He watched her turn from him and leave, his gaze admiring the dark shine of her hair, its length braided now in a long rope, hanging down her back. She put on such a facade of professionalism, he thought. And he had the unholy urge to tumble the starch out of that rigid spine.

"What? No good night kiss?"

As if his words had stung, she jerked and halted

her retreat. "I may change my mind about staying here after all. My reputation doesn't appear to matter to you at all, Mr. Lawman." She turned her head and he was struck by the dark look of disapproval she shot in his direction.

His words were conciliatory as he backtracked. "On the contrary, Nurse Whitfield, I'm very concerned with your reputation. In fact, I'll even give you leave to walk home, right now, if you think any differently."

"Don't tempt me," she said sharply. And then as if she thought better of it, she paused in the doorway. "I won't be leaving, McBain. Not tonight, at least. I'll put up with you for another day and see how things go. I told you I need the money that nursing brings me, but you need to understand that while I'm working on a case, I *will* be in charge."

"Even when your patient is the law in town?" he asked mildly, wishing she would turn to face him.

"Even then," she said, looking over her shoulder at him, her eyes narrowed, her color high, as if his actions had embarrassed her mightily.

And perhaps they had, but he could not find it in his heart to apologize, for the sight of her, flustered and pink-cheeked, did his heart good. The woman was looking better by the minute. And his grin appeared unbidden, drawn by the fire that dwelled deeply within the woman he watched. A fire he fully intended to sample before many more days had passed.

THE MAN IS IMPOSSIBLE. For a moment, Anna was torn between marching out the front door or smothering the lawman with his pillow. She shook her head. Either way, she would not be doing her duty as a nurse, and she scorned the idea of either option. So far as the sheriff was concerned, she must work to get him well enough to cope on his own. And given the strength of the man and the obvious determination he possessed, it shouldn't take more than a couple of days. A week at the most. She'd stick it out, bear with his childishness and keep his wound clean and his stomach fed.

The sound of a muffled chuckle followed her into the parlor and she sat on the sofa, sliding her shoes from her feet. She'd forgotten to get a sheet or quilt from the closet in his room, so the lightweight throw on the back of the sofa would have to do. There appeared to be a flat spot on the sofa that promised comfort and she wiggled her body against the high back, drawing up her knees beneath her dress for warmth. Although the temperature was still fairly warm outdoors, there always seemed to be a chill in the air that pervaded the night of late.

Her clothing would be a wrinkled mess by morning, but she planned to walk to the Owens' house and change her dress and under things before the whole town was up and moving.

From the bedroom, she heard his voice, caught the sound of his muffled groan as the bed shifted and the whole frame squeaked. He'd turned over, and no doubt his shoulder had protested the move. Another day or so would make a difference, she knew, for the wound was healing rapidly. Apparently the sheriff was a healthy man under ordinary circumstances, for his body was eager to be back to normal.

The sound of a rooster crowing awakened Anna and her eyes flickered open, noting the pale light of dawn through the front window. Swinging her legs to the floor, she stood, yawned and stretched lazily as she scanned the floor for her shoes. One toe stuck out from beneath the sofa and she bent to pull them from their hiding place. Not a sound issued from the bedroom and she wondered if she could leave the house and do her errands before he awoke.

Leaving without letting him know was out of the question, she decided, lest he awake and call for her. With a sigh, she went into the kitchen, lifted the lid of the cookstove and was relieved by the coals that still glowed. She'd forgotten to bank the fire, but luck was with her apparently, and she placed logs from the box behind the stove into the cavity, watching as fire licked eagerly at the bark.

The reservoir held warm water and she scooped a panful into the basin in the sink. In a matter of minutes, she'd washed her face and hands and sleeked back the sides of her hair then headed for the bedroom.

A quick rap on the doorjamb was met by a growl of displeasure from the bed. "It's too early to be up and around," the sheriff said.

"I'm going to walk home and get my clothing changed, McBain," she told him. "And then I'll stop by the Emporium and get food for your kitchen. It shouldn't take me longer than an hour or so altogether. Go back to sleep for a while." Her footsteps took her across to the bed as she spoke and one cool hand was placed on his forehead, her palm registering the lack of fever.

"Will I live?" he asked, his lids opening far enough for her to see the sharp, dark blue tint of his eyes.

"Afraid so," she answered tartly. "At least until I get back. I'll change your bandage before I fix your breakfast."

"I'm hungry already," he said, his impatience obvious. "The bandage can wait. Breakfast can't." He watched her, apparently noting her intent to leave. "I let you sleep all night," he said, as if he'd managed a great feat.

And so he had, she thought. But then, the house was quiet, with no rattle of bedpans or whispers from the nursing staff to keep a restless patient awake and on edge. "I'll warrant you didn't open your eyes till I knocked on that door. And you've recuperated enough not to need middle-of-the-night care."

His grin was quick, his eyes wide open now, and she stepped back from the bed. No man should have the ability to look so handsome, so appealing, while lying in a sickbed. Even in her limited experience as a nurse, she'd never seen another patient so well endowed, so fascinating as the man before her.

Nonsense. Pure nonsense, this business of evaluating the man on the basis of his looks. Anna turned her back and left the room, aware of his eyes following her. Once out the front door, she relaxed. Making monkeyshines with a lawman was the most insane thing she could possibly do. Even being friendly with the man was a mistake. The past, the mess she'd left behind, was reason enough to keep her counsel inviolate, to stay in the cocoon she'd formed for herself in this town.

But the long, muscular body, the dark hair and the stunning blue eyes of the man called Aaron McBain filled her thoughts as she made her way in the early morning light to the house on the edge of town where all her earthly possessions were stored.

CHAPTER THREE

AARON HAD SEEN HER somewhere before. As sure as he knew his name was Aaron McBain, he knew that her face was familiar. He had no recollection of her size or the long, elegant lines of her body, and if he'd seen her in the flesh at some other time in his life, he would not have forgotten the attributes she possessed. For surely Anna Whitfield was about the most womanly, attractive bundle of femininity he'd ever come across.

His thoughts bordered on the impure as he considered how long it would take him to steal a kiss from her rosy lips.

Aaron laughed at himself. Some heroic lawman he'd turned out to be, no matter what the town fathers thought. His father had been a patriot upholding law and order and teaching his son to apply the letter of the law to his daily life. But he'd let a bank robber get the drop on him, and then had watched as the felon had been cut down by a bullet from Miss Hattie Cooper's little derringer.

That elderly lady had been depositing her money in the bank when the gunman had appeared, and, contrary to public opinion, Hattie Cooper was not shy and retiring as most folks thought, for after giving the sheriff a chance to overtake the robber, she'd apparently decided he'd needed a bit of help, and accordingly had stepped back from the counter and shot the hooligan in his tracks. Not fatally, but painfully, thereby gaining the undying thanks of Aaron McBain, he thought as he drifted off to sleep.

The sun had made its way over the roof of the house next door when he heard the sound of his potential friend's voice at his front door. "It's me, McBain. Anna. I'll be in there in just a few minutes."

He smiled, shifted in the bed and winced, aware of the pain in his shoulder. Yet, more aware of the woman who spoke his name in such an offhanded way, listening to her footsteps as she made her way through his house. She'd begun by calling him Sheriff, then had apparently considered and rejected the use of his Christian name to settle on the more casual McBain. His smile turned into a grin of pleasure. She had a way about her, that was for certain.

ANNA UNLOADED THE BOX of foodstuffs she'd brought from the Emporium. The proprietor had found the items she'd required, batting not an eyelash at her purchases. For the first time since making her residence in Ottawa Falls, she'd swept into his establishment bearing a grocery list, and if he was curious about where she was taking the food she purchased, he hid his interest well.

"We got some fresh butchered chickens, ma'am," he'd said, and Anna had nodded quickly.

"That would be fine, sir," she'd told him, thinking of a kettle of soup for the invalid under her care. And perhaps a piece of fried chicken for herself.

Now she eyed the limp carcass of the chicken and realized that it must be chopped into parts for the kettle. Cooking had not been a big part of her education, but living in a well-to-do household all of her life had made her privy to countless cooks and housekeepers.

If she remembered right, chicken soup began with a large kettle and a generous amount of water. She peeled and sliced an onion from Sheriff McBain's pantry and in moments she'd washed the chicken, cut it into an assortment of pieces and dropped most of them into the simmering water with the onion.

A sack of noodles and several carrots, gleaned from the backyard garden, would complete the recipe, if she was remembering properly.

A coffeepot awaited filling and she pumped

water from the red pitcher pump at the sink, then added a handful of coffee grounds, and, as the storekeeper had instructed, threw in a pinch of salt. "So's it won't be bitter," he'd told her, pleased at being asked his own method of brewing coffee.

He'd sent her on her way with a wide grin, a small slab of bacon and a pound of pork sausage in her basket, along with a dozen eggs, all wrapped nicely in a sugar sack, adding a round of butter from a collection on his countertop. "Miss Cooper brings in butter twice a week for me to sell," he'd told Anna. "Makes a tidy bit, she does, what with her egg business and running a boarding house." His smile had been beneficent. "She's kinda a heroine in town, what with shooting the bank robber and maybe saving the sheriff's life, you know."

"I'd heard about that," Anna had answered as she'd checked her purchases and dealt with the money owed to the store owner.

Now she thought again of that lady whose talents apparently included shooting straight and making butter fit for any man's table. "Thank you, Miss Cooper," Anna murmured beneath her breath as she turned out the flat measure of butter into a dish she'd found in the cupboard. The bacon was laid out to cook in a large iron skillet and three eggs set aside for frying once the bacon was done.

"McBain, are you awake in there?" she called out, hearing a series of bumps and muffled imprecations from the area of the bedroom.

"Yeah, I'm awake, and about halfway into my pants. But I could use a hand, Nurse Whitfield," he called back.

Anna rolled her eyes and wiped her hands on a clean dish towel she'd located. "I'll be right there," she answered, and with a last look at the bacon, edges already curling nicely in the skillet, she moved quickly from the kitchen.

He was standing, swaying a bit, but definitely upright, and his trousers were pulled to his waist. He'd apparently begun the buttoning process and given up on it, once he'd realized his buttons and buttonholes didn't match up right. Anna went to him, sitting to face him on the side of the bed. He stood before her and she undid the botch he'd made, then redid the buttoning quickly, her fingers careful to edge the fabric from his body, lest she come in contact with whatever dwelled beneath the fly front.

Not that she was a shrinking violet, but rather a once-burned, twice-shy refugee from a tarnished marriage, a past unspeakably besmirched by fear and scandal. The mystery of a man's conformation was old news to her, but she had a vague feeling that McBain's own physical makeup was a long way from the last male she'd had contact with.

Enough of this. The past was just that—a time best forgotten, its years hidden by a fervent hope for her future.

"I'll get your shirt, McBain," she said. "A clean one, I think." And so saying, she opened his dresser drawer and sorted through the clothing there. "I'd say someone else folds things for you," she commented. "The looks of these shirts show a woman's hand."

"My wash lady," he said, frowning at her as she approached with a blue-and-white striped specimen in her hand. "That's my good shirt," he told her. "I don't wear it for everyday."

"Well, you are today," she announced, "just as soon as I put a clean dressing on your wound." The necessary items for his care were on the bedside table and she motioned to the bed, pausing until he relented, sitting on the edge of the mattress, awaiting her ministrations. She was deft, efficient and only too aware of the masculine body she tended. His chest was broad and muscular, the line of dark hair centering it a temptation for her fingers.

McBain bore up bravely as she worked at his wound, accepted the touch of cool hands and the firm yet feminine feel of her skills as she wound the bandage into place. Her scent reached him, her breasts only inches before his face, and he closed his eyes, attempting to keep his male libido under control. The woman seemed to have no notion whatsoever that she was messing with a man who'd been too long without a female in his life.

Anna looked down at the sheriff's shoulder. The wound was clean and dressed with salve, the bandage in place, and she was about six inches from a man who tried vainly to hide his physical reaction to her. And at that thought, she shook her head, ashamed of the images that flooded her mind.

Holding the shirt before her, she unbuttoned it, then held it behind him to accommodate his wounded shoulder. Carefully, she slid one sleeve the length of his arm, allowed the back yoke to lay across his shoulders, then circled him to lift his other arm into the other sleeve. "That'll do," she said efficiently, her fingers busily straightening the collar.

"Now if you'll stand up, I'll match up your buttons and buttonholes." He obliged her by acceding to her instructions and she readied him for his meal, doing up his shirt and tucking it into his trousers with a deft hand. By the time the chore was complete, she was breathless and flushed and wished fervently that the sheriff had offered to do at least a bit of the buttoning and tucking himself. His body was lean and hard, muscular and tough and yet there was about him a core of gentle manhood she glimpsed on occasion. "Your breakfast is on the back burner," she told him, chancing a glance into his dark gaze. "Come out to the kitchen when you're ready to eat." And was given a quick nod in reply.

She escaped to the kitchen where she slid the bacon back on the hottest part of the stove, guaranteed it would cook rapidly, and then turned the pieces, taking them from the grease to drain on brown paper as they turned crisp and cooked to perfection. *At least I can fry bacon and make a decent pot of soup.*

And at that thought, she smiled, settling the plate into the warming oven while she tended to the eggs. From the bedroom, she heard footsteps and then he appeared in the kitchen doorway, features pale, but looking to be well-rested. His blue eyes were sharp, taking stock of the table, the food being cooked and the woman who worked in his kitchen.

Doing her best to ignore his scrutiny, Anna broke the eggs into the hot grease, one at a time, and heard the sizzle of the whites as they turned brown around the edges. It was the way the cook had made her breakfast at home, in those long-ago years before she'd made the biggest mistake of her life. Now she watched as the grease spattered and the eggs cooked quickly. From the oven she brought bread she'd sliced and toasted and centered it on a small plate, then placed it on the table and turned back to the stove.

A round spatula from the pantry seemed a perfect size to turn the eggs, and she put it to use then quickly lifted them from the pan, lest they become too done, too hard to allow the yolks to run a bit on the plate. "Two for you, one for me," she said, sliding his plate before him on the table.

"Only one for you? I thought I had plenty of eggs, Anna. You can certainly eat anything in this house that appeals to you." She thought he frowned as he spoke and she hastened to reassure him.

"I'd really thought to cook three for you, McBain, but considering that you're in the midst of recuperation, I thought you probably hadn't worked up that much appetite. I never eat more than one egg for breakfast. But I thought a big man like you would want more."

He settled in his chair at the table and his expression lightened. "Aha!" he exclaimed. "Lacy eggs, just like my grandma used to fix."

"Lacy?" she asked, peering down at the plate before her. "Never heard them called that before."

"My grandpa used to ask for them every morning. Grandma fixed them in the bacon grease, the way you did and the heat was enough to bubble up the edges and make them crispy. We enjoyed them, probably because Grandpa did."

Anna folded her hands in her lap and bowed her head for a moment before she picked up her fork.

"You needn't pray in silence, Anna. But since you did, I hope my food received a blessing equal to that on your plate." He picked up a piece of toast and buttered it, then offered it to her. "Jam, too?" he asked.

A container on the table held strawberry jam, and he pushed it in her direction, a gesture she accepted with a smile. "Thank you. I love strawberry. I used to pick the berries from the yard when I was small and helped clean them for jam."

"You had a good life, didn't you?" Aaron had the urge to find what made this woman so attractive to him, whether it be her beauty, or perhaps simply the strength and independence she exhibited. Whichever it might be, he was well on his way to leading her astray. And wasn't that an old-fashioned idea?

As if she had thought out her answer to his query, she nodded. "Yes, you could say I had a good life. My childhood was wonderful. My parents were well-to-do and my mother doted on her family. She made everything fun for us, and we ran wild pretty much all of the time. I learned how to climb trees before I went to school, and there was always croquet in the summer and sledding in the winter." A note of longing had crept into her voice, and she laughed softly.

"Just an everyday, normal childhood, I suppose."

"And what about your life after that?" he asked.

Her gaze rose to meet his and she felt a flush creep up her neck to stain her cheeks. "I married." It was a statement that offered no explanation and she hoped against hope that he would expect no more than that. Fork in hand, she punctured her egg's yolk and dipped her toast into the golden well.

"How old are you, Anna? I know you're a woman full-grown, but at the same time you have a sense of innocence about you. I find it hard to believe that you've already lived through a marriage."

"Well, I have," she said sharply, as if she would end this conversation before it went any further. "I'm twenty-seven," she told him, "and if you really must know, my husband is dead, so my marriage no longer exists."

"I wondered," he said, lifting a forkful of egg to his mouth and picking up a slice of bacon. "You don't wear a wedding ring, and you haven't introduced yourself as Mrs." Both of which were to his advantage, should he succeed in steering her toward his bedroom, and eventually his bed.

"My title has been Nurse since I came here," she said. "It's been quite a while since I wore my married name." And then she paused, realizing she'd left herself open for more questioning.

"Whitfield isn't your married name?" He seemed only mildly curious, and she shook her head.

"No, it isn't. And as far as seeming young and innocent, I'm neither, McBain. I lost my innocence years ago, and I'm too close to thirty to be considered young."

"Some women have the quality of youth," he said slowly. "It doesn't seem to leave them, no matter how many years they live. My mother is one of those women. She was young at sixty, when I saw her last. Of course, the fact that she was happy in her second good marriage may have had something to do with it. She'd been a widow for a number of years, and things were rough for all of us for a while after my dad died." His father had been a deputy sheriff who'd died upholding the law. These days were much improved for his mother, who lived in Texas with her second husband, a well-to-do businessman who led a nice, safe life, causing his family no worry.

"I'm sorry," she said quickly, thinking how difficult it was to lose a parent, especially when family was so precious and in his case probably not living nearby. "Are you from back East?"

"No, Texas is my home. At least it was, years ago."

"And now? Have you lived here long?"

Some way, she'd turned into the questioner and

he didn't like it. He'd begun to find out an assort-, ment of facts, and she'd neatly turned the tables on him, dredging his past into the present with little effort. He seldom spoke of his family, or his life before his time here. He'd thought to seek other work, but try as he might, it seemed that the life of a lawman was his destiny.

But then, he'd done his share of questioning, too. For his instinct told him that Anna Whitfield kept to herself a great deal. She hadn't mentioned friends or even acquaintances here in Ottawa Falls, and if her story regarding the parts of her past she'd made him privy to were in fact truth, the last several years had not been easy for her.

They finished breakfast quickly and Anna proved to be adept at clearing up and taking care of the dishes. He thought to offer his help, but decided it was more enticing just to watch as she moved about his kitchen, setting things to rights. She moved gracefully, a fact he'd noted in the hospital, and her hands were those of a lady, elegantly fashioned with long fingers and neatly kept nails.

"You know your way around a kitchen," he said idly as she wrung out the dishrag and hung it over the edge of the sink board. The skillet awaited her touch and she wiped it with a bit of brown paper and then the damp dishcloth, not placing it in the dishwater.

"It doesn't take a whole lot of intelligence to wash and dry dishes." Her eyes slanted a look of humor at him as she put the skillet into the oven for storage. "I used to think it was a privilege to help in the kitchen at home when I was a child. That was before I knew it was just a part of women's work."

"It strikes me that much of what goes on in life is women's work," he said dryly. "At least all the distasteful things like laundry and changing baby diapers and such."

A look of abject longing flooded her mobile face, and he felt that he'd said something hurtful to her. Surely not the remark about laundry. Maybe the baby diapers bothered her. Perhaps she'd had a child....

"Did I say something wrong?" It seemed he could read her like a book, Anna decided, realizing that her quick punch of sorrow had drawn his attention. The child she'd carried for only six months had left an indelible imprint on her heart and she yearned for the day when the pain of its loss would no longer strike her at odd moments.

"No, of course not," she said quickly, unwilling to share her most private, sorrowful memory with a man who was still, essentially, a stranger to her. And she gave him credit for recognizing that she would not speak longer of her past, for he rose from the table and waved a hand at the parlor door.

"I have several books you might be interested in reading," he told her, "and the weekly newspaper is on the library table if you'd care to look at it."

"Would you like to sit on your chair for a while? Or are you ready for an hour lying down in bed?"

"Later on, perhaps," he said, leaning against the doorjamb for a moment, his gaze intent on her.

The thought of sharing the parlor with him for an hour or so this morning was appealing, but she wanted no continuation of the prodding and poking he'd instigated in the kitchen. Her time with McBain was going to be limited, for she'd about decided to begin plans for moving on. Her next visit to the rooming house where she lived would see her packing the essentials she'd carted across the country—no little mementos, no pictures, no personal souvenirs of a life, only the basic clothing needed for survival, a coat for cold weather, a shawl for warmer evenings and the assortment of powders and creams she was not willing to get rid of in order to save on the weight of her luggage.

"Please join me, Anna." McBain phrased it almost as a command, waiting till she should walk past him into the small hallway that connected the rooms in this house. She seemed hesitant, and he sensed she was upset with herself, with the bits of information she'd volunteered into his hearing.

Nothing that would give away important details, no names mentioned, only memories of childhood and that one hesitant moment when he'd hit a sore spot, and she'd reacted like a horse with a stone in his shoe. A wince of pain, an adjustment in the lines of her face, her composure shaken by something he'd said.

But she was following his lead, entering the parlor, seeking out and examining the small selection of books he owned. Anna's fingers touched the spines, as if she read the titles with the weight of her fingertips, and she took one from the shelf, holding it in both hands, inspecting the cover and opening the front pages.

"You're interested in government?" he asked, noting the tome she held, a study of congress and its doings, the responsibility of the house of representatives and the power of the government over the people.

She glanced up, a secret sort of smile twitching her lips. "Not really. But living in the eastern part of the country makes one more aware of the goings-on in Washington. My father spoke often of his opinions and his family was a captive audience at the dinner table."

"Was he a government figure?"

She shook her head. "No, not a member of congress or the president's staff. Just a citizen who worked for the honor of supporting his party and sometimes helping to push laws into effect."

"But it wasn't your cup of tea, I suspect," Aaron said, thinking that Anna was not the type to be involved with the paper-pushers in the Capitol.

"It certainly isn't now. I had my share of proximity to the workings of this country. Now I'm satisfied to settle back and act as a citizen, letting others get all excited about laws and amendments and such."

"How about proximity to a lawman, Anna? Does it bother you that I've been sworn to uphold the law of the land? That I'm a part, a small part, I grant you, but nevertheless a representative of the law, right here in Ottawa Falls?"

Her eyes widened and for just a moment she seemed stunned by that thought. And then she shook her head quickly. "Of course not. To me you're a patient, whether you wear a star on your shirt or carry a Bible on Sunday. I look beyond the manner in which a man or woman lives their life when I see them as patients. I'm only interested in getting you healed and back to work as soon as I can."

She cast him a look he could not interpret; perhaps a bit of disappointment touched those gray eyes. "I probably will never see you again after the next few days."

"You think not?" He grinned, watched as she responded to his lighthearted words, and then closed the newspaper he held. "I had in mind a different sort of relationship with you, once we've gotten beyond the patient-and-nurse stage."

"I don't have relationships with my patients." Her voice was firm, but her mouth trembled as she shot him another glance, as if to see how he would react to her words.

"You're having one with me, right now. You're cooking for me, sleeping on my sofa, tending my wound and washing my dishes. Only one item on that list qualifies as a nursing chore."

"I beg to differ, McBain. I'm taking care of you, providing rest and nourishment."

"And a big dose of medicine you apparently aren't aware of," he continued. "You feed my soul, Anna. I'm rather attracted to lovely things. Art and music qualify as such, and so do you. I've enjoyed just watching you, appreciating you as a woman." *More than you can possibly know.*

She blushed, a slow peach cast to her skin deepening as he watched. "Don't give me reason to leave you, McBain. I'm here as a nurse. If you make more of it than that, I'll be obliged to take my leave."

He leaned forward in his chair as if he might capture her hand, draw her closer to him, but she drew back on the sofa, out of reach. "Don't go, Anna," he asked softly. "I'm not trying to insult you, only explain the attraction I feel for you. I'm not trying to make advances toward you, for I've no intention of harming you in any way. I like you. I like the way you look, your conversation, the way you move about in my house."

He trailed off, sensing that her level of discomfort was rising as he spoke.

"You're a good man, Sheriff McBain," she said, a sad smile touching her full lips. "But I've no intention of forming any sort of friendship with any man. I'm more interested in finding work that will suit me and making a life for myself."

"I thought nursing suited you quite well, and you've made a life for yourself right here."

She shook her head. "This is a stopgap, a resting place, just a bump in the road. I won't be in Ottawa Falls for an extended time, only long enough to add to my nest egg, long enough to make a few decisions."

A sudden thought struck him, a vague remembrance of her face in a painting or a drawing that portrayed her. "Are you on the run, Anna? Is someone after you, someone you're afraid of?" he asked quietly—and watched as the peach hue of her complexion turned ashen.

Her laugh was forced and harsh, and unlike the woman, it unsettled him. "What on earth would make you ask such a question?" She rose and put the book she held on the shelf, her back to him, her shoulders squared as if she expected a barrage of questions and was preparing the answers.

"Just curiosity, I suppose," Aaron said. "You aren't very forthcoming about your recent past, and I feel a sense of hesitation when you speak, as if you fear revealing too much about yourself." He was silent, awaiting her next move. "I won't hurt you, Anna. When I'm here with you, I'm just a man, not the law. If you want to talk to me, I'll listen, but I won't pry."

"If you go that route, we'll have a problem, McBain. I'm not about to divulge any mention of my affairs." She turned to face him and her eyes held his, a look of such pleading assailing him that he rose from his chair to face her. She was only a few steps away, mere inches of space, but a chasm stood between them as she held out one palm, warning him to step no closer.

"Am I not allowed to touch you?" he asked. For he felt a yearning to do that very thing, as if he might awaken the woman who was hidden beneath the flesh and bone of Anna Whitfield.

"We have a professional relationship, McBain," she said tartly, her hands gripping her skirts, her chin lifting as if to provide a barrier he would not cross. "No more than that."

The woman didn't know him and obviously

didn't recognize her own need. For, as if waves of emotion stormed him, he felt the yearning of a fellow creature who sought sanctuary, a female who felt stranded and insecure. There was no option, no way Aaron could ignore what was so patently exposed before him.

He reached for her, drew her off balance and held her tightly to his chest, ignoring the pain engendered by his action. His arms surrounded her, his head bent, his cheek pressing against hers, and he was silent for a moment. Until he felt the unmistakable dampness that crept between the soft skin of her face and his own whiskered countenance. One hand lifted to her cheek and he wiped away tears that fell from her lashes, then leaned back a bit, the better to see her.

Eyes closed, she bent her head, until his lips were pressed against the clean line of her forehead. He pressed a soft kiss there, a touch that offered comfort and inadvertently brought his masculinity into an alerted state of being.

She smelled of soft things, lilacs perhaps, the scent of spring flowers in her hair, although she wore no such fripperies as cologne, had made no attempt to attract him. But the texture of her flawless skin alone invited his lips to travel to her temple, and from there down the line of her cheek, more dampness catching his attention.

"You're crying," he whispered, and she inhaled, as if she would withdraw the evidence of her suffering. "I feel I've done something to upset you, to cause you pain, and I don't know what it is," he said, feeling helpless in the face of her sorrow.

"You've done nothing wrong," she said, releasing her hands from their position against his chest. Now she fished in the pocket of the apron she wore and brought forth a small hankie. It was inadequate for the tears she'd shed, but she made a valiant effort to wipe her face, obviously embarrassed by her lapse, by the tears that gave away her fragile emotions.

"I'm all at sixes and sevens," she told him, drawing a deep breath. "I've got a few decisions to make and haven't known how to plan my future. I suppose it felt good to lean on someone else for a minute." She pushed back from him, but he thought the action was reluctant. "I'm all right now, McBain. Honestly, I am."

Stepping back from her a bit, he looked down at her upturned face, the trembling lips that spoke the lie, and could not resist the silent invitation she offered. His mouth took hers, and his embrace turned to capture, for the first time taking advantage of a female, holding her still for his kiss, his arms sliding to keep her in place, lest she retreat from him. And she allowed it, did not struggle against his hold. He needed this—the feel of soft flesh beneath his lips took his breath—and he ached to know the texture of her mouth, the secrets hidden behind those lush, curving lips.

He'd thought to kiss her lightly, to offer comfort and then release her. Instead he took comfort of his own, slanting his mouth across hers, insinuating his tongue between her lips until she relaxed, allowing his intrusion. And yet, it was more of an invasion, for he conquered every part of the sweetness she owned, her tongue and teeth, the soft, vulnerable flesh of her cheeks and mouth, her lips and even the ridged roof of her mouth. As if he could not leave any part untouched, he held her close, one big hand against her head, the other circling her back, holding her in place for the exploration he'd instigated.

And, wonder of wonders, she did not fight him, only clung to his neck, once her hands were freed from capture against his chest. She turned her head as he silently bid, his hand beneath her chin, holding her, his grip not painful, but firm. He had no yearning to force this woman, to take what she was not willing to give freely, and yet he used all his powers of persuasion, his aim being to please her, to perhaps incite her to some level of arousal, in which she might return his kisses, press her body more firmly against his and give him the warmth he sought.

She'd never been kissed in just this way before,

Anna realized. No other man had claimed her so fully, so tenderly, without attempting further advances that would spoil the moments of pleasure she sustained. She'd been kissed by a man who considered himself an expert at the game, early on, in the courtship she'd received from John Carvel, the senator from Pennsylvania.

But once married to him, kissing had not been a part of the wooing process. The physical advances at his hand had been brief, painful and mortifying, for the most part. She'd been used, had been forced to mate as might an animal, cornered and afraid, yet at the mercy of the larger predator who sought her favors.

And though she was certain Aaron McBain would not bring this bit of seduction to a culmination, he left no part of her untouched where he sought to bring pleasure to them both. His hands only held her against him, his fingers not squeezing or pinching her flesh. For she was cuddled in his arms as if she were cherished by the embrace that held her. His heat penetrated beneath her clothing, warming her from the outside in, and at that thought, she could not hide the smile she knew bloomed on her lips. Her face was buried against his, and then he released her mouth and she turned just a bit, seeking the vulnerable place beneath his chin, there where his throat pulsed with the heartbeat he could not seemingly control.

He was aroused, of that she was certain, and yet he did not push against her, did not forcefully bring his condition to her attention, but only held her firmly, as if he would somehow keep control over the masculine urges that possessed him.

"Are you all right? Anna, have I hurt you?" His concern radiated from his mouth to her ear, and she heard the rumble of his words through the chest wall that supported her.

She could not speak, could only turn her head a bit, an imperceptible motion meant to soothe his fears. For she had not been injured, had not felt the harshness of hands on her body, only the welcome warmth of kisses and caresses that gave comfort to her feminine heart. And now she must draw back, must look up at the dark eyes that would search hers for answers, must let her gaze so imprint upon her mind the face and features of this man that in days and years to come, she would recall this moment, would remember the first time she'd been cherished by a man's hands and body, with no fear of cruel invasion or assault on soft flesh.

Aaron felt the stiffness melt, knew the feel of feminine flesh warming against his own, met her soft gaze as she looked up into his eyes and then scanned his features as if filing that one long look away into her memory, lest she not ever again stand so near him, lest she never again feel the warmth of his arms.

"I can't let you go," he said, tightening his hold, feeling no resistance, for he sought any trace of pressure from her. If she pushed him aside, he would release her, if she begged for freedom from his touch, he would give it. Not willingly, but because he would do nothing to harm her, to bring fear to those gray eyes, distaste to the calm features that lent beauty to her face. It struck him that though he had thought her to be lovely, she was not traditionally pretty, not a classic beauty, but instead possessed a clear, limpid quality of features that lent themselves to an unforgettable vision of perfection.

Surely somewhere, some man looked for her. Somewhere, her family grieved her absence, and surely there was a gaping hole where once she had spent her days and nights, where she had lived a life containing friends and family. Someone must be seeking her—

His mind stood to attention as he put a name to the face before him. Susannah Carvel, wife of Senator Carvel, who had been murdered in his bed just three short months past. The face on the Wanted poster in his office was duplicated before him, the curve of eyebrows, the straight line of her nose, the fullness of her lips.

"I have to go to my office for a while," he said, fearful of his face showing evidence of his thoughts. Unwilling that she should know the direction of his mind.

"Not alone, you won't," she said firmly. "I can go and find anything you need and bring it back to you, or I'll take you myself and wait for you there."

"It's only a short walk," he told her. "I don't mind the company if you'd like to go along."

"I thought you were tired, that you planned to lie down for a while," she said, as if doubting his need for exercise this morning.

But he denied her notion, shaking his head. Indeed, he would not go without her, lest she take it in her head to run from him during his absence. And that was a dire possibility. She was primed to run, he could feel it in her, could sense the almost animal instinct that ruled her now.

"I feel well enough to walk over there right now. Just let me get my boots on."

"All right, I'll help you," she said quickly. "I'll comb my hair and put it up first."

"Not for my benefit," he told her, his admiring look taking note of the waves she hadn't yet put in place this morning.

"I can't parade around town without my cap, anyway. I'm going with you as your nurse, so I'll have to look the part."

His nod was unwilling, but he couldn't take a chance on upsetting her in any way. Too much was at stake, so he merely nodded and released her hands, looking toward the front door where his boots awaited him. And beyond the door was the sidewalk that would lead to his office, where a Wanted poster awaited his eyes, a poster he'd noted, read and reread just weeks ago, his interest taken by the young appealing woman whose face had been copied on dozens of such posters and sent out to lawmen all over the country. The likeness was flat and lifeless, but the real woman stood here before him, and he recognized that the artist had not been able to capture the fresh beauty she bore, the clear eyes of innocence, the small smile of pleasure brought to her face over the past half hour. By the kisses of Aaron McBain.

The kisses she might think were treacherous, should she discover that he'd found her out.

CHAPTER FOUR

THE POSTER WAS THERE on his desk, beneath the town newspaper, apparently the last item of interest that had snagged his attention before the sounds of a robbery had brought about his recent hospitalization. No one had touched his desk; no one had rifled through his papers and, as he'd suspected, no one else had seen the poster he sought out upon entering his office.

Lest Anna see him scooping it up into his possession, he folded it into the pages of his newspaper, then doubled the front page upon itself and tucked the slender publication beneath his arm, till he should sit in his chair and relax this evening. She watched him from the doorway, her eyes taking in the bare essentials that comprised his office, the desk, the leather chair that held the image of his body in its ancient padding, the nails on the wall where he hung, at various times, his hat or gun. Now the keys to the cells behind the office hung in solitary splendor. His gun was on a belt around his waist, his hat tilted over one eye as he rose from the desk and looked up at Anna.

"Seen enough?" he asked. "Not that there's much to look at in a sheriff's office. Just the tools of the trade."

"I was noticing the posters on the wall over there," she said, waving a negligent hand to where he'd pinned several sheets of paper, each of them bearing the likeness of a man currently wanted by the law. "They all look like mean, hateful creatures, don't they?"

He scanned the papers she'd included in her survey and nodded. "Some folks look evil, and then there's those who don't seem to suit our ideas of criminals. Those who wear innocence like a cloak, and seldom show any evil inclinations to the rest of the world."

"Have you met any like that? Criminals who don't act the part?"

He met her gaze with eyes that delved deeply beneath her surface. "I've met some who didn't deserve the title of criminal, or murderer or thief. Usually they're vindicated by the truth, but sometimes there's one or another who'll keep on running instead of facing their problem and getting things cleared up."

She lifted her chin and tossed him a defiant look that quickly faded to despair. "Maybe there are those who fear not being believed. Those who have no friend in which to confide, or perhaps no proof of their innocence."

With a shiver, she seemed to shrink within herself and was silent again, as if she knew they were both discussing one person in particular. "I'd be ready to listen, should such a person ask for my understanding," he said softly, his voice carrying to where she stood, and then noted the quick jolt of her body as his invitation struck home. She turned and met his gaze, her own eyes seeming faded and weary, the flesh of her face appearing almost transparent, as though she had lost what little strength she possessed in that moment, as if she could barely remain upright on her feet. She paled, even as he watched, and her eyelids fluttered.

"Anna?" He spoke only her name, and then as if tempted beyond his ability to withhold her name any longer, he spoke it aloud. "Susannah?"

She jerked wildly, her hands flying upward to cover her mouth, the gray hue of her eyes turning to steel, darkening almost to midnight-black, widening in fright as her body turned toward the door.

"Don't run from me," he warned her, his words harsh, and then he stepped toward her, one long stride after the other, until he was against her back, taller than she, looking over the top of her head, noting an errant lock she'd not been able to tame into place.

"I haven't moved," she said. "Maybe I'm just taking my last look at freedom." Her voice taunted him, and she laughed, a brittle sound that made his throat ache. Turning toward him, as if on a pivot, she faced him, head-on. "How long have you known?" Her eyes were not frightened, for she surely knew he would not harm her.

"I had suspicions from the start. I didn't know where I'd seen you, but once I began going over the possibilities, I realized your face was on a poster in my office." He gripped her hand, sliding his fingers upward to her wrist, and she was held in a vise she could not have escaped had she tried.

"I'm not running, Sheriff," she said, looking down at his long fingers that measured the fine bones of her arm. "My first concern is getting you home and into your chair. Besides, it wouldn't do me any good to try escaping you now."

"No," he said musingly. "It wouldn't. You'll not be more than arm's length from me from now on, Susannah."

"What will you do to me?" she asked, and the flicker of her eyelids told him of her fear.

"I don't know." He straightened his hat atop his head, indecision riding him. "I just don't know. But while I figure it out, you won't be out of my sight," he told her quietly.

She thought how amazing it was that his voice became more menacing as it lowered in volume. How the intensity of his words magnified as he murmured his threats.

You won't be out of my sight. Not for a moment did she doubt his words. He was the essential lawman, hard-edged and cautious, a man not given to pity. Perhaps she could hope for mercy, hope it was within his power to feel some small bit of sympathy for her problems.

"You can't know what has happened to me," she said quietly, not attempting to pull from his hold. Her neck had bent, like the broken stem of a flower, as if her head were too heavy to hold upright, and her chin drooped almost to her chest as she opened her mouth to speak.

"Don't look so defeated. You're a strong woman, or you wouldn't have come so far. Whatever has happened to you is in the past, and you've overcome the urge to run and hide. If you hadn't, you wouldn't be here now."

"I'm here because I thought I was safe," she blurted out harshly. "And then I met a man who has access to my past and will use it against me."

"Will I?" At his soft query, she lifted her head

and met his gaze, noted the icy sheen of indigo-blue eyes and the stark, harsh lines of his face.

"You know you will. You're a lawman, sworn to bring criminals to justice, and I fear I qualify as one of your enemies."

"No, you're not my enemy, Susannah," he said, his voice skimming the syllables of her name. "I find you to be an enigma, neither friend nor foe. But for sure, I have no intention of causing you hurt or pain."

"And do you think sending me back to Washington will be a bright and happy experience for me? That I'll be welcomed with open arms by the police there? And then exonerated by them for even thinking I might have killed my husband?"

"Did you?" He retained his grip on her wrist, but his other hand lifted to her chin, tilting her head upward until he could look fully into her face.

No. I couldn't kill anyone. Anna swallowed the urge to speak the words aloud, and as though he demanded honesty, he refused to allow her gaze to veer from his.

She'd wanted John dead, and might even have taken his life had things gone on long enough. If her aching soul had not found peace when she'd seen his life's blood pulsing from his body. Would she have done it herself, given more abuse?

Her honest heart berated her, and she knew the depths of her hatred for the man she'd married.

Yet, she recalled, as though a load had been lifted from her shoulders, she'd felt lighter. Free. And she hadn't cried, except for the tears she'd shed for herself. For the frightened woman who had borne cruelty as if it were her due. For the pitiful creature who had clung to her dignity, attempting to hold together a marriage that had been doomed from the start.

"Did you feel safe once you realized he was dead?" McBain asked. "Would you have pulled the trigger if you'd had the chance?" He looked into her eyes, his own holding her gaze, and she knew him for what he was.

Uncompromisingly honest, a man of honor.

Perhaps I would have killed him, if that woman hadn't done it in my stead. And so she found she could not tell the lie that trembled on her lips, and so sought out the uncertainty of truth as she knew it.

She shook her head. "I might have killed him, if things had been different. I wanted to, but I didn't. I went that night to tell John I was leaving our marriage. No, I didn't hold the gun or fire the shot that killed him. But I'm glad he's dead. I saw the woman who shot him, heard the sound of him falling on the floor, saw his blood flow." Her eyes closed then, and to her abject dismay and mortification, twin tears ran from beneath her lashes and made trails down her cheeks, falling on the bodice of her dress.

"I was there when he died. If I'd been holding a gun in my hand I might have been the one to shoot him."

"But you didn't have a gun?" The question sounded casual. Its intent was obviously not. Aaron spoke again. "According to the paperwork I received, he was shot in the back. Were you behind him?"

"No, never. He was in bed with his mistress." The word trembled on her lips and she drew a deep breath as if to rid herself of the label she'd put on another woman. "I came in the room and saw them, heard them talking, and things were blurred from then on. He'd written me a note, asking me to come to Washington, and I went. Like an absolute fool, I went. Maybe I'd hoped we might make a civilized end to things, but…" Her pause was long and she lifted her gaze to his as if she'd lost track of her story.

"Then what happened?" Aaron asked, the words barely spoken aloud, fearful that he might frighten her, cause her to cease her toneless recitation.

"I'm not sure what happened, only that I saw her raise her hand with the gun in it, heard the shot fired."

She shuddered, her eyes dark against the pallor of her skin. "I almost took along one of John's guns with me," she confessed, as if her intent left her open to guilt. "I even took it from his desk," she said woodenly. "And then I put it back. I thought I wouldn't have whatever it takes to take another life. But I didn't want the temptation in my reticule."

She looked up at him, and her eyes held desperation now, a frightening darkness that fixed her gaze on some unseen memory. "He deserved to die, but…I didn't kill him. He cheated me and he cheated the people who'd voted for him. He even cheated the woman he'd brought into his bed that night. He'd told her he would marry her, and when she demanded to know his intentions, he laughed at her.

"He laughed," she repeated, the thought of the man's cruelty seeming to shatter her calm.

For her eyes filled with tears, her face twisted grotesquely and she uttered a low moan, a sound of abject desperation. It was more than he could withstand, and he reached for her.

The mouth he'd kissed, the lips that had returned his caress, were pale, drawn taut against her teeth, her jaws gripped in a spasm of horror, as though she saw and recognized that scene in Washington once more. She was limp in his arms, her legs not able to hold her upright. Her weight rested against him, and he could only hold her thus, wishing vainly for some words of comfort, some sound of acceptance that would give her the knowledge that he was with her. That he would not turn his back on her.

She struggled to stand upright, to hold her weight on limbs that trembled and he loosened his grip on her waist, releasing her from the embrace he'd forced upon her. "Can you stand alone?"

She nodded. "I'm fine." And then she crumpled again, her tears flowing freely. "No, I'm not, am I? I'll never be fine again." The soft tones of her voice elicited his compassion as could nothing else have done. The hopelessness of her words nudged him into a declaration of intent, and he spoke quickly, damning the instincts that bade him be silent.

"I'll help you, Susannah. Whatever it takes to get this whole thing straightened out, we'll do it together." And yet, there remained doubt. He'd told her he believed her, but perhaps his belief was tinged by his attraction to the woman. Right now, he'd believe black was white if Susannah said so, so greatly did his masculine need rule him. As a lawman, he must back away from his certainty of her innocence, use his keen senses to consider the story she'd told him.

As if Susannah felt his reticence, she shuddered once and then stilled in his arms. "A man is dead, McBain. I didn't pull the trigger. I didn't even possess the gun. But I have no proof of my innocence, and neither have you. Only my memories of that night. I don't know who was in that bed with him, though I suppose you might be able to discover her name, her last name. He called her Bettina, I remember that much. It doesn't seem likely to me that there are very many women by that name in Washington. She was blond, and I think she had blue eyes." Her laugh was brief, mocking. "I don't think that will do an awful lot of good, will it?"

"You might be surprised," he said, his voice thoughtful as if he assimilated everything she had said, filing it neatly into little slots in his mind. "Whatever happens, I'll do what I can, Susannah. Will you trust me?"

Can I trust myself to be unbiased, to be competent? Or will I blindly accept her words as truth? Her trust was somehow essential to him and yet, if he were to question her story, if he doubted her words, did he have the right to ask for her trust?

"Do I have a choice?" she asked bleakly. "I have no one to turn to, McBain. Only you." Then as if another thought had found its way into her mind, she asked a question of him. "Is there a price on my head?"

He cleared his throat. "Of course there is. There's always a price on a Wanted poster. And that may be to our benefit."

She froze in his grip. "In other words, you'll at least come out of this with a few dollars in your pocket."

"That's not what I said. If there's a price on your head, it simply means that you're worth something to those who are looking for you. And it may mean that we can use it to our benefit. That someone in Washington wants you badly enough to seek you out."

"I have a better idea." She lifted her chin proudly. "Why don't you just turn your back and I'll walk out that door and you can pretend you've never seen me?"

He shook his head. "There's no way on God's green earth I could ever remove your existence from my mind. I'm up to my neck in this thing already, and forgetting that you exist is not possible."

"I'm easily forgettable, I'd think."

"You haven't the faintest idea what you're talking about," he said, denying her claim.

She jerked from his hold and stood apart from him, not fleeing, but trembling as if she considered that very thing. "I'll not be railroaded into prison. If ever a man deserved to die, it was John Carvel, but I didn't kill him, no matter what the facts suggest. I might have wished him dead, but…" Her fist touched her left breast and she shivered, her hand trembling.

His eyes narrowed and his mouth tightened as he offered her an ultimatum. "Don't try running, Susannah. I'll be after you so quick, you won't know what hit you. I've no intention of letting you go."

"Why?" She assumed a look of arrogance and he smiled at her bravery, at the pride of the woman, at the beauty of her countenance. And hid his reaction, cherishing her sensuality as he considered the woman who had softened in his embrace, melted in his arms.

"Why?" His brow quirked as if he mocked her, as if the single word of her query amused him. "Because you made a big mistake when you let me kiss you. An even bigger one when you kissed me back, when you leaned against me and allowed me to feel the warmth of your body."

She flushed, the peach tint of her complexion turning a deep rose, her eyes glistening with tears she made no attempt to hide. "Only one of several mistakes I've made, McBain."

"Maybe it wasn't a mistake," he said thoughtfully, making no attempt to hide his admiration for her flushed countenance, her shimmering eyes. "Maybe it'll be the smartest thing you've done thus far." Seducing a lawman might be in her best interests, after all.

"And what makes you think that?" Arrogance turned to anger as she met his gaze, wiping her eyes with a bit of fabric from her pocket. "I wasn't trying to entice you."

"Do you think I don't already know that?" And his mind did indeed believe her rigid stance, the defensive words she spoke. And yet a suspicion lingered in his lawman's mind. Might she be a woman who would cast doubt on her guilt by allowing a man intimacies?

No matter. She was the woman he wanted, and her kiss had given him a heated pleasure she seemed to share. Not as if it were a planned allowance of intimacy on her part, but as an answer to his own need. It had not been a mistake, but a window into what might take place in the time to come.

"We need to consider something, Susannah. Marriage might be in your best interest right now. Marriage to me. The fact being, if you were my wife, I couldn't testify against you, should it come to that. Even if I had some sort of proof of your duplicity, I couldn't legally be held responsible if I remained silent." Not to mention that the state of matrimony with Susannah as his partner filled him with an emotion akin to happiness.

He repeated his offer, making it more of an order than a request. "Marry me, Susannah."

"If I were married to you…" She laughed aloud. "I don't think so, McBain. I've been in one such mess already in my life. Tying myself down to a man is something I'll not risk again."

"Not even for the chance to stay out of jail?"

"Not even." Her jaw was firm, pugnacious in its pose, and he thought she looked like a banty rooster defending herself from him.

"You wouldn't like prison, Susannah."

"No doubt I'd hate it," she agreed. "But if I head west from here instead of depending on you to clear my name, I shouldn't have to worry about it."

"I told you earlier that you'll be next to me from now on. I meant it."

"You surely don't mean to involve yourself in all my private moments," she said, forbidding him entry to her personal life.

"One way or another, we'll be like Siamese twins," he told her. "Believe me, I'll be with you night and day."

She turned from him and walked through the office door, down the single step and onto the board sidewalk. Behind her, she heard the door slam shut, and before she could move either right or left, he was there, one long arm around her waist, holding her firmly to his side.

"Stop this. Don't touch me," she whispered harshly. "You're embarrassing me, right here in the middle of town."

"Then take my arm and walk beside me," he said, the words a command. He waited a moment and imperceptibly relaxed as she nodded her head and lifted her hand to slide it inside his bent elbow.

"Now what?" she asked.

"Now we go home and you fix us something to eat."

"You know what I mean. What are you going to do with me?"

"I'll send out a wire in the morning and find out just who is after you, and try not to raise too many questions. Whether or not I'll be given the information I want is still in doubt, but I'll try."

"And in the meantime?"

"Nothing. Absolutely nothing. We'll walk back to my house slowly, and nod and smile if it seems appropriate, and wait until morning."

"And then you'll keep me with you and eventually watch as the law trundles me off to prison."

He looked down at her, and his smile was tender. "I have no intention of letting you go to jail, sweetheart. I can think of better uses for you."

She pinched her lips together, fearful of what he might say if she questioned his theory, even as she recognized his attempt to lighten her mood.

"I haven't been a rousing success at anything I've set my hand to, thus far, McBain. As a senator's wife, I was socially inept, unwilling to turn a deaf ear or an unseeing eye to the games played in the Capitol. As a woman fleeing the law, I fear I've made a miserable mess of things. But I know for certain that when John was shot, I was not the one who pulled the trigger. I was in front of him. The only person behind him was the woman, Bettina." She closed her eyes, clutching tightly to his arm, lest she fall.

"I didn't even earn my salt as a nurse. I still can't imagine why they took me on at the hospital when all the experience I listed was nothing but a bundle of lies."

"I know why they took you on, sweetheart," he said quietly, slowing his pace to match her own. "They were desperate for good nurses, since most of the members of that profession come from the dregs of society. I'll bet they snatched you up in a jiffy. I doubt they even asked for references, did they?"

She shook her head. "No, as a matter of fact, all the director of nursing asked was how soon I could come to work." Her smile was bleak. "They really must have been desperate."

"You were like a gift from heaven. At least to me. Do you know, I thought I'd died and gone to heaven when I woke up and saw you looking down at me? I'd have sworn you were an angel."

"Apparently, far from it," she said flatly. "The only thing I had going for me was that I hated suffering of any sort, and knowing that I could relieve pain or anxiety in a patient gave me a reason to go to the hospital every day and act the part of a nurse."

"You weren't putting on an act. You have

healing hands, the touch of an angel of mercy, as nurses are sometimes called."

"And so you wanted me to tend you at home. Still think it was a good idea?" she asked.

"One of the best I've ever had." His words were sure and certain.

"Even knowing the worst there is to know about me?"

But, did he? What did he know, with any degree of certainty? That she was the most appealing woman he'd met in a month of Sundays? That he wanted her in his bed, with a throbbing desire he was finding it difficult to put out of his mind? Certainly there was no guarantee that she was the personification of innocence. Much as he wanted to have total faith in her, his rigid adherence to the law would not allow him to accept her word without some sort of proof of her honesty.

She'd shed the look of despair and now a gleam of pride lit her eyes. Aaron drew a breath, relieved that her backbone was once more in place, that she was not ready to give up without a fight. "You don't even know me, McBain," she said, tilting her chin defiantly.

"Maybe I've only been privy to the worst parts of your past, Susannah, but I have yet to sample the best you have to offer," he said, bending his head to speak more directly into her ear.

She honestly looked puzzled and he silently cursed the man who had so readily torn her ego to shreds. The woman should know, without a doubt, that she was lovely, appealing to a man, and had much to offer, should she so desire. And he lived now in the hope that she might offer herself to him one day. One day soon.

But if that day should never come, he would still defend her, protect her and somehow help to free her from the hands of the law, and if he found proof of her veracity he would welcome the opportunity to defend her.

His own ideas about the death of Senator Carvel left Susannah free of guilt, and if there were some way of proving her innocence, he would find it. On the other hand, should she be spinning a story for his benefit, he would see to it that justice was served. Wouldn't he?

They reached his house and turned from the sidewalk, Aaron opening the gate and leading her up the walk and then the single step to the porch. The door was unlocked and they entered the hallway and from there to the parlor.

"McBain?" She lifted her gaze to meet his as he turned her into his embrace. "I need to think about all of this, your thoughts of marriage…" She hesitated, a long pause following the word that had fallen from her lips. "I don't think that part is a good idea.

I don't ever want to marry again, and I certainly won't marry anyone just to find a way out of this mess. I couldn't take advantage of you that way."

"Well," he said slowly, lifting her chin with a long finger, "while you're thinking of the problems ahead, just include this on your long list." His mouth settled over hers carefully, with no trace of force or coercion, only the soft pressure of need. She was trembling in his arms and he would not have it, would not allow her to fear him. "Kiss me, Susannah. Give me your mouth, know that I'll never hurt you."

His whisper was warmth to her lips, a breath of persuasion to her heart, and she opened to him, allowing him the entry he sought. His arms were firm around her, his hands holding her where they would, giving her no choice but to endure his touch, and yet it was no trial to feel his warmth, to know the promise of strength and comfort he offered. She accepted him, twined her arms about his neck and leaned into the kiss he offered.

Too soon it was over and she inhaled deeply, aware suddenly that she was plastered against his body, her breasts flattened against his broad chest, her hips nestled against his erection. Almost comforting, nearly a welcome force against her, she knew the surge of an aroused man as he slid one hand to her hips and pressed her more firmly in place.

"Just stand still for a minute, Susannah," he whispered, his tone that of a man who seeks comfort, a man asking for nothing more than this moment of tenderness between male and female, two persons who are willing to take from each other, for a small particle of time, without thought of what tomorrow might bring.

She could not deny him what little he asked of her, and so remained in his embrace, finally leaning her head against his chest in an attitude of full submission, his heartbeat sounding in her ear, his arms enclosing her in an island of peace.

SUPPER WAS EATEN SILENTLY, each of them aware of the unspoken commitment they had forged between themselves, a promise to be kept, a union of spirits to be cherished. Susannah, for she would henceforth be known by her Christian name while in his presence, was filled to the brim with the knowledge of his need of her, and was even more so aware of just such a yearning that dwelled in herself. A yearning she feared would bring her to his bed.

"I've frightened you, haven't I?" Aaron asked quietly as he pushed his plate to one side, his meal completed.

Susannah looked up at him, shaking her head slightly, unwilling to admit to him the fear that held her captive. "No, honestly. I'm not afraid of you, McBain. Only what I feel for you."

"Well, that's encouraging at least," he returned, a half smile tugging at one corner of his mouth. "Can you tell me what it is you feel?" His hand snaked across the table and he lifted hers from where she'd clutched at her napkin with trembling fingers.

Tears formed in her eyes and again she shook her head. "I don't even know. Only that I'm grateful to you for giving me shelter. For making me feel safe for the first time in months, years perhaps."

"Is that the best you can do? I had more in mind an attraction for me, as a man. I'd hoped you might yearn for my touch, might feel just a trace of the longing I have to hold you, to possess you, to lie with you in my bed and own you as my lover."

She felt the flush creep up her cheeks, knew that she could not lie to the man, could not deny the warmth of her feelings for him. "For the first time in my life, I've found a man I think I might learn to…admire, McBain. I lived with a man who said he loved me, but knew it for a lie. He was cruel, vicious sometimes, arrogant always. He possessed a mean streak that frightened me beyond measure. He made my life a living hell on earth for years, until I reached the end of my forbearance, and knew finally that I could no longer live in the prison he'd made of our home."

"He abused you?" Aaron asked, his eyes darkening with a rage she knew was not directed at her, but rather the man she'd married seven years ago. "Did he strike you? Leave bruises on you?"

She nodded, unwilling to confess to the horrendous fights she'd survived, the painful blows she'd weathered with a stoicism John had despised. "He was cruel, McBain. Just leave it at that."

"Did he rape you?" His mouth was taut, his nostrils flaring, as if he would seize and destroy such an evil being.

"Rape isn't possible inside the marriage structure, I was told," she confessed, unwilling to admit to being such a victim.

"Rape is always possible, whether it occurs between a husband and wife or two strangers. When a man forces himself on his wife, it's abuse of the worst sort. The law may consider that the husband has rights, that his wife should not deny him the marriage bed, but when it occurs, it's wrong."

"I didn't have the chance to deny him anything," Susannah said bluntly. "He just took what he wanted without warning, without my..." Her voice softened until Aaron could barely hear the words she spoke. "Without my being aware of what was to take place. In the middle of the night, or afternoon or whenever he was angry at some insignificant thing that he blamed me for. It didn't take much to turn his anger against me, to make me toe the mark, as he said."

"My God," Aaron said, the words as yearning as a prayer. "How could you live through such abuse and yet retain the innocence you wear?" He stood from his seat and rounded the table quickly, giving her no recourse but to rise as he tugged her hand and lifted her from her chair.

His arms circled her gently, his mouth touched her forehead with a whispering kiss and he bent low over her as if he would shield her from all harm, as though he ached to possess her and yet knew he had no right to her body—or her heart.

She was cradled against him, her arms around his waist, holding him tightly, even as he bent his head to whisper words of comfort against her ear. Outside, darkness had fallen, the night birds called from the trees in the yard, and as he reached for the lantern over the table, then blew the flame into oblivion, she felt the peace of his embrace infuse her with an emotion she could not describe.

Love? Perhaps. Yet she had not known him long enough to feel so deep a yearning, had she? How long did it take to recognize love for another human being? How quickly could a woman find love in a man's arms, even knowing that there was no future for herself with him?

Aaron led her from the parlor, through the

doorway and into his bedroom, taking her without words, without explanation, to where his wide bed awaited them. There he placed her on the mattress, eased her shoes from her feet and tugged a pillow beneath her head. Straightening, he looked down at her in the dim light from the window.

"I'm going to lie down beside you, Susannah. I don't want you to fear me, for I won't attempt to make love to you. I only want to hold you and sleep beside you tonight."

He waited for a reply, as if he must be given permission for what he had offered her, and she could not find it in her heart to deny his need.

Her arms lifted to him and she smiled, her lips trembling, her abject need for his presence surely obvious to the man. It seemed she was able to deliver her message, albeit silently, for he sat on the edge of the bed and tugged off his boots, wincing as he felt the pain of flesh pulled taut, of stitches strained to their limit. Then he turned to lie beside her, knowing that physically he would not be able to claim her as his own, that he was not capable of more than sleep tonight.

His arm found its place beneath her head and his other hand turned her to face him, allowing whatever distance she should choose to remain between them. But she could not remain apart from him and nestled closer, inviting his arms to enclose her. And enclose her they did, for with a sigh of thanksgiving, he fit her to himself and held her as though she were a priceless bit of crystal, a valuable possession to be cherished.

"Sleep, Susannah," he said softly, his head bending to allow him access to her face. His lips spent a hundred kisses across her brow, on her cheek and then beneath her ear where the warmth of her life's blood flowed and beat in an unceasing measure. "Nothing will harm you here," he murmured and then simply held her close as she slipped into a deep, dreamless sleep.

Nothing will harm you here. Only a man who is sworn to betray you, should he find evidence that would brand your story as an untruth.

CHAPTER FIVE

"I'M ALL WRINKLED," she said crossly, brushing at her dress. It was morning, and she'd wakened in his arms, looked through sleepy eyes to find him watching her, only inches separating their faces. Quickly, before he could hold her to himself, she slid to the edge of the mattress and arose, looking down at the dress that had been used as a sleeping garment.

"I'll fix some breakfast, and then change my clothes," she decided aloud, and he nodded his agreement, even as a smile chased across his face, his amusement at her flustered condition all too apparent.

She sailed through the doorway, and he was left alone to consider the night just past. It had been uncomfortable at best, he decided, sleeping next to a woman he wanted with every fiber of his being. He'd been careful not to press her closely against himself, lest she recognize his arousal and thus fear his need of her. Now, he arose just moments after she reached the kitchen, listening as she clanged the lid atop the stove, recognizing the sound of wood being added to the fire he'd carefully banked just hours past.

The lid clanged back in place and he heard the oven door open, knew the sound of his skillet being lifted from within and then placed on the top of the range. Her footsteps crossed the kitchen and he knew she headed for his pantry where hung the slab of bacon she'd purchased from the Emporium.

Recognizing that it was too heavy for her to lift down from the meat hook, he quickly rolled from the bed and headed for the door. "I'll lift the bacon down for you, Susannah," he called out. "Wait for me to do it."

She had turned to face him as he strode in the kitchen door, her eyes wide with amazement and her hands propped on her hips. "How did you know I—"

"I heard you cross the kitchen floor and I knew you'd put the skillet on to heat already." His explanation was firm and logical and she stepped aside as he neared the pantry door. With a quick lifting of his arm, he grasped the bacon slab and brought it into the kitchen. "Where do you want this?" he asked, holding it before himself.

"On the sink board," she said quickly, reaching in the kitchen dresser drawer for a long knife. "Are you sure you didn't strain your shoulder, doing that?" she asked, eyeing him closely.

And though he felt a pinching pain, there on his other arm where the bandage covered his wound, he shook his head. "I'm fine."

He placed the bacon where she'd directed him and sat down at the table, watching as she honed the knife on a crock before she tackled the bacon. It sliced neatly through the meat, and in moments she had filled the skillet with eight slices. Immediately, it began to sizzle and she snatched up a fork from the drawer, ready to turn it as it browned.

AARON HAD EATEN WELL, then pushed his plate to one side, watching Susannah as she rose to carry their dishes to the sink. She filled the dishpan with water from the stove's reservoir and then turned to him, as though she felt the intensity of his gaze.

"What are your plans for the day?" she asked, glancing at him as she tossed a dish towel over her shoulder. "In my opinion, I think you need to rest a bit after the walk to town yesterday. You're pushing yourself too much."

"Is that your professional opinion? Or are you trying to rid yourself of my presence, suggesting I spend the morning in bed."

"I can only speak as your nurse. When you exert yourself to the limit, as you did yesterday, you have to make up for it by pampering your body, allowing it to recuperate."

"So my morning will be spent in bed?" he asked, as if he would not argue with her.

She nodded firmly. "The doctor should be coming by today to take those stitches out of your shoulder. And that's going to take a lot of starch out of you, if I know anything at all about it."

She turned to him, frowning as if she were getting her day in order and sorting out her chores in her mind. "I'll have enough to do, cleaning up the kitchen, then fixing your dinner and sweeping the floors, without worrying about you getting into trouble. I thought I might take a good look at your garden and see what's available to add to your supper later on."

"The tomatoes are ripening, I believe," he said, his tone just a bit prideful, as if his gardening skills were worth bragging about. "You'll find that the green beans should be ready to pick. The first planting is doing nicely, and the second will be ready in two weeks or so."

He watched as a smile twitched at her lips.

"I'll be sure to appreciate your hard work while I'm picking the beans."

"And I'll appreciate yours while I smell them cooking," he answered politely, his eyes feasting on her as she moved about his kitchen.

She made short work of the dishwashing chore and wiped the oilcloth-covered table with quick sweeps of her cloth. "You about done with that coffee?" she asked as he lifted his cup a final time to his lips.

"It's empty," he told her. And as she hesitated, looking at the pot on the iron range, he spoke quickly. "I've had enough for now, Susannah. I'm off to my bed." He rose, pushed his chair beneath the edge of the table and grinned at her as she watched him. "Want to join me?"

His cocky attitude had the desired result as she flushed and shook her head quickly. "I think you're mocking me, McBain. I'd appreciate it if you were more circumspect in your behavior."

"Wow, that's quite a mouthful," he said, laughing a bit. "I was only hoping you'd keep me company during my nap. Maybe sit beside the bed and talk to me till I go to sleep."

"I thought I'd made it plain that I have work to do, if I'm to earn the money you've promised me."

He grimaced a bit. "I'll leave you to your work, Susannah. And you may take your wages from the wallet in my desk. Just figure out your usual pay from the hospital and double it for the time you've been with me. I don't want to take a chance on rousing your anger and hearing you threaten to leave me."

"Doubling my pay won't be necessary," she said stiffly, as if his words had surprised her.

"It's necessary to me. I expected to pay well for the privilege of having a private nurse at my disposal."

A knock at the door startled them both and Susannah quickly left the kitchen, crossing the parlor to the front door where the doctor waited.

"Come in," she said, stepping back to allow him room to enter the house. "The sheriff is waiting for you."

"I thought I'd stop by on my way to the hospital," the young doctor told her. "I hoped you'd remember that this was the day to remove those sutures."

Dr. Grissom approached McBain, who watched him warily. "Is this gonna be as painful as it sounds?" he asked as the doctor opened the small black bag he carried.

"Just a pinch when I pull the thread out."

"Multiplied by how many?" McBain asked dryly.

"You've only got eight or ten stitches there." The doctor adjusted his spectacles as he began the task of unwrapping McBain's shoulder.

"I see your nurse has kept this clean as a whistle," he said, looking down at the area with approval.

His hands were gentle as he slid the scissor blade beneath the silk thread he'd used to sew up

McBain's flesh and clipped the first suture. With a pair of long tweezers, he pulled the silk from its place and continued on to the next.

"You're very brave, Sheriff," Susannah said, her voice a teasing sound in his ears as the wound was freed from the thread that had bound it together. McBain looked around at his shoulder, craning his neck to better observe the doctor's work.

"That's what they pay me for, ma'am," he returned smartly.

"Well, you won't be so spry when I have to clean that up good with carbolic salve," she told him. "It might burn a bit."

He shot her a look that promised retribution. "I'm sure I can handle whatever you send my way, Nurse Whitfield."

Susannah grinned, opening her own bag to retrieve the salve and fresh bandages. By the time she'd finished her work, Dr. Grissom had taken his leave and she was once more alone with the sheriff.

"That wasn't so bad, was it?" she asked him, inspecting her bandage and deeming it passable.

He shook his head. "I told you I heal fast. In another week, you'll never even know I was wounded." He rose then and began buttoning his shirt, allowing it to hang free of his trousers.

"I'm going in to lie down for a while. I'll take your advice, ma'am, and spend an hour in bed."

She nodded her head in acquiescence and watched as he left the kitchen. He'd made it quite simple for her, she decided. He'd told her to take her wages from his wallet, and she'd do that very thing.

Accepting her pay from him, she would have sufficient money to catch a train to the west. Or perhaps she might rent a horse from the livery stable and ride north to where the Wyoming border promised a hiding place, should he come after her.

The country she considered escaping to was riddled with small canyons, a town or two in which she might find shelter, and the promise of employment if she found a likely spot to tarry.

She waited until the silence from the bedroom told her he had found his place on the comfortable mattress and pulled the quilt over himself. Waiting long enough for his weary body to settle down and his active mind to slow its paces long enough to sleep, she finished her chores and went to his desk.

The wallet remained untouched where she had replaced it after taking enough for his supplies. Now she counted out a sufficient amount to pay herself for the days spent in his company, and doing as he'd bid her, she doubled the bills in her pocket. Guilt assailed her as she considered what she was about to do to the man, but her sensible mind told her she had no choice. If she were to escape his hold on her, it must be now.

But first she felt a need to provide for him, to make him a meal for the late afternoon, when she would not be here to provide him the nourishment his healing body required. The beans were ready to pick, as he had said, and in minutes, she had gathered a full pot of them. Sitting on the back stoop, she snapped them, removing the stems and filling his largest kettle with the results of her work.

Returning to the kitchen, she put the beans into the basin, covered them with water and rinsed them clean. Locating the bacon grease she'd kept aside in a crock, she poured a generous amount into the kettle, sliced up an onion into the sizzling grease and cooked it till the onion slices were transparent. The basin of beans was added quickly, enough water to cover them included, and the kettle was pushed to the back of the stove to simmer. A piece of ham hock she'd purchased from the butcher would eventually cook from the bone, the meat flavoring the beans nicely, and the small whole potatoes she added to the simmering brew would complete the one-dish meal.

As the cook back home had said, "The longer you simmer it, the better." Hours over a slow heat would cook the beans to a fare-thee-well and provide McBain with a meal and some to spare.

Her guilt at leaving him in the lurch appeased somewhat, she gathered her belongings, sorted out the items she could get along without and packed the remainder into her valise.

A quick peek into the bedroom assured her that his sleep was deep and the window open far enough to ensure fresh air. He looked young, helpless almost, as he slept, one arm over his head. He'd removed his shirt and the white bandage on his shoulder marred the physical perfection of the man, making him seem vulnerable to her eye.

The urge to let him know she was leaving swept over her and she subdued it, knowing he would not allow her to go, would instead attempt to halt her departure, and in so doing might harm himself. The results of her care of him and the strength of the healed area where the doctor's stitches had been would not hold up should he battle with her.

As if the words were spoken aloud, she heard them in her mind. *I care for you...too much.* And leaving him was one of the hardest things she'd had to do; taking her last look at the man brought tears to her eyes.

The words echoed through her head. *I care for you.* Perhaps she should be honest and call the feelings she held for him by their proper name.

Instead she took a final look at the man she'd come to know during the past few days. Silently, she gathered up her belongings, her valise and the shawl that would take the place of a coat. Over her wrist, she slung the handle of the small bag that contained her money and a white cotton handkerchief, an item she knew she would be using to mop up the tears she was guaranteed to shed before the day was over.

The front door opened silently and she slipped from the house, hastening down the front walk to the road, where she stowed her valise behind the fence, out of sight of anyone who might pass by in the next little while. From there, she walked quickly to the end of town where the livery stable awaited her, her shawl draped over her shoulders, her pocketbook in hand.

The blacksmith who owned the business looked up as she approached and smiled admiringly. "Good afternoon, miss," he said nicely. "What can I do for you?"

"I need a horse to ride, or maybe a buggy might be better. I'm going visiting for the rest of the day." She pulled some coins from her pocket. "How much will it be?"

"I can rent you a buggy for today and tomorrow both for half a dollar, and that way you won't be obligated to return it tonight, in case you decide to stay over with your friends. I'll be leaving early today, and you probably won't be back till after I've gone home anyway. My wife's havin' company for supper and told me to be home before sundown."

Susannah lowered her eyes to the coins she held, pleased by his words. The fact that she wouldn't be returning the buggy tonight, or any other night, was a great deception. But in order to escape, she needed to have a day's travel under her belt before McBain should call up a posse to find her.

The blacksmith took the money she held, and she spoke hastily. "Keep fifty cents for a deposit and I'll collect it from you when I return your conveyance, sir."

He agreed readily and went inside his stable to find her the transport she required. In five minutes' time, she had climbed into the buggy and lifted the reins.

"You know how to handle that mare?" the blacksmith asked, watching her closely.

"I used to take my father's horses out daily in the park, back east. I can handle the reins."

"Yes, ma'am," he said agreeably, watching as she turned the buggy and headed back the way she had come, on the road that would eventually lead north, out of town. The horse he had been shoeing awaited his attention and he turned back to the forge, picking up the horseshoe he'd been forming and continuing his work.

The day was warm and Susannah removed her shawl, placing it on the seat beside her, then directed the mare toward the sheriff's house. She slid from the seat, collected her valise and tossed it on the back of the buggy, rapidly climbing once again to the high seat, where she picked up the reins and directed the mare north, heading out of town.

It was almost too easily accomplished, she thought, this escape she had set out upon without much forethought. Only the fact that she must separate herself from the lawman who was a threat to her freedom had allowed her to leave without sufficient planning. Where she would go and what she would do when she arrived at a destination were both questions she set aside to be answered later.

For now she had become a thief, absconding with a buggy she had no intention of returning to its owner, and should McBain follow her, he had one more reason to toss her into a cell. She shivered as she considered that idea, imagining the stark, barren cells behind his office in the jailhouse. They would no doubt contain the bare essentials, a cot, perhaps a rudimentary bucket for her to use when the occasion arose, and not much else.

Criminals were not pampered in such surroundings. And Susannah Carvel was a criminal, now on the run from two separate law-enforcement agencies.

AARON AWOKE SLOWLY, his body rested, his senses alert to the silence in his house. Susannah was cooking, for the appetizing aroma of bacon or ham whetted his appetite. Perhaps she'd picked green beans and was even now cooking them for his supper. He rolled carefully to the edge of the bed, sat up slowly, wincing as the pain in his shoulder seized his attention, and then stood, gripping the bedpost to gain his balance.

"Susannah?" He called her name and knew, even as he did so, that she was not in the house. A quality of silence, a premonition of unwelcome solitude, the absence of her presence—he felt each element surround him, knew with a jolt of fear that she had left.

That she had gone from this place and was not planning to return.

Entering the kitchen, he spotted the kettle on the back of the stove, steam rising from the contents and the source of cooking odors becoming readily apparent. He peered within the kettle and saw the results of Susannah's efforts. His garden was no doubt bereft of green beans, but his kitchen was filled with the aroma of the supper she had left for his benefit.

He closed his eyes for a moment, ruing her departure, knowing that he must begin a search for her, if only to fulfill his duties as a lawman. His tendencies as a man were to haul her back to his home and settle her to the extent that she would no longer be tempted to leave his presence. And how he would accomplish that, he had no idea.

Tying her to the bed came to mind as a viable option, but he sensibly set it aside and searched his mind for another route he might follow.

First, he had to find the woman, and that, in itself, was not an easy problem to solve. She wouldn't have tried to walk away, so she must have somehow found a conveyance of some sort. She probably possessed the ability to ride horseback, but that option didn't seem likely. Susannah would no doubt travel by train or, given the opportunity, by buggy. And the only likely spot for her to obtain that sort of vehicle was at the livery stable.

Aaron's gun belt was in the bedroom, his gun in the holster, bullets kept handy atop his chest of drawers. In moments, he had once more become the law in Ottawa Falls, garbed in dark trousers, his badge pinned to his vest, his gun at his right side. Pulling on his boots was a chore, but he persevered and in a few minutes was ready to take his leave.

But first, he pulled open his desk drawer, noting without surprise that his wallet lay where he'd left it and that it contained a good amount of cash. He'd known she would not steal him blind, had known she would only take what she had coming to her.

A quick stop in the kitchen earned him a loaf of

bread, already wrapped in a dish towel, and a hunk of cheese he'd left in the icebox. He looked down at the floor, where the ice had leaked out, melted into a puddle beneath his feet, and shrugged. Time enough to clean it up when he returned. He might even make Susannah do the chore, so aggravated was he by now.

His wallet went into his inside pocket, a clean handkerchief into his trouser's pocket, and his hat on his head. The front door was left unlocked, the beans still cooking on the stove, where the fire would burn itself out in a couple of hours. Maybe he'd be back by then, ready to eat his supper. And at that thought, he smiled dryly, knowing it would not be so.

The walk to the livery stable was short under ordinary circumstances, but today the road seemed long before him, the flaming forge and the blacksmith who manned it appearing as the light at the end of a dark tunnel. Stubbornly, Aaron continued on his way, wishing he had his horse beneath him instead of having to rely on his own noticeably weak legs.

"Hey there, Sheriff," Ellis Monroe hailed him as he approached the open forge, waving a long pair of pincers in greeting. "You lookin' for your horse? I thought you were all stove up, recuperating in bed from your wound. What you doin', wandering around town?"

"Looking for someone to saddle my horse, Ellis. I'm about to set out on a search."

The blacksmith peered at him thoughtfully and nodded. "Would this have anything to do with the young woman who left here about an hour ago with one of my buggies and a mare?"

"Which way did she head?" Aaron asked briefly, relieved to know that Susannah had at least had the good sense to rent a buggy instead of setting off afoot.

"Back towards your place. She stopped there for a minute or two and then set off again, headin' north, out of town."

"If you'll saddle my gelding, I'd appreciate it," Aaron told him.

"Would you do better to find a couple of fellas to ride with you, Sheriff? I kinda hate to see you ridin' off alone."

Aaron waved aside his doubts and headed for the interior of the stable. "I'll be fine. I've been lying around long enough. It's time to get out in the fresh air and get a little exercise."

Ellis followed him, passing him without haste and leading the black gelding from his stall. He halted long enough to pick up Aaron's saddle, then quickly tossed a saddle blanket over the gelding's back and put the saddle in place. The horse stood placidly, seeming to be a calm, orderly sort of creature, until Ellis fitted him out with bridle and bit.

Once the black felt the weight of the man who owned him atop his back, knew the hands that held his reins, he became another creature altogether. He pranced, his tail swishing impatiently, and his whinny rang out.

"Always amazes me how that horse knows you, Sheriff," Ellis said. "He acts like a sleepy slug standin' there in his stall, but once he sees you and feels you in his saddle, he's a different animal."

"He's just been resting up for a long ride," Aaron said with a laugh. He turned the gelding toward the wide open doors of the livery stable and rode him into the open. "Anybody wants to know, I've gone on a long ride," he said, casting a warning look at Ellis, a look the blacksmith seemed to understand.

"I understand, Sheriff. Lots of luck to you. She's not going to travel very fast with that buggy. You oughta catch up with her in an hour or so."

"Thanks, Ellis. I'll see you when I get back."

CHAPTER SIX

THE TRACKS IN THE DUSTY ROAD could have been from any number of wagons or buggies, several vehicles having obviously passed this way in the past hours. Riding to one side of the road, where the horse had better footing, Aaron kept the animal to a rocking lope, a gait that would cause the least amount of pressure on his shoulder. He was far from comfortable, but well rested, and knew he was capable of riding for hours in pursuit.

"Fool woman," he groused under his breath. "Don't know what she thought she'd accomplish by takin' off that way. She might have known I'd come after her. And by the time I catch up with her, this damn shoulder of mine will be poundin' like a son of a gun."

He rode rapidly, not as hard as he might have under other circumstances, but at a pace that would guarantee her capture, maybe by nightfall. "Hope she's got enough sense to stop somewhere for the night," he muttered. "Hell, she probably doesn't even know how to light a campfire."

And then he laughed at his own foolishness. Susannah was capable, had known exactly how to light the fire in the cooking range. A simple campfire wouldn't be beyond her ability to cope with. But he doubted she had food with her. If she got hungry enough, she'd be happy to share his supplies. Bread and cheese wasn't much, but it sure beat going hungry.

It was almost nightfall when he spotted a buggy about a quarter mile ahead. Even as he watched, the vehicle pulled off to the side of the road and a woman climbed down from the seat. She looked neither right nor left, only walked to the mare's head and led her into a grove of trees.

Aaron turned his gelding toward the grass that grew along the road, seeking shelter amid the trees, lest Susannah turn and look back to where he rode. He was within fifty feet of the buggy when he halted and leaned on his saddle horn, seeking her whereabouts. She'd taken the bit and bridle from the mare, replacing them with a rope around the animal's neck, then had tied the rope to a large tree. Grass grew deep around the area, and the mare was knee-deep in her evening meal, barely looking up as Aaron approached.

Beyond the animal, kneeling on the ground,

Susannah was up to her elbows in her valise. Whether a flicker caught her eye or she heard his approach, she looked up to where he stood, her eyes wide and startled, her complexion pale in the fading light.

"McBain." She spoke only his name, and he came closer, standing over her as might a man who had finally found his prey.

"Would you like to tell me why the hell you left?" he asked, attempting to hold his voice to a dull roar.

She winced and looked away, but he would not allow it, bending to grip her chin, tilting her face up in order to peer into her eyes. His hand was harsh against her skin, perhaps because of his anger, and she flinched visibly beneath his touch. But he was adamant, holding her thus, bending to speak his query again.

"Why, Susannah? Why did you leave me that way? Didn't you know I'd follow you?"

She shook her head, an almost imperceptible movement. "I'd hoped you'd let me go, McBain. I took nothing from you that didn't belong to me. I have money from your desk, but no more than you told me to take. I didn't even take food from your kitchen, and I was just wishing I had." She smiled, a movement of her mouth that touched him, so much did her lips tremble.

"I have some food with me," he told her. "I've even been known to share."

Susannah lowered her eyes, her chin still caught in his grasp. "I can miss a meal or two. I've done it before."

"No doubt. But you won't tonight," he said, his voice low, almost a growl in the lowering darkness. And she thought he sounded like a beast, angered by his betrayer.

That she fit the description was no comfort to her soul, for she knew he would somehow or another take his anger out on her. And for that she could not blame him. She'd betrayed him by leaving, had broken his trust and thereby deserved his anger.

"Have you a quilt or blanket in that bag?" he asked, releasing her from his grip. She nodded, digging deeper to the bottom of her valise where she'd long ago placed a light covering, should she need it on her journey.

She'd set off from Washington barely prepared for a journey, but had had the good sense to stop in Philadelphia for a small amount of clothing. Fitting what she could into the bag, she'd carried it during the long journey across the country to Colorado. Now, the quilt she'd thought to bring on this venture was pulled into view and she clutched it to her bosom.

"Spread it out on the ground," Aaron said

gruffly. "We'll sit on it for now and eat." Her fragile skin bore the marks of his fingers and he felt a rush of remorse that he should have marked her thus, and he reached for her face, tilting it to the side to catch the last light of day in the quickly darkening sky.

Whether she feared his presence or simply was too weary to make a fuss, she did not argue, but returned his scrutiny, then did as he'd directed, settling on one corner of the quilt, as far from him as could be accomplished. Her shawl was once more pulled over her shoulders, the evening turning a bit chilly, since the sun had found its place below the horizon.

"I'm really not awfully hungry," she said softly.

"I'll bet you're wishing you had a bowl of those beans you left cooking," he told her, lifting a brow as he watched her shrink into the shawl and pull her dress down over her raised knees.

She nodded. "I've thought of them several times over the past hours. Why didn't you stay there long enough to have a bowl yourself instead of coming after me?"

"You're more important than the whole damn kettle. I knew I had to catch up with you by night, or you'd be in a peck of trouble on your own."

"I've been on my own for a long time. I don't need anyone to look after me."

"No?" He looked as if that were a debatable subject, she thought, his frown registering his doubt of her ability to survive on her own. "And what would you have done if some bunch of scallywags had shown up and made themselves at home?"

She shook her head, knowing she could not come up with an answer that would satisfy him.

"Don't you know what can happen to a woman alone out here in the wilderness?"

"No, but I'm sure I'm about to find out," she said, turning her gaze from him.

He dropped to squat beside her. "I thought you had better sense, Susannah, than to think I'd hurt you. I told you I'd help you, that I'd take care of you. Didn't you believe me?"

She was silent, recalling his solution to the problem, and then spoke cautiously, choosing her words with care. "I didn't think that marriage would be a good idea, and you seemed set on the idea." *Marriage is a trap.* The words swam in her mind and she feared for a moment that she had spit them in his direction. And perhaps she should speak them aloud, for they were surely lodged in her mind, along with the experiences that made her doubt any man's integrity.

"I don't know where you got the idea that I would want to fall into another marriage, Aaron," she said quietly, fearful of hurting him, knowing that he felt affection for her. "I've lived with a man, lived with the fear of his strength, and spent my tears night after night, dreading what he might do to me next." She looked up at him, aware of his silence, his look of confusion.

"I'm not accusing you of being that sort of person, Aaron, only telling you that it will take much to turn me into a wife again. I don't know why you thought I'd agree."

"It was the only thing I could come up with on the spur of the moment," he admitted. "And I still think it would work. I'm not a man like the senator, but I don't have any way of convincing you of that."

He bowed his head as if he could not longer look into her gaze. "You sure can't run around the country by yourself, girl. You're asking for trouble. I want to take care of you and keep you safe. In order to do that, I'll have to marry you and make you legally mine."

As though another thought entered his mind, he met her gaze once more, his voice harsh, his demeanor more demanding. "And by the way, what were you planning on doing with the buggy you rented from Ellis? He's gonna figure out right quick that you're not bringing it back, and then what will he do?"

"Well, he can't tell the sheriff about it, that's for sure," she said, her words snippy and sarcastic. "My hero has chased me down, it seems, and left the whole town of Ottawa Falls without protection from the bad guys."

"You've got a smart mouth. Did anyone ever tell you that?" he asked, reaching to touch the lips that would not remain silent, even as a chuckle broke through and gave notice of his amusement.

"I've gotten into trouble over it, more than once," she told him, thinking back to occasions she'd tried hard to put into the past.

His frown darkened his visage, as if he caught her meaning. "I'm sorry, sweetheart. I think I shouldn't have reminded you," he told her, taking the loaf of bread and the packet of cheese from his saddlebag and placing the repast between them on the quilt.

The offer to partake of the sparse rations he'd brought along was tempting. Susannah unwrapped the bread, thankful that she'd sliced it before putting it away earlier in the day, and shot him a grateful look. The cheese was in a large chunk, but he rectified that in short order, using the knife he carried to cut it into smaller bits and pieces.

"Now tell me you're not hungry," he said, taunting her gently as she felt saliva fill her mouth.

"I'm not hungry," she said obediently and then smiled a bit, making a lie of it when she picked up a piece of the cheese and took his knife from him to cut a thick slab of bread in half. He took possession of his weapon when she'd finished and sheathed it quickly.

"Afraid I'll use it on you?" she asked smartly.

"No, that's the least of my worries. Anyone who took such good care of a wounded man as you did wouldn't be about to inflict more damage unless there was no way out of it. And trust me, Susannah, I'll not give you reason to stab me."

"I couldn't do that anyway," she said quietly, picking up a piece of bread and tearing off a bite-sized piece. She glanced up at him, realizing as she did so that night was falling rapidly, for his features were almost hidden in the shadows. "Thank you for the food. I lied when I told you I wasn't hungry."

"I know," he answered, biting into a chunk of cheese, holding her gaze with his own.

She watched him, her eyes seeking out the signs of weariness she knew he must be doing his best to conceal. "You should be home, resting. I'm sorry you felt you had to follow me, McBain. I'm just not sure you came after me because you're a lawman or because you—"

His words cut her short. "You know why I came after you, Susannah. And being a lawman hasn't much to do with it right now. I don't want anything to happen to you. I'm here to look after you, till we come to some sort of agreement."

She stifled a sob, blinked back tears that threatened to fall, grateful for the darkness that hid her from his scrutiny. The man was impossible. He was concerned about her safety; his own welfare had been put into limbo while he followed her all afternoon and evening, and now he spoke of an agreement they should make. A way to keep her safe. And for a moment, she wondered just how *safe* she was with him.

"I'm taking you home, Susannah. We'll go back to Ottawa Falls, and then decide our next move. But know this, what we do will be as man and wife. You will marry me, since traveling with you requires it. Otherwise, we'll travel as lawman and prisoner, and I don't want to do that."

"You aren't giving me much choice, are you, Mr. Lawman?" Her words were biting, her jaw firm and set as she faced him across the blanket.

"I can't afford to. I want the privileges of a husband, Susannah. I won't settle for less, and let me tell you, girl, you owe me that much."

"I don't see how you figure that," she told him, belligerence in every word.

"I'm willing to put my reputation on the line for you. I'll be leaving a job I enjoy, a town where I'm known and respected, all to save your neck and get you cleared of charges. For that, you owe me."

"You don't have to do any such thing. Just let me go. Let some other lawman find me someday. That leaves you off the hook, and you can stay right here in your nice safe job in Ottawa Falls. I won't be around to disturb the peace or give you grief."

His hands moved swiftly, and she stood no chance of retreat. He turned her beneath him, sprawling across her on the quilt, his heavy body holding her down, his fingers gripping tightly to her shoulders as he bent to her.

"You've been giving me grief since the day I met you, Susannah. I've been like a randy kid, wanting to touch you, needing to put you in my bed, wanting you in my life. The list goes on, and I'm not proud of the power of my need for you. I should be able to be neat and tidy about this, place you in a compartment and label you as a criminal, and then treat you as such."

Aaron shook his head, allowing his mouth to touch hers, as if he required the sustenance of her kiss to continue his tirade.

It was a merging he had not expected, for he'd been dead certain that she would not give in gracefully to his advances. Instead, her lips softened beneath his and her body melted into his larger, harder frame, as if she were meant for just such a blending. A sound of pain was born in her throat and touched his lips, a cry of need such as he'd never heard from her.

"Susannah? Have I hurt you?" He lifted his head and watched in the ghostly light of the full moon as her eyes opened to meet his. Overflowing with tears, they shimmered like the stars that gathered overhead to watch.

"No." It was a definitive answer, leaving no doubt she was far from angry, relieving his mind from the fear of having caused her physical pain. "You've never hurt me, McBain. I know what it is to fear a man, and though I live daily with that memory, I can't find it in me to dread your touch or be repelled by you in any way." She inhaled sharply, a shivering breath that seemed to give her strength, for she freed her arms from his hold and lifted her hands to meet at the nape of his neck.

"I wish I could say that I don't want to be with you, Sheriff," she whispered, "but I'm not that good a liar. I fear you'd see past my fabrication too easily, so I won't even attempt to tell you that you're not what I want in my future."

"And is there desire in your feelings for me, Susannah?" he asked, his heart beating double time, it seemed, so great was his joy at her words. "Will you marry me and trust me to take care of you?"

"Ask me again in a week or so," she answered. "I won't give you an answer now. I don't know if I'm capable of making such a decision. Not with you lying over me, and the darkness around us sheltering us from the rest of the world. Not when I yearn so badly for the feel of your body against mine, your skin touching my breasts and your kisses giving me the pleasure I crave."

His hand measured the width of her chest, his fingers resting lightly on her breast. The palm of his hand cupped the soft flesh and he held it within his grasp with care, as if he possessed a treasure beyond price. A soft groan rose from his chest and was buried against the fabric of her dress as he bent low to brush his cheek tenderly against the firm rounding of her bosom.

"Have you ever known pleasure in the act of loving?" He lifted his head from her for a moment and spoke softly, asking the question without hesitation, and then wished fervently that he might recall it as he felt her retreat from him.

"Don't make me give you chapter and verse of my marriage. Not now, McBain. Later, I may be able to confide in you to that extent, but not now. I feel exposed and...perhaps *afraid* is the best word."

"Afraid of me?" he asked quietly. "Fearful of my touch on you?"

"You know better," she said quickly. "Perhaps it's my past I fear, for sure I hate to admit how cowardly I was, remaining married to a man who abused me, a man who never cared for my comfort or satisfaction in the marriage bed." She bit her lip, as if holding back words that begged to be spoken. "I lost a child because of John's cruelty. My baby was born dead and his father was glad of it."

"What did he do to you?" As though he had the right, his words were a demand.

"He forced me to bed with him, kicked me in the belly when I wouldn't give in." She sobbed quietly, her memories crowding around and smothering her. "He said I was fat and ugly and he hadn't bargained for a baby. He needed me to help further his career and no one was interested in seeing a woman with a big belly, attending parties and going out in public."

She whispered her pain and he bent closer to hear the words she offered. "I was afraid to tell the doctors about his beating me, the scandal would have been more than I could bear. And now I wonder why I was so frightened about a stupid thing like scandal."

"I think your fear went further than that, Susannah. You feared for your life if the true story was made known, didn't you?"

She stilled, like a fawn caught in lantern glow,

her eyes wide, her breathing fractured. "He threatened to kill me, more than once, if I didn't do as he demanded. He said my baby's death was my own fault, that I should have obeyed him."

"The sad part of it is that women don't have a lot of options in marriage. But I'll tell you this now, and then we'll not bring it up again until the proper time comes. You will find no fear in our bed, Susannah, only the pleasure that comes with a loving relationship between husband and wife. I can promise you that. I swear it, in fact. And should we make a baby between us, it will be loved and cherished by its father as well as you."

He held her close, his heartbeat vibrating against her own. "The thought of making a baby with you makes me ache, Susannah. I want all there is in marriage for us, all the joy and hope and love we can find. And the passion we'll find together."

"Is that what you want of me now? Passion? Tonight?" she asked, her mouth trembling as she asked the question that would leave her vulnerable to his greater strength and the force of his need. And if it was, what would she lose by acceding to his need? Certainly not her innocence.

"If you're not willing to wait, I'll understand, McBain." *Even though I fear what might come to be, between us.* Shamed by the thoughts that would not subside, the panic as she thought of what pain a man could bring to the marriage bed, she trembled beneath him.

He groaned, dropping his head to lie beside hers, his mouth touching the flesh beneath her ear, that fragile bit of skin that yearned for his breath against it. "Don't tempt me so, love. I'd like nothing better than to undress you right now and show you what our marriage will give you. But I won't do it. You deserve better than the hard ground beneath you when we make love. At least for the first time. It will be in a bed, between clean sheets, in a place where we have privacy and comfort, where I can spend a whole night making you mine."

"I don't know what to say." Her voice was broken and she sobbed beneath her breath.

Sorrow for the tears she shed brought pain to his heart, for he wanted only joy and happiness for her. But he feared that he could offer neither, not until he was able to free her from the fear of capture, from the stigma of appearing on a Wanted poster tacked to a thousand walls all over the country.

His hands brushed her breasts again, his fingers touching and testing the firm flesh beneath her clothing, and his warm breath penetrating the fine material of her bodice as he laid his face once more against the plush rise of her bosom. "I want to touch you properly, Susannah, without all the layers of fabric in my way. But I'll wait. I won't do anything to dishonor you, no matter how badly my body craves to be close to yours. No matter how dearly I would love to find all the soft, secret places nature has bestowed on you. It's enough for now that I've touched you, that my hands have known the sweet warmth you'll one day offer me as my bride. Until then, I'll do my best to be patient, until you're ready to be mine."

"Will we sleep here?" she asked softly. "Or will you force me into that buggy tonight and drag me back to Ottawa Falls as your prisoner?"

"We'll stay here and cover up with half of your quilt. That makes our bed rather small, but I can stand it if you can," he said, his smile visible through his words.

"You'll have ruined me by morning."

"And you think that worries me? You think I haven't already considered that?"

"I suspect you've considered this from the first. That you would somehow lead me to the place where I'd feel obligated to marry you. But I have no reputation to uphold, McBain. I lost it the day I walked into your house and then spent the night on your sofa. The whole town knows I've been living with you."

"You make that sound unsavory, somehow. As

if you've been sinned against, and I never intended that, Susannah."

"No, what you intended was that I would find myself in the position of either marrying you or branding myself as a fallen woman."

"If you're a fallen woman, I'll be happy to be the man who places you upon a pedestal, ma'am."

"I've never wanted that, McBain. I've only wanted to have a husband who would respect me and care about me."

"And you don't think I'll fill the order?"

She was silent for a long minute, and he tightened his grip on her, holding her closely to himself, as if he could somehow make her know his commitment was something she could rely on, that his intentions were of the most honorable sort.

"You'd be a good husband for the right woman. I just don't know if I'm that woman."

"Leave that part up to me," he said, the words rough-edged and spoken in a husky voice that made her shiver in his grasp.

"Now, close your eyes, sweetheart, and let me pull this quilt over you. I'll keep you warm," he promised softly. "And in the morning, we'll go home."

CHAPTER SEVEN

AARON DROVE THE BUGGY HOME, his horse tied to the rear, Susannah snuggled against his side. He felt encouraged by the time they'd spent together, felt he had forged a bond between them that could be built upon and made to grow. Susannah had given him more than he'd expected, much more than he'd dared to hope for. Her response to him was honest, her kisses and the warmth of her body beneath his had given him only a taste of what his future might hold, and he plotted silently as the mare headed back toward Ottawa Falls.

"I'll have to find someone to take my place for a few weeks," he said, planning aloud as he considered the days that would unfold into months before this thing had been seen to completion.

"Is there someone available?" She turned to seek his gaze, and he smiled as he nodded.

"I have a deputy already, and though he's not been called on to do a whole lot, he's a capable man. Walt Turner's his name, and he's holding the fort now while I've been lying around, being lazy. I'll talk to the mayor and see if there's a problem with asking Walt to take hold for a few weeks."

"Do we have to let the mayor know where you're going?"

"I don't see any way out of it," Aaron said slowly. "He'll need to be able to reach me should there be an emergency, but I don't have to give him a lot of details."

"When will you wire the law in Washington and let them know that you've taken me in custody?" She spoke the query stiffly, as if the words were painful, both to speak and hear aloud.

"As soon as I get back in town. There's something you need to know up front, Susannah. I'm not alone in this. I have a friend in the capital, a U.S. marshal. We'll have someone on our side, someone who has some influence, someone I trust. But in the meantime, we've got other fish to fry. First we've got to get this rig back to Ellis, so's he won't be thinking you've run off with his property."

"He said the money I gave him was good for two days, so there shouldn't be a problem."

"That's a relief," Aaron said with a grin. "I didn't want to toss you in a cell tonight while Ellis wrote up a complaint."

"Would you have? Tossed me in a cell, I mean?" Her eyes were wide with apprehension.

"I'd have stayed right there with you, sweetheart. Do you think I'd leave you to languish in the jail all by yourself while I trotted home to a nice soft bed?" He sighed and cut a sour look in her direction. "I wouldn't have a choice, Susannah. If Ellis had signed out a complaint against you, I'd have put you in a cell in a heartbeat. I'm sworn to uphold the law, like it or not."

"Well then, we'd better hope that Ellis is in a good mood when we show up, although I don't think he'll quibble about me keeping the rig overnight."

"I'll take care of it, Susannah. I'm just givin' you a hard time of it, makin' you think you'll end up in jail. I'd much rather have you home in my bed with me."

"That isn't going to happen, McBain. Not now, at least. We aren't married, and we may never be, so don't be counting your chickens."

"You're a killjoy, did you know that?" His eyes sent a message of laughter her way, Susannah decided, denying the words he spoke. "I only want to keep you where I can find you, any hour, day or night, and if that means you sleep in my bed, then, so be it."

He lifted the reins and slapped them lightly against the mare's back, spurring her into a lope, a pace that would find them back in town by noon.

"We're going to be the talk of the town, you

know. Riding in from who-knows-where in the middle of the day, just the two of us."

"Once we're married, they won't care about our little jaunt," he said with a chuckle. "And that's going to happen, quick as a wink."

"Quick as a wink?"

"Just as soon as we can get the preacher involved, and locate a couple of witnesses, we'll tie the knot. I don't want any grumbling from you about it, either. I'd just as soon make this official by tomorrow."

Susannah subsided into her corner of the seat, her brow furrowed as she considered his words. He'd not given her a choice, only told her what would happen, and she could not find a valid reason to argue with him. "Am I not to have a say in anything? You seem to have it all planned out, McBain, and I'm not sure I like it, not one little bit."

"Maybe I forgot to mention the main reason for this, Susannah. We're getting married so I can take care of you, keep you close to me without making you look like a woman of ill repute. I won't travel all over the country with you, with handcuffs keepin' us together. If that's the way you want it, I'll reconsider the whole thing, but trust me, you won't feel very comfortable looking like a prisoner onboard the train."

"I may not look like one, but a prisoner is exactly what I'll be. I have no guarantee that you'll not turn me over to the authorities in Washington and walk away. The reward might be well worth your while, after all."

"That's why you're going to marry me. I told you I can't testify against you if you're my wife, and... Aw, hell. You're not listening to me, Susannah."

"I suspect I'm a little bit in the dark here, McBain. I never thought I'd marry a man in order to save my neck from the hangman's noose. I had in mind a more—"

"A loving relationship?" he asked, cutting her off in the midst of her meandering.

She ducked her head, embarrassed to hear the words she had only considered in her mind, fearful of speaking them aloud. "Now that you mention it, a bit of feeling between husband and wife wouldn't be amiss."

"Oh, I have feelings for you, Susannah. I'm not gonna blurt them out right here and now, but give me a day or so and you'll be well aware of how I feel about you."

"A man can make love to most any woman, I understand, given the opportunity," she said. "I'd really like to think that there was more to it than that."

"You want me to tell you I love you?"

She shook her head. "Of course not. I don't want you to ever lie to me, McBain. Especially not about something as important as that."

"I care about you, sweetheart. You know that. I wouldn't be putting my reputation on the line if I didn't. I think we can have a good marriage, once all this claptrap is done with. After we prove your innocence and haul buggy back here, we'll have a nice ordinary marriage, just like half the other folks in town."

"I don't want a nice, ordinary marriage." She knew her words were harsh, her attitude stubborn, but the thought of living a lie with a man who might never come to love her was frightening. She'd already been down that road, and the marriage bed without any real element of affection being shared between husband and wife was not appealing to her.

"Then how about a hot and heavy romance between two people? No one would know but you and me, and I'll never give away any secrets."

"Now you're teasing me," she said, feeling the flush rise to cover her cheeks.

"Maybe. A little, anyway. But know this, Susannah. That wedding license is gonna give me the right to make love to you more than once a week or so."

"Do we have to talk about it?" Her eyes were

closed, her cheeks burned and she feared to look at him, not knowing what to expect next from the man.

It seemed he would take pity on her and his arm encircled her shoulders as he pulled her across the seat to settle close beside him. "No, we can wait till tomorrow night, sweetheart. I'll even blow out the candle before I come to bed."

"I'm afraid, McBain." The words were stark, a blunt warning of what was to be.

"I expected that. I can make promises till the cows come home, Susannah, but you'll have to just wait and see what happens. I don't expect you to believe me about this, but I'll do my best to make you happy to be my wife."

"When will we leave for Washington?" Her voice sounded weak and puny, she decided, certainly not that of a woman who was grimly determined to prove herself innocent. She cleared her throat. "I still don't like this whole thing, McBain. I keep thinking there must be another way around it, other than putting yourself into a marriage you had no intention of being involved in. You've only known me for a few days, and—"

"That's long enough to make up my mind about something as important as this," he said forcefully. "I knew when I opened my eyes in the hospital and saw you bending over me that I wanted you with me. I was willing to settle for your presence in my home while I recuperated then, but now I'm planning on a much longer relationship. I've never met a woman before who appealed to me the way you do. And I'm not letting you go, so just get over all your fussing about it. It's gonna happen."

THE KETTLE ON THE BACK of the stove was cold, and the beans were limp, an unappetizing mess, Susannah declared.

"No, I don't think so," Aaron said, lifting a stove lid to place short logs within. "We'll just get a fire going and heat things up. It was cool enough last night so we don't have to worry about the meat spoiling. Besides, the ham is smoked meat and isn't likely to spoil so quick. You'll see. It'll taste just fine."

Susannah only shook her head and went to the bedroom to change her clothes. She felt scruffy after sleeping in the same clothing she'd put on yesterday morning. If McBain wanted to eat day-old beans and ham, she'd not put up a fuss. There was still bread in the pantry and cans of peaches she could open for supper. He could eat his beans for dinner, since it was noontime and past, and she'd concentrate on the next meal to come down the pike.

A knock at the back door interrupted her thoughts and she hurried out to answer the summons. A lady stood on the stoop, and without being told, Susannah knew it was Hattie Cooper.

"Hello, there," Susannah said, swinging the door wide, the movement a subtle invitation for the lady to enter the kitchen. "You're Mrs. Cooper, aren't you?"

"*Miss* Cooper," Hattie said quickly. "Never found a good reason to give up my freedom for the sake of cleaning up after a man. Not that there aren't a few of them around that would probably be worth the effort." She peered beyond Susannah to where the doorway stood empty. "Where's the sheriff? Still abed after having that bullet dug out of him?"

"No, he's in the parlor, I believe," Susannah said. "I was just about to fix him some dinner."

"Well, don't let me stop you," Hattie said, pulling a chair from the table and seating herself. "I just ran on by to see if there's anything I can do to help out. They told me at the mercantile that you bought some of my butter, and I want you to know that from now on, I'll bring a bit by every week. The sheriff don't have to pay for butter so long as my churn works."

"Thank you," Susannah replied, taken aback by the lady's blunt attitude. "He'll be pleased to hear that, I'm sure. And so long as you're here, do you know anyone close by who bakes bread and might sell me a loaf or two?"

"I sell bread and cinnamon rolls out of my kitchen three days a week. No sense in going any further than that for whatever the sheriff needs."

"I'm not fully familiar with the town. Whereabouts do you live?"

"Next street over, toward the stores in town," Hattie said. "The old gray house that sits back from the road. There's always a calico cat or two in the yard. Can't miss the place."

The woman was friendly, Susannah thought, and beyond that was owed a debt for her straight shooting in the bank when McBain had been wounded. She spoke her mind quickly, wanting to express her own thanks.

"McBain tells me you saved his neck with your shooting ability. I surely appreciate it, Miss Cooper."

"He's got to you already, has he?" Hattie's eyes sparkled as she spoke. "He's a handsome one, he is. Lots of women in this town would like to get their hands on him, but he don't look around much." She tilted her head and her look was appraising. "I'll bet he's given you the once-over, hasn't he? Wouldn't be surprised if he took a real shine to you."

Susannah grinned. There was no helping it. The woman was irrepressible and right on target. "He seems to like me well enough," she said agreeably.

"Enough to marry the girl," Aaron said from the small hallway. He leaned on the doorjamb and grinned at Hattie Cooper. "Hey there, Miss Hattie. I'm sure glad to see you. I've been wanting to pick a bouquet of flowers and bring them by your place, but the only yard worth scalping is yours and I decided that toting your own flowers up to your doorstep wasn't the best idea I've ever had."

"You're a scamp," Hattie said, blushing at his words. "You can come pick my flowers anytime you want to, Sheriff. I'm just glad I had my gun loaded that day. Never thought I'd shoot a man with it, but it never hurts to be ready for anything. I feared I'd be upset about making the fella bleed like a stuck pig at first. But then I thought I'd rather see him bleed than you, and he'd already done the damage on your shoulder by then, so I didn't feel a bit sorry for the man."

"Well, you have my thanks, ma'am. You just keep that gun loaded and in your reticule. You never know when it'll come in handy." He grinned at her, his liking for the woman apparent, Susannah decided. "You're not interested in being a deputy, are you?"

"A woman? You want the town after me, McBain? Bad enough I shot a fella. If I was to be carrying one of them big guns like yours, they'd shun me, that's for sure. I'll bet you can find another deputy, should you need one, just by looking around a little. I'd say Walt Turner does a pretty decent job for you. You don't need but one deputy anyway, with a town as peaceful as this one."

"You're probably right," Aaron said with a sigh, "but I'd have enjoyed seeing you all togged out with a holster hanging down your side and a pair of britches on."

"McBain!" Susannah spoke his name with emphasis. "Don't be insulting Miss Hattie that way. She's not about to wear men's clothing no way, no how."

"He was just funnin' me, girl," Hattie said with a chuckle. "McBain's a good man, and we get along just fine." She looked back at Susannah. "I'll be going now, but I'll bring by some bread and rolls tomorrow, just like I said."

"We'll be taking a trip in a couple of days, Miss Hattie. If you'd like to keep an eye on the house while we're gone, I'd take it as a personal kindness. And I think Miss Susannah has a question she'd like to ask you, a favor, now that I think of it."

A favor. Her mind was blank, and then the grin McBain wore prompted Susannah's memory. "I'm going to need someone to be my witness for a wedding," she told Hattie. "Would you stand beside me while I speak my vows? I'd surely appreciate it."

Hattie blinked as if stunned by Susannah's words. "While you speak your vows?" And then she grinned. "Brave girl, you are."

"It's not as bad as all that," Aaron said, tossing Hattie a chiding look. "I don't want the woman to get away, so I've kinda rushed her into this. We'll be leaving for a couple of weeks right after the wedding."

"And that's why I'm going to be watching your place for you. I can do that, and I'd be pleased as punch to stand as witness for this pretty woman." She shot Aaron a look that might have stung, if she weren't possessed of such sparkling eyes and rosy cheeks. "You think you can find somebody who'll stand up for you, McBain? Got any friends here-abouts?"

"Yeah, I'll either ask Ellis down at the livery stable or my deputy, one or the other."

"What time you going to do the deed?" Hattie asked.

"I'll stop by the parsonage in the morning and see if we can make arrangements for a wedding on short notice," Aaron said. "Susannah needs to stop by the Mercantile and find a new dress to wear and then we'll see when the preacher has time for us."

"You ought to let some of the townsfolk know about it, Sheriff," Hattie said. "They'd sure enough like to be there to give you their blessings."

Susannah looked doubtful at that, but Aaron seemed to be considering the idea.

"Might not be a bad thing at that," he said slowly. "The folks hereabouts have been good to me. I'd hate to have them think I didn't want to include them in our wedding." He turned to Susannah hopefully.

"What do you think, sweetheart? Can we give it a day or so and let folks know what's gonna happen?"

One glimpse of the smile on Hattie's face made up Susannah's mind. "I might as well get in good with the neighbors right off," she said. "Let's talk about Friday afternoon. What do you think, Hattie? Will that give us enough time for a wedding and a short reception?"

"Sure beats you gettin' hitched and then running off together. The folks hereabouts will appreciate being let in on the celebration. They think a lot of our sheriff."

"Well, that's settled then," McBain said with a sigh, as if he were pleased to have the decision made. "Let's say on Friday then. Just about dinnertime, probably about one o'clock. The afternoon train leaves for St. Louis at five, so we'll have to do some fancy footwork to get ourselves to the station by then."

"I'd think we better reserve the dining room at the hotel for the reception," Hattie said. "You'll want to have punch and sandwiches for folks who come to the wedding. They won't like it if you just make tracks for the train station when they're all set to celebrate."

And so it was that the women in the general store were told the next day of the coming wedding. Susannah blushed when the storekeeper showed her the available dresses she might choose from, turned even pinker when his wife brought out an assortment of nightgowns that ranged from staid flannel to wispy bits of lawn and batiste.

With a grin, Hattie chose one of the latter, a pink confection with lace and ribbons decorating the front bodice, a long gown with little substance to the fabric. In fact, Susannah had a vision of McBain peering through it as if it were but a pane of glass, so delicate was the shimmering material.

She took the bundle in one hand, her dress and new petticoat and the nightgown Hattie had convinced her was perfect. The ladies who gathered around her in the store were friendly, curious and they seemed more than ready to see their sheriff married. They looked her up and down, and their eyes told her that they deemed her suitable for the illustrious man who kept law and order in their town.

In fact, by the time the ordeal was at an end and Hattie and Susannah were walking home, they had both resigned themselves to a festive occasion, not

at all like the quiet affair Susannah had thought the
wedding would be.

A stop at the hotel guaranteed them the use of the
restaurant on Friday afternoon, and Susannah
ordered an assortment of sandwiches and fruit to be
a part of the buffet table. The hotel owner told her
he would see to it that they had a punch bowl that
would have no bottom, and one of his girls would
see to serving it to all the folks who attended the
party.

Later that evening, she settled down in the parlor
with Aaron, letting him know the cost of the party
and all that the hotel owner had offered.

"How much was your dress?" Aaron asked as
her words came to a halt.

"I bought it," she told him. "Along with new
underwear and a nightgown."

Her face flushed as she spoke the words and he
laughed aloud. "I can't believe you're blushing
because you bought a new nightie. You probably
won't be wearing it for long, anyway. And why am
I not being allowed to pay for your things?"

"You'll be stuck paying for me for the next forty
or fifty years. But until the day of the wedding, I'm
still my own woman, and I can manage to buy my
own things."

"You're taking the fun out of it. I'll just have to
go into the general store when we come back. Or

maybe we'll stop at a large store in St. Louis and I'll get you some fancy duds there. I'm looking forward to dressing you, Miss Whitfield. I want you in some bright colors and pretty prints."

"I tend to stick with dark tones, blues and grays."

"Not when you marry me, you won't. I want to show you off, and the best way to do it is to tog you out in bright colors and pretty styles. I'm marrying a beautiful woman and I'm planning on dressing you up in fine style."

"I've had beautiful clothing in my life, and I found that it didn't make me happy. Living with you, in this house, is almost guaranteed to give me a wonderful life, McBain. I can't ask for more than that. Fancy things aren't important to me. Money is only good so long as it's used to buy the things we need. Beyond that, I have no use of it."

"You're a rare woman, sweetheart," he told her, rising from his chair and making his way to where she sat, looking up at him.

His hands were warm on her waist as he drew her into his arms, and he held her close, as though he could not stand any space between their bodies. "I want you next to me for the rest of my life," he said, bending to her and whispering the words in her ear. His mouth coaxed her, his hands beguiled her and he reached to the light, blowing out the flame before he led her to the bedroom, where she changed his bandage, applying the plaster with deft fingers and gentle hands. When she finished, she sat on the bed.

"I'll have no reputation left at all," she said, watching him as he knelt before her, sliding her shoes off and then pulling back the sheet and quilt, fluffing her pillow and offering her a space in his bed.

"We'll be married before folks have time to start talking about us. Just three more days and we'll be Mr. and Mrs. McBain, and it's gonna be a long three days, let me tell you, love."

She removed her dress and lay down on the mattress in her petticoat and shift, pulling the bedding up over herself. McBain slid from his shoes and stockings, and made his bed on top of the quilt, drawing an extra cover from the closet over himself as he settled down near her.

"I'm removing myself from temptation," he said with a grin. "I figure being under the covers with you would be asking for trouble, so I'll stay right here and behave myself for the next three nights. Then you'll be all mine, Susannah. I'll have to dream about you, I suspect, because holding you in my arms will be awfully tempting."

"You can keep my back warm. I'm not worried about you losing your famous self-control. Just lie down there and curl up behind me. We've slept this way before."

He did as she'd asked and sighed contentedly as his arm slid around her. "So we have, sweetheart. And it was almost as hard that night to leave you alone as it is tonight."

"I'll bet this town has never had such a scandal as we've tossed them. I'm surprised they even look me in the eye. The ladies in the Emporium were kind, very friendly in fact. I was a little afraid they'd give me the cold shoulder, staying in your house and all."

"Once they heard we were going to be married, it probably made all the difference in the world. A few words spoken by the preacher will turn you into an eminently respectable woman, Susannah. Just wait and see."

THEY SLEPT WELL, AND WOKE early, hearing Hattie in the kitchen, the stove lids clanking and the smell of the fire being coaxed into flames.

McBain was on his feet in seconds, donning his shoes and pulling a clean shirt from the dresser drawer. He looked back at Susannah. "I'll be out back for a bit. You'll have privacy to get dressed without me hanging around." With a grin, he was gone, and she arose slowly, reaching for her wrapper.

Hattie looked up as she entered the kitchen. "I

figured McBain would rise and shine when he smelled the coffee boiling. I've got the biscuits in the oven and the sausage ready to cook for gravy. Anything else you'd rather have?"

"I'm not about to complain, not when you're being so efficient, Hattie. I just want McBain to take it easy for the next day or so. He thinks he's all healed up and ready to go full tilt. Being gone for a week or so will be good for him, make him take things slow."

The back door opened and McBain shot a quick look at Susannah. "The grass is wet out there. Your shoes will get damp if you don't stay on the path."

"I'll be right back," she told Hattie, then made her way off the back porch toward the outhouse. McBain had planted morning glories on the eastern wall and they wove their way over long strings he'd tied to the roof and then allowed to stretch to pegs in the ground. It gave the bare wooden building a charm it did not deserve, yet provided a bright spot in the yard.

Completing her early morning duties, she wandered back into the house, washing up at the sink, and then setting the table as Hattie brought a bowl of sausage gravy from the stove, along with the pan of biscuits. Coffee was poured into their cups and the three of them sat down together, comfortable with their own company.

"I've got a number of things to do at the office today," McBain said, cleaning up his gravy with half a biscuit and then drinking the last of his coffee.

"Don't be rushing around," Susannah called after him as he left the kitchen, heading for the front door. "I don't want you to be messing up your shoulder."

"You're nagging him already," Hattie said with a laugh. "You'll make a fine wife for the man, girl." She sobered and cast a long look at Susannah. "I don't know just who you are or where you hail from, but I don't blame McBain for staking his claim on you, young'un. He needs a woman to keep him clean and well fed, not to mention a girl who'll love him and have his babies one day."

"You're making me blush, Miss Hattie," Susannah said, protesting the woman's words. "I just happen to be available and I think the sheriff thinks it's time to have a wife in his home."

"There's more to it than that. I don't know what his reasons are altogether, but I'll guarantee you he's champing at the bit to get you well married and in his bed."

"Now I'm really blushing," Susannah said, flustered by Hattie's remarks.

"No need to. Good loving's a part of marriage, and I'll warrant that Aaron McBain is a prime candidate for the job of husband. He's a good man, girl, and he'll give you lots of pretty babies one day.

"Now, I think I'd better be on my way," Hattie said, "afore you get any pinker in the cheeks. I've about wore out my welcome, I fear."

"Never," Susannah told her, reaching out to hug the diminutive woman. Spare and slender, Hattie Cooper might have been getting on in years, but she was agile and spry, and on top of that, she was the hero of the town, should anyone ask Susannah her opinion.

The kitchen was quiet without Miss Hattie's dry humor, but Susannah had much to do in preparation for McBain's dinner. The kettle of soup she'd made was heating up nicely, the bread ready to take from the oven, and she added a handful of coffee to the pot, along with the requisite pinch of salt. Bustling around the room, she felt more than ever a housewife, setting the table for their meal. The soup was about done, only needing to be dished up, when she heard him come in the front door. His first request would be for coffee, she'd be willing to warrant.

And sure enough, he tipped his head in the direction of the stove as he took his seat five minutes later. "Any coffee in that pot? I can get along without, but it sure would taste good if you've got some made."

"Can't you smell it?" Susannah asked, carrying the pot and a pair of cups to the table.

"Yeah, I guess I can. I was just too busy, sniffing you and that pretty soap you use."

"You've smelled it before."

"I know. It just about did me in, the other night when I was layin' on top of you and investigating the side of your neck, there by the side of the road."

"Is that what you were doing?"

"No, not entirely. I was doing my best to investigate all the parts of you that weren't covered up with clothes."

She darted him a censuring look. "You managed to do that all right. And some parts that *were* covered up, too."

"I wasn't going to mention that, but since you brought it up, I'll just elaborate on it a bit."

"Oh, no, you won't," she said, lifting the coffee-pot she held in a threatening gesture.

He smiled at her, an arrangement of his mouth that brought a small dimple into being on his right cheek. "Do you think I'd insult you, Susannah? I thought I'd be allowed to tease you while we're alone in our own kitchen. And I wouldn't do anything to embarrass you."

"Liar." She spoke the single word with a flourish of her coffeepot, sweeping it high over his cup to pour the dark brew into it. "You've already embarrassed me a couple of times. Just talking the way you are right now is enough to make me turn red, and you know it."

"But not in front of anyone else, Susannah. I'd never cause you to be ashamed of me in front of others. And should I deliberately cause you pain in company, I hope you'll have the good sense to bash me over the head with whatever's handy."

"You mean, like the coffeepot?" she asked mildly, pouring her own cup full and returning the pot to the stove.

"Preferably some item that isn't filled with hot liquid," he said, revising his stand. "Maybe a pillow or some such thing."

"You'd like that wouldn't you?" she asked, recognizing his jibe as teasing. "If I were to attack you with a pillow you'd probably…"

Her pause was long and he grinned, bringing the dimple to her attention again. "I'd probably what?" he asked, rising from his chair.

"Well, it's for sure I wouldn't scare you any. No matter what I used for my so-called attack."

"No, you won't scare me off, lady, no matter what tactics you use. I'm planning on hanging around for a lifetime, and you'd better get used to the idea."

CHAPTER EIGHT

BEDTIME ARRIVED SOONER than Susannah was ready for it. Wasting no time on dithering, McBain nodded toward the door of his room and spoke bluntly.

"Get yourself in there and ready for bed, sweetheart. I'll give you time to crawl under the covers before I come in."

She felt the flush climb her cheeks, deciding it was getting to be an everyday event, this blushing his remarks instigated. "I feel like I should sleep on the sofa," she said, casting him a look that begged for his understanding.

"Maybe," he said. "But I want you where I can get my hands on you, in case you think about running off again. You'll sleep in my bed, Susannah. And no arguments please."

She gave in, a bit ungracefully, managing to show her indignation with a flip of her skirts and the lifting of her chin that told him she was not happy with his issuing of orders.

And he only laughed, his chuckle following her

as she marched across the bedroom to find her nightgown in the bottom of her valise. She stepped behind the screen in the corner of his room that shielded the porcelain slop jar from sight, and stripped from her clothing with quick movements that threatened the very seams of her dress.

Feeling a bit more comfortable with the nightgown safely pulled over her head, she looked down at the yards of fabric as the weight of cotton material fell about her figure, keeping her form from his eyesight. Made of flannel, the gown was too heavy for the warming weather, but she had packed it because she had no idea if she would have blankets available to her on this journey.

She needn't have worried, she decided, watching as McBain stripped from his clothing, retaining only his drawers as he crawled into the wide bed behind her. He'd slept in his clothing last night, but seemed to be readying her now for the intimacies of marriage. She clung to the edge of the mattress, her head buried in the feather pillow, waiting to see where he would deign to spend the nighttime hours. And soon found that his intentions involved being as close to her as he could get.

His arm wrapped around her waist, he tugged her back against his chest and belly, giving her no chance to protest, only holding her close, his hand beneath her ribs, his forearm supporting the weight of her breasts. She shifted in his grip, but to no avail, for he only held her closer, growling a protest when she would have moved from his embrace.

"Cut it out, sweetheart. Just lie still and go to sleep. I'm not about to jump on you, not unless you tempt me beyond reason."

And just what that meant, she had no idea. Surely the man didn't think she was playing the flirt with him; certainly he must know that she was only attempting to allow propriety a small space in this bed.

But it seemed that propriety was the furthest thing from his mind, for his hand shifted to cup her breast, his fingers tracing the crest that formed beneath his touch, and a murmur of satisfaction touched her ear as he bent his head to press his lips to her neck.

"McBain, please…"

"Please, what?" he asked, his whisper muffled as he spent a myriad of kisses on her flesh.

She shivered, the feel of his breath warm against her skin, his hand hot against the soft weight of her breast. "I want to be able to speak my vows to you on Friday knowing that we haven't anticipated them."

"I'm only teasing you, *love,*" he said, his voice lending a wealth of meaning to the word he chose to name her. "I won't push you into any more than this, just holding you, touching you a bit."

"I must sound like a child to you," she whispered. "And I'm far from it. I'm twenty-seven years old, McBain, but when you touch me, I feel like a rank amateur at this game. I don't know what to expect from you, and as much as I trust you, I doubt your ability to behave yourself, given the fact that—"

His laughter surprised her, his arms tightening around her as he settled into place behind her. The nudging of his arousal made her only too aware of his need, but there was within her an element of trust that overcame her doubts, and she knew suddenly that the man would not attempt to coax her or bring her to a completion of this blending of their bodies.

"I can wait for you. So long as I know you'll speak the words on Friday, I can hold back the desire that is alive between us, love. We'll wait, just as I said."

Susannah felt the relaxing of her muscles, the softening of her body against his as she heard his whispered words, knowing that he spoke the truth, that she need not fear a seduction tonight. Yet, *fear* was not the right word to describe her feeling. For that signified a dread or a horror of the act of loving, and she looked forward to that with McBain.

And yet, there was another factor to face. The

knowledge that fear would be present in some form when they were wed, that the memories of the past would overwhelm her and she would not be able to give as readily as she ought to the man who would be her husband.

And more than words could say, more than feelings could describe, she wanted to be all that McBain deserved on his wedding night, yearned to be sweet and submissive and loving in his bed. But her body seemed not to cooperate with her desires.

For the memory of other nights, other beds was alive, even now, in her mind. She dreaded the thought that she would be unable to respond to McBain as she should. That he would be repelled by her wariness, that he would lose patience with her trepidation.

"McBain?" She spoke his name softly, drawing his attention.

"I'm here, love," he said, his whisper warm against her skin.

"I'll try to be a good wife. I really will. I just hope you can be patient with me."

"I'm the very soul of patience," he said wryly. "Can't you tell?" And even as he spoke, she felt again the nudge of his arousal against her bottom, knew the thrill of his arms possessing her, his body shielding her from all harm.

"I hope you don't forget those words over the next couple of days."

AARON FELT PRIDE CLOTHE HIM as he beheld his bride. She was a vision in a soft blue dress she'd obtained at the Emporium.

Just an hour since, she'd pressed the wrinkles from it in the kitchen with a pair of sad irons that had heated on his kitchen range, then donned it carefully and not sat down, lest she be wrinkled in the church when she faced the parson and the man who would be her groom. Her skirts were full and stood out from her with the aid of a mountain of petticoats, he was certain. Her waist seemed tiny in comparison with the rounding bosom above and the cascading fabric below. And all in all, the resulting picture she presented to him was one he could barely keep from touching and caressing. His hands actually itched to hold her, his fingers twitching as he recalled the feel of soft flesh beneath them, the rounding of her breasts and the way his palm fit the circumference of her waist.

He knew the feel of those full breasts, knew the softness of her flesh beneath his hands, and felt the familiar fullness in his groin that seemed to accompany each occasion he had to look at her so minutely. She was lovely, not a porcelain beauty, untouched by life, but a woman seared by the fire of experience, a female whose worth was determined by the obstacles she had overcome, the trials she had faced and survived.

And yet there was, beneath the strength and courage she owned, a fragile, vulnerable creature who could be hurt beyond measure by the expectations of the man who was to be her husband. That he held her happiness in his hands was a fact Aaron could not deny, a fact he had pledged to honor, for should he not allow her to express her deepest fears, her direst memories, he might damage the bond between them as husband and wife. Damage it before it became a reality.

And to that end, he determined to give her all the time she needed to accept him, to welcome him into her bed. He stood beside her in the small chapel, taking her hand as the parson instructed him, sliding the simple gold band upon her finger, a ring he'd purchased on a trip to the Emporium without her, only Ellis along to guide him in his choice of a wedding ring for his bride, just yesterday.

Now her fingers trembled in his, and he looked down at the slender arrangement of skin and bone that formed her hand, the soft flesh that covered her palm. It was the same feminine hand that had tended him when he'd needed most to feel compassion from another human being. He recalled the touch of those slender fingers on his brow, the cool contact of her welcome fingers brushing the hair from his eyes, the smile she spent on him, as though she would somehow refresh him, relieve his pain with just the power of healing hands upon his body.

And she'd done just that, had taken him home. How a woman who had proved herself to be so filled with kindness and caring could ever be considered a criminal was beyond his ability to conceive.

As her husband now, he vowed to spend every waking moment seeking to find the truth behind the death of the senator from Pennsylvania.

THE RESTAURANT AT THE HOTEL was filled with their guests when they arrived, and Susannah felt herself blushing at the remarks made by the ladies who greeted her at the door. Aaron was the subject of many jests and cheers as the menfolk congratulated him.

The punch bowl was filled to the brim with a flavorful batch of some pink concoction that complemented the sandwiches and the sliced fruit the hotel had provided. The owner had insisted on making the reception a wedding gift to the sheriff and his bride.

They circled the room, visiting each table of guests that vied for their attention. McBain had one long arm about Susannah's waist; she blushed at the advice tossed her way, and he had a proud look that would not be denied. Families sat together at round tables, the children dressed in their Sunday best, behaving as well as could be expected at such a festive occasion.

"I can't believe you invited all these young'uns to the party," Mrs. Hitchcock said in Susannah's ear as she bent close to speak to the woman. Wife to the hotel restaurant owner, Mrs. Hitchcock was well aware of her prominent place in the social order of Ottawa Falls, and now she looked about her at the tables that held both parents and children alike.

"It must have cost you a pretty penny to feed all the children," she said pertly, her smile avid as she awaited Susannah's reply.

"The sheriff wanted the families who have supported him so well to be present at our wedding, and if it involved a passle of young'uns, so be it. They're a big part of the town, and McBain says they'll be the citizens of tomorrow."

"Hmm, well that's one way of looking at it, I suppose," the regally dressed lady commented, tossing a glance at the man they discussed as he neared the table.

"Susannah." His voice speaking her name gave Susannah a thrill of pleasure and she turned to him with a smile. "Are you about done with your visiting?"

"I will be soon," she said nicely, rising from the chair she'd occupied next to Mrs. Hitchcock. "We were just discussing how wonderful it is to see all the families turn out for our party. The church was almost full, wasn't it?"

"They wanted to get a good look at the woman who captured our sheriff's attention," Mrs. Hitchcock said. "Some of us were getting downright worried that he wouldn't take the proper step and marry you, my dear." Her smile seemed smug to Susannah's mind, but she deliberately overlooked the woman's remarks.

"Oh, I had no doubt about his intentions, right from the first. The sheriff is a good man, very well brought up and a gentleman from the word go."

With a wave of her hand, she rose and took her leave, Mrs. Hitchcock gaping like a floundering fish on a riverbank as McBain led his wife to another group of townsfolk.

"See what they think of us?" she whispered to him as he bent low to catch her words.

He only laughed, his big hand forming against her back, the bulk of his big body providing shelter for her smaller form. She melted against him, pleased at the role of being a submissive woman, even though the title fit her poorly.

It was enough that the town thought she was docile and easily molded to the proper design, so long as Aaron McBain knew of her independence and the strength of her character.

"You're a scamp," he announced in her ear. "Just eatin' up all the stuff people have been telling you, about how beautiful you are and how lucky you are to have me for a husband."

"They're right on at least one count," she told him, gazing up at him from limpid eyes. "I'm surely a lucky woman to have you. Maybe *blessed* is more the word I want. For I thank God every day for bringing you into my life, McBain."

He seemed barely able to keep his hands still, his fingers clenching against her side, his long body edging closer to her as they walked among the friendly folk who ate and drank and enjoyed the party.

The ladies gathered around her after the food had been demolished and spoke to her of tossing her small bouquet of flowers into their midst. She climbed the curving stairway, midway to the second floor and then turned to view the women gathered below. The unmarried ones were front and center, awaiting their chance at catching the posy of spring flowers, fresh from Hattie's garden and tied with a blue ribbon.

Susannah tossed it high in the air and watched as the younger women, most of them girls still less than twenty years old, fumble for the prize. A slender blond girl, Susie O'Brien, won the prize and was covered with blushes as the ladies called out to one of the young men who was watching from near the door.

Hattie's voice in Susannah's ear spoke the reason for the commotion. "Susie there is pretty near engaged to Tom Lincoln. They've been courting for almost six months. Probably be having a wedding before winter sets in."

"I'm glad she caught it then," Susannah said in a low tone. "She certainly looks happy about it, doesn't she?"

"Not near as happy as you look, missy." Hattie's eyes misted as she turned Susannah in her embrace and hugged her tightly. "You make me wish I'd had a girl like you of my own," she said, swallowing her tears. "Only thing that would have made my life complete, would have been having children of my own. Guess I'll have to settle for looking after yours when they start to arrive."

"Hattie!" Susannah's voice held amusement as she spoke her friend's name. "I won't be worrying about that for a long time."

"You never know about these things. Might be a baby right around the corner for you. By this time next year, you could have an armful."

Susannah smiled, thinking of the joy inherent in having a child, and bent to kiss Hattie's cheek.

"You'll be the godmother of any children we have. And I'm hoping for at least three or four."

"That sheriff looks like a mighty potent man, sweetie. I'll bet you he'll have you pregnant every two years or so for a while. He'll make pretty babies, that's for sure. With your good looks and his dark coloring, they ought to be beauts."

Susannah laughed, blushing at Hattie's words. Below her, she caught sight of McBain, his dark hair gleaming in the light that shone through the open hotel door.

"Are you about ready to go for a train ride?" he asked. The reason for their trip east was a secret they had not shared, even with Hattie, and now, hearing his words, Susannah felt a moment of dread as she considered what they would find at the end of the road.

THEY WERE ALONE at the house once more, readying for the trip, Susannah checking over the things she'd packed in her small valise, Aaron placing the odds and ends of her belongings in his suitcase, along with his own clothing, his shaving gear, his paperwork that would open doors for them on this journey.

Susannah worked slowly, mindful of the limitations of time, for their train was to pass through Ottawa Falls in an hour. If the truth be known, she would rather have stayed right here and cooked a

meal for him in his kitchen, would have preferred
to spend the day in cleaning and cooking, the hours
in pretending she was a simple wife, and he was a
simple man, beginning their lives together. Instead,
they would don the faces of anonymity and join a
hundred other passengers en route to St. Louis,
and from there they would travel to the nation's
capital.

Aaron took long moments to send a wire before
they boarded the train, and she stood beside him,
aware that it concerned her. "Just letting my U.S.
marshal friend Sam know what's going on," he
told her. "I've given him our schedule, so he can
keep track of everything and let us know if there
are any problems."

She nodded, anticipating the trip, yet dreading
the outcome, should it not be as Aaron thought
likely. Nonetheless, they were on a honeymoon of
sorts, traveling as husband and wife, as Mr. and
Mrs. Aaron McBain. No, not as Mr. McBain, but
as a sheriff, a lawman, escorting a prisoner to her
fate. There were no handcuffs to be seen, but as
surely as she knew they existed, tucked into his belongings, she knew that he would use them if the
need arose, if she should rebel against his authority.

And yet, she felt all the anticipation any bride
might feel, facing her wedding night, knowing that
the dawn would bring about a new relationship

between them. She trembled, feeling his arm tighten around her waist as he led her to the private compartment they would have for this journey to St. Louis.

The door closed with an audible click behind her and he turned the lock before he faced her. "Finally alone, Susannah. Tell me, do you feel married?"

She scraped up a smile, knew even as it twisted her lips that it was a mockery, for she felt more like crying in his arms, and this was not as it should be. No matter the circumstances, she was a bride and he the groom who expected better than this from her.

So the misty eyes she raised to his were not filled with fear or concern, but only with the anticipation of a bride who awaits the pleasure of her new husband. "Will we wait until dark?" she asked quietly, and felt a quick relief as he nodded. "And in the meantime?" she asked.

"We'll eat supper in the dining car and act like newlyweds are supposed to act. We're on our honeymoon, so far as anyone else is concerned."

"And what about us? Should we consider this a breathing space before the storm ahead? Or is it a time to share, just the two of us?" She thought her voice sounded almost as a plea, and rued the thought that he might think she begged of him these hours they would spend in this small room, beginning their marriage in the face of danger and trials yet to come.

"No matter what else ever happens in our lives, tonight will be ours to savor and enjoy, sweetheart. I've never had a wedding night before, and I hope this will be totally opposite to whatever you experienced seven years ago."

Her thoughts flew to the wedding day so long ago. A lifetime it seemed: a happy bride, expectant and glowing, a man who had promised joy and happiness and a forever to be cherished. The reality of the night that followed made her shiver as she recalled the embarrassment and pain of her initiation into wedded bliss, the cruel words of rejection as she failed to meet his standards. Standards set by the train of women he'd known and bedded over his wild years. Memories she rejected in favor of the reality of the present.

For now there was Aaron, and his tenderness. She slid her arms around his waist, leaning into him, as if his presence were precious to her and she could not resist this moment of pure intimacy. "It will be perfect," she whispered to him, lifting her face to his, her mouth finding his with inborn accuracy, as if she'd been created for this moment, as though all of her life before now was but a preface to what would pass between them in the hours to come.

They ate a meal that neither of them was truly aware of, chewing and swallowing, stealing tidbits from each other's plates as several other passengers watched and smiled at the two who were so obviously in a world of their own. "I feel like a honeymooner," she whispered, tasting the meringue on her dessert. It resembled a cloud, and she relished each bite, feeding Aaron a goodly share as he watched her enjoyment with dark eyes that measured her and deemed her ready for the night to come.

CHAPTER NINE

TENDERLY TUCKING HIS HAND beneath her arm, McBain led her to their compartment and closed the door, locking it to ensure their privacy and then easing her into his embrace.

"Shall I blow out the lamp?" he asked softly, his need to watch her in the dim glow that fell on their bed a viable force within him.

"Not unless you want to," she answered and he smiled, thankful that she was not unwilling to be without covering before him. For his first intention was to remove her clothing, to seek out the sleek lines of her body beneath the folds of her garments. Her dress buttoned down the back, and he turned her from him, his fingers making short work of the small pearl buttons. He pushed the dress forward, allowing it to fall down her arms and from thence, the weight of the fabric taking it to the floor.

He lifted her from the circle of blue, unwilling to wrinkle or mar the beauty of her dress, for he hoped she would wear it again tomorrow for his pleasure. He bent to lift it from the floor and placed it carefully atop the upper bunk, smoothing the wrinkles from the bodice with careful hands.

Her petticoats were next and he untied the tapes that held them around her slender waist, watching as they gathered at her feet, leaving her in the briefest bit of batiste and lace, the chemise he had chosen for her at the Emporium while she'd awaited the pressing of her dress. It fit her to perfection, her breasts outlined by the tucks and darts that formed its shape, and he lifted one hand to touch the rounding splendor of her bosom, willing to await the unveiling of her beauty until she should deem it to be proper.

It seemed that his bride had no qualms about him seeing her flesh, for she unbuttoned the dainty garment and slid from it with a shrug of her shoulders. He caught it up from the floor as she stepped back from the silky bit of seduction and he placed it on the top bunk with her dress.

She bent then to remove her garters, fancy little bits of fabric, with lace and silk ribbons that tied in dainty bows. Her stockings were white, silky and soft, and she slid them down the length of long legs and then off, where they lay in shimmering circles on the floor. He bent to pick them up and smiled at her, his eyes lighting with anticipation.

"I'll think of what you're wearing under your

dress each time I look at you tomorrow," he whispered, his fingers loathe to leave the soft silk he held. But before him was the glistening reality of his bride, and he knew not where to place his hands, fearful of frightening her with his ardor. So the stockings were relegated to rest on the dress and petticoats she'd shed so gracefully only moments before.

He needn't have worried lest she be frightened of his touch. Her own hands were busy with the tie he wore, sliding it from beneath his collar, then unbuttoning his shirt and removing his cuffs and collar, stripping the white garment from him with hands that trembled as they moved against his body.

"I want to see all of you, McBain. I want to know you, to feel your skin, your arms and legs, your chest and the way this line of hair grows down your chest to your waist." Her hand trembled there as she undid his trousers. "And beyond your waist," she whispered, sliding her hands behind him to free him from the restriction of his drawers.

The touch of her hands against the flat line of his backside was almost his undoing, and he wondered at the innocence of the woman who touched him. She'd been married, but still bore the sense of innocence he'd first found so appealing in her. Now she touched his body with fingertips that trembled against his flesh. Her breath caught as he groaned aloud, and she hesitated, allowing her hands to lie where they were, altogether too close to the part of him that made itself known in a mighty way.

"I thought last night when you got into bed with me, that tonight you wouldn't be wearing these," she said, her face flaming as she slid the undergarment from him.

"I don't want to frighten you," he said, grasping her hands lest she discover the part of him he'd kept from her, unwilling to make her dread the joining of their bodies. He knew he was on the very edge of his control, not only because he'd been long without a woman, but because he wanted so badly to make this night one of beauty for her.

She touched him, eased her hand around the increasing size of his arousal and measured him with the slender length of her fingers, the warm cup of her palm holding him with such intimacy he could barely contain himself. "Not now," he said, removing her hands from him, lest he disgrace himself before they'd barely begun this journey.

He sat on the edge of the lower berth and drew her closer, his gaze drawn to her breasts, those enticing, firm bits of feminine charm that had attracted him from the first. She was all woman, warm and welcoming, and he closed his eyes, lest he pounce upon her as might a randy youth with his first woman.

For indeed he felt the quick need for completion, the yearning to touch her flesh, to discover the hidden secrets of her femininity. Yet he would not rush her to an embrace she was not ready to accept.

Easing her onto the mattress, he lay beside her, lifting to view the beauty he'd uncovered, reaching to touch the flesh he'd yearned to own and, finally, bending to take the small, budding crest into his mouth. She moaned, a low, soft sound of pleasure that was accompanied by her hand on the back of his head, her fingers pressing him closer to the prize he had claimed.

He lifted for a moment, seeking her gaze, and his own was solemn as if the words he spoke were a vow he would honor no matter the urgent need to take her that possessed him.

"I won't hurt you, Susannah. I only want to love you."

"I know that," she said softly, and her eyes echoed the meaning of the words she spoke, telling him silently of the trust she offered, of the gift of her body she bestowed upon him. His hands were warm, his breath a flash of fire as it moved over her, his kisses intimate and burning against the fragile flesh he took as his own. He buried his nose between her breasts and inhaled the scent of her, the sweet feminine aroma that was so uniquely a part of her, and then he moved lower, to where she would one day carry his child, and his kisses blessed the cradle that would give sustenance and support to the children of his loins.

He wanted to hold all of her at once, yet somehow restrained the desire to possess her until she should be ready for his body within her own. His fingers moved to her thighs and thence to the warm, damp place he yearned to enter. It was enough in these moments that she allowed him to touch her, to pet the soft tissues that were only a part of her feminine self. His fingers slipped into the channel that awaited him, and he carefully felt for her readiness, his heart rejoicing as he recognized the heat of her arousal.

She was moist and ready for him, her woman's flesh hot to the touch, and he could wait no longer, his hands brushing her breasts and belly, his body rising over hers, his male member seeking out the sanctuary she offered. For but a single moment she stiffened, her body taut with what could only be fright or apprehension.

He soothed her with his mouth, kissing her face, nuzzling every warm spot he could find, her throat, the tender place beneath her breasts. Even the bend of her elbow and the nape of her neck were not spared the touch of his lips. He would not have her fear him, or shudder at the touch of his masculine parts against her. If need be, he would wait; not willingly, but patiently. For this he could be patient. For Susannah, he could control the passion that drove him to the goal of completion.

And so he loved her, almost silently, carefully, always mindful of her past experiences in this realm, fearful himself of doing anything that would remind her in any way of the man who had so abused and misused her body. His hands moved with care, exploring the curves that formed her, seeking only her trust. And in that he was success-ful it seemed.

For his reward was a softening of her flesh, a welcoming heat that seemed to envelop him, and a return of his caresses as she turned her face to his, seeking out his mouth, blessing the length of his throat with tiny, biting kisses that told him of her readiness for this joining. And then she lifted her arms to him, accepted him into her body with a joy he could not help but acknowledge.

She was tight, whether because of lapsed time since her last encounter with the *noble* senator or because of the tension she tried so hard to hide. It made no matter, for he entered her carefully, with small, measured thrusts, seeking the depths of her, and yet in no hurry to explore the extent of her woman's secrets. She would be his for all the years to come. Tonight was but a preface to many such nights, many such times of discovery.

He shivered, thrilling to her newfound eagerness, feeling the proof of her need for him, even as he sought and claimed the depths of her womanhood, even as he possessed the warmth she offered, accepting the caresses she spent on his body, the kisses she shed upon his face and throat, and then across the width of his chest.

His hands coaxed her to join as a partner on this journey and she seemed unsure of herself as he bade her come with him, his fingers moving carefully against her woman's flesh, his need for her held in abeyance as he sought her pleasure before his own. As a flower unfolding its petals before him, she accepted his touch, rising beneath him, her breathing shattered by the immensity of her climax and he growled his satisfaction against her throat.

Then with a groan that spoke first of need, then fulfillment, he sought and found his own share of their mutual pleasure just moments later.

He would not, indeed, could not, release her from his embrace, only held her tighter to himself.

"I've needed you so badly and I've been so afraid I'd frighten you." He lifted from her and looked down at the woman who returned his smile with joy glowing from her eyes, with happiness forming her mouth and with hands lifted to touch him as if he were a priceless object that had just come into her possession.

"McBain…" She was hesitant, and he waited patiently as she gathered her thoughts. "I don't know what to say, how to tell you what I feel."

"You don't need to, sweet. I think I married an innocent, didn't I? A woman who had no knowledge of her own ability to receive pleasure at a man's hands. Am I right?" And without waiting for her answer, he bent to her and kissed her, deeply and with all the love he could express with a single blending of their mouths.

"I never knew there was such joy to be found," she whispered. "I never knew, McBain."

"You've given me…" He paused, unable to finish his thought. "More than I ever thought I would find in a woman," he said finally.

She closed her eyes and held him close, and when he would have rolled from her, she would not allow it. "No, stay, please," she murmured, her arms capturing him, binding him with the strength of her love, unwilling that he should leave her just yet.

"Just let me roll to one side. I won't let go of you," he told her and shifted their position so that her head was on his shoulder, her body still entwined with his, her heartbeat still matching the rapid beat of his own.

They were silent for long moments and then he nudged her a bit, speaking the words he had held back until this time, seeking the answer his hungry heart yearned to hear. "Did I please you, Susannah? I tried not to give you any pain or distress. I know I was a bit rough. But I had been so long a time without warmth in my life that I fear I rushed you. And I was determined not to, you know. I wanted so badly to make this night good for you."

"It was wonderful, love," she whispered. "Never think that you rushed me, or displeased me in any way. It was perfect. In fact, I fear you won't ever be able to replicate such an occasion." She looked up at him and her smile was teasing. "But I'll be happy to let you try."

THE TRAIN STATION in St. Louis was huge, larger than any Susannah had ever seen, save for the one in Washington. But her memories of the night she'd departed Washington were vague, and she settled in to enjoy her time here in this magical place where east and west met and merged, where trains headed in all directions and people were carried hither and yon by the wonders of modern transportation.

In the privacy of their new compartment for the trip to Washington, they settled in for the re-

mainder of their journey. Though Susannah
dreaded the ordeal to come, she felt infinite trust
in Aaron, knew he would be with her. They'd
barely found comfort in the seats, their fingers
entwined as they watched the crowds bustling on
the station platform, when a knock sounded at
their door.

Aaron rose and stepped across the small room,
opening the door with caution, then wider as the
conductor spoke his name. "Sheriff McBain? I
have a wire for you, sir." He stood in the doorway,
holding a paper in his hand, looking past Aaron to
where Susannah sat waiting. "This just arrived and
I thought I wouldn't be able to catch you before the
train left. I think you'll want to read it right away."

With a nod to Susannah and a small salute in
Aaron's direction, the conductor disappeared down
the corridor, and Aaron shut the door.

"What do you suppose it is?" Susannah asked.
"Who would know we were here?"

Aaron read, silently and quickly, then lifted his
gaze to meet hers. "It's from the powers that be, by
way of my friend with the government, the marshal
I told you about. We're heading back home, sweetheart. It's not safe for you in Washington. They'll
be sending a man out to Ottawa Falls immediately,
and I suspect it will be the very man who sent this
wire, Sam Peterson."

A shiver of apprehension ran the length of Susannah's spine and she felt a chill encompass her body. "Someone is out to get me."

Aaron nodded. "Looks that way. I was afraid of this very thing, Susannah. But if Sam is the agent they're sending to help us, you'll be in good hands. He's a Texan, and I'd trust him with my life." His single stride brought him to her side and he gripped her hands firmly, drawing her to her feet. "Let's get moving. We'll have to hurry before the train leaves." Their luggage in hand, he led Susannah from the compartment and toward the exit from the car. The conductor awaited them and offered his help as she stepped down to the platform, Aaron close behind.

"There'll be a train leaving for Denver in an hour," he said, making Aaron aware that he knew what their needs were. "I'd suggest you take your wife with you to the ticket agent's office, sir. She might be lost in the rush of passengers on the platform."

"I appreciate your concern," Aaron said, his hand on Susannah's elbow, then sliding around her waist as he led her toward the glassed-in enclosure where the agent sat, his visor in place, his shirt-sleeves rolled up precisely to just below his elbows. With a keen look, he nodded at Aaron, then bent to the papers he held in his hand.

Without explanation, he had readied two tickets for Ottawa Falls, and Aaron surrendered the ones he held that would have taken them to Washington. "Can I do anything for you, sir?" the agent asked, obviously aware of the message Aaron had received. "There's a room available for your use if you like. You can wait there until your train is ready to board."

"Thank you. I'd appreciate that," Aaron said, mindful of Susannah's exposure on the platform. Should anyone be watching them, be aware of who she was, they were an open target where they stood. With a quick gesture, the ticket agent motioned toward a door just six feet or so from where Aaron stood.

"You can go right in if you like, sir. There's a sofa and several chairs and you can hear the announcements of arrivals and departures from there."

Without speaking, only giving the man a nod of appreciation, Aaron steered Susannah into the private area designated for their use. A small window looked out upon the station, and he watched from there as the train pulled away, heading for Washington.

Keep Mrs. Carvel isolated from the general public, and under guard. An agent will notify you within forty-eight hours of your next move.

Short and sweet, it was a warning he'd almost

expected. They'd known that once Susannah's whereabouts were a thing of record, she would be at risk, and they couldn't expect much of a safe window of time. Several of those involved with the coal magnates had an inside track with someone, and the news of her whereabouts was probably already in the wrong hands.

Other federal agents were on the trail of the shady individuals seeking her, intent on doing her harm. A feeling of relief swept through Aaron. If he could keep her safe in Ottawa Falls, even if only for a few days, perhaps more help for Sam would arrive. He didn't know how Sam would feel, knowing his bosses thought he needed a hand, but Aaron felt that if an agent were sent to give him aid, he'd welcome it.

"What will we do, Aaron?" Susannah perched on the edge of a chair near the door, her face ashen, as if fear possessed her. And well it might, for she was in danger, and too intelligent not to be aware of the powerful figures who sought her.

"It looks like someone is giving you credit for more knowledge than you possess," he said quietly. "Did the good senator confide in you, Susannah? Did he tell you what he was up to?"

She shook her head. "No. I was his hostess, but aside from dressing up and looking presentable, my duties were few and far between. I knew he had contacts that took him into secret meetings, and the men who came to call would spend hours at a time in his study with him. But I didn't know much about them, usually he introduced me, but beyond their names, I was in the dark. I did know that he had a lot of dealings with the coal industry, and he had certain arrangements with some of the mine owners. But I tried my best to stay away from his shenanigans."

Aaron stood apart from her, his back rigid, his shoulders squared, his sharp gaze scanning the crowd that flowed across the platform. "We'll need to make a file, Susannah. I want everything you can remember down in black and white. I need to know everything you know, names, dates, places."

"I'm afraid I'm not going to be of much use, Aaron. But it sounds like someone thinks John confided in me, doesn't it?"

"I'm sure we'll find out just what's going on, sooner or later. And sooner is my guess," he said. He touched his hat brim with one long index finger, pushing it up a bit, then that same hand dropped to where his gun was snugged firmly in its holster. He drew it out, reached into his pocket and she heard the click of cartridges as he loaded two empty spaces.

Susannah closed her eyes, aware suddenly that her husband was a walking weapon, that he would not hesitate to use the gun in his hand for her protection. And yet, she dreaded the thought that he might be called upon to do that very thing. That he might be forced to shoot, perhaps kill a man, should she be threatened. Sworn to uphold the law, pledged to protect her, not only as a citizen, but as his wife, he stood between her and danger unknown.

"Might as well relax, Susannah. It's gonna be an hour or so before we leave here. Why don't you settle down on that sofa, put your feet up maybe."

"I can barely breathe, and you want me to take a nap." She blurted the words at him roughly, and then blushed as she recognized the anger that drove her. "I'm sorry, Aaron. I'm not upset with you, just with the mess I've gotten you into. You'd have been better off if you'd never met me, never had anything to do with me."

He turned his head, his eyes dark and discerning as they swept over her. "I beg to differ with you, Mrs. McBain. You may be a lot of trouble to me right now, but once we get over this patch of rough road, we'll be fine. I'm planning on spending a lot of years with you, lady. And if last night was anything to go by, I'm planning on enjoying every one of them."

Flustered, she covered her hot cheeks with her hands, the palms cold, her fingers trembling, her flesh chilled by the fear that coursed through her veins. "Don't talk like that, Aaron. I'm afraid I wasn't nearly as experienced as you thought. Even being a wife for seven years, I was in new territory last night, and if I left you wanting..." She closed her eyes, sensing his regard as though his gaze were a flame and she the tinder he sought to engulf in his warmth.

His laughter stunned her, and she shot him a glance of astonishment. "Are you making light of me?"

"Never, sweetheart. I'm only amazed that you are so naïve, so unaware of your own power over me." He smiled, the laughter gone, only a look of tenderness remaining as he turned the full force of his attention on her. "You made me a happy man, Susannah. I thought I'd made that clear to you, but it looks like I'll have to repeat the message. You'll find that I'm very happy with you, more than satisfied with your response to me."

"John said—"

"I don't give a damn what the good senator said. Neither about you or to your face. He didn't know what kind of a woman he had, and obviously didn't appreciate you. He's gone. A thing of the past, and well forgotten, as far as I'm concerned. You're a warm, loving female, and I intend to make you totally aware of that fact, whenever I get the chance."

She laughed softly. "Now I'm really blushing, Aaron. I may have let myself in for more than I bargained."

"Too late now, sweet. You're stuck with me." And with that he turned back to the window, but not before she noted the satisfaction he made no attempt to hide. His dark eyes crinkled at the corners and his dimple was exposed, tempting her with the tiny crease in his cheek.

She rose and approached him, sliding her arms about his waist, leaning her head against the solid width of his back, pressing her ear to catch the pulsing of his heart, smiling as the beat picked up speed at her touch. "I don't mind being *stuck* with you, Sheriff McBain. In fact, I'm looking forward to the train ride back to Ottawa Falls. I just think your words are a bit too descriptive. *Stuck,* indeed."

He laughed again, a full-bodied roar of enjoyment at her statement. "I hadn't looked at it that way, Susannah. Thanks for bringing it to my attention." And then he chuckled again, as if the double meaning of his descriptive phrase tickled his fancy. He turned in her embrace and enclosed her in the strength of his arms. His head bent to her, his mouth touching her temple as if he blessed the tender spot with his kiss.

"You shouldn't be standing in full view here, sweet," he told her. "Just get your little fanny back over there to the sofa, and let me keep an eye on things." His tone was tender as his mouth brushed against her skin, his hand pressing her forward into his embrace. She felt the strength of his arousal rise against her and knew a moment of pure pleasure that this strong man was vulnerable to her.

The next half hour went by quickly, Aaron keeping watch, Susannah curling in the corner of the sofa, better able to relax now, slipping off her shoes as she awaited word of their imminent departure. It was not long in coming, for Aaron stepped to the door, responding to a muffled announcement that failed to penetrate the walls of the room where they waited. He opened the door a crack and she heard the announcement clearly. Their train would be arriving forthwith and they could board almost immediately.

Aaron reached out a hand to her and she responded, rising and stepping close to him, his big body hiding her from view. "I'll get our satchel, sweetheart, and, in a few minutes, we'll be on our way."

The walk across the platform was without incident and a smiling conductor welcomed them onboard, instructing them as to the direction of their compartment. Again, they enclosed themselves in the small room, and Aaron locked the door, guaranteeing their privacy.

Susannah sat near the window, pulling the curtain to one side, yet keeping in the shadows lest she be seen from the platform. "I don't like having to hide," she told him. "And I'm afraid this is only the beginning."

"We'll eat supper, here in our room," he said. "I'm not going to expose you in the dining car. I'll ask the conductor for a tray of food."

"Another picnic?" She grinned as she recalled the cheese and bread they'd shared by the side of the road only a few days since.

His lips twitched as if he, too, recalled that event. And then his words verified the fact. "At least we won't have to lie on the ground and stay warm with but a light quilt to cover us." His gaze flitted to her and he grinned. "There's a lot to be said for a real bed, sweetheart. And we'll take full advantage of ours tonight."

SUSANNAH WENT READILY into his bed that night, yearning for his warmth beside her, aching for the feel of strong muscles and the total attention a man could bestow on a woman, surrounding her. He told her in specific detail what there was about her that merited his love, described the small things about her that gave him pleasure, and offered the knowledge that his life was enriched by her presence.

Her fear that their coming together on their

wedding night might have been but a single occasion of marital bliss soon was banished—put into limbo by the tender possession of her body. A fear forever set aside as she basked in the joy of Aaron McBain's gentle touch upon her body, and in the place of that fearfulness she learned of the overwhelming passion he brought to being in her body and spirit. A passion she allowed full rein, and a joy she reveled in.

SUSANNAH LOOKED FORWARD to returning home, knowing that the ordeal in Washington was to be set aside, indeed perhaps might never come to pass. Should she be forced to confront officers of the law in Ottawa Falls, it would be on McBain's home ground, and he would be with her. Aaron made it clear that his position as a lawman would protect her, but she'd feared that his badge would mean little to the high-powered men in Washington. Now she rested easy, sensing Aaron's confidence in her and the knowledge that his presence gave her an equal amount of assurance.

He faced her now, in the privacy of their compartment, his visage once more that of a law officer, his warmth subdued as he stated his need for knowledge.

"I'll have to know more about your place in the senator's life, sweetheart." Aaron's words were calm and easy, but bore a strength of will that Susannah recognized. He would not allow her to leave out anything that might give aid to their pursuit of her innocence. Though his phrasing might be termed an invitation to confide in him, she was aware that he would probe the depths of her mind to gain every detail of her memories.

"I can only tell you what John allowed me to know," she said, aching to comply with his demand, but dreading to dredge up the recollection of her past. She looked at a spot over his shoulder, not willing to meet his gaze as she spoke of the darkness she'd escaped.

"There were so many men, Aaron. Men who played games with people's lives, who bought and sold favors among politicians. John, apparently high on the list of those who could be bribed, was contacted by numerous men who sought his help.

"There was a string of them, big, bold…" She paused, remembering the host of brawny businessmen who had frequented the house in Washington.

"Sometimes they came in the middle of the night, their voices loud, John always offering them drinks and entertaining them in his study. When they arrived earlier in the evening, it was usually for dinner, an occasion meant to introduce them to other members of Congress. John expected me to play his hostess, and…"

She closed her eyes, unwilling to admit to being manipulated by the man who would have offered her body as a bribe. Unable to put into words the disgust she felt when she remembered the line of greedy, avid flesh hunters who had darkened the doorway of her home.

Gathering her courage, determined to give Aaron what he asked for, she spoke again. "I know that money changed hands, that John lived far above his means as a senator. Sometimes he sent me from the room, saying that business was beyond my comprehension and I would be bored by their conversations." She laughed, a bitter sound that held no trace of mirth.

"He wasn't trying to protect me. He just didn't want me to know the sort of things he was involved in. And I was glad to be forbidden that knowledge. We lived forever on the edge, John with his underworld contacts and I with my fear."

"Did you fear for your life? Or his?" Aaron pressed her, his voice deepening as he encouraged her to continue.

Susannah inhaled deeply, her mind searching for the facts he sought. "I knew he was being paid by the coal magnates. They didn't want the workers to strike, and John was given the task of buying votes and convincing other legislators to support the cause of the mine owners. But my life wasn't on the line, so much as my—"

"He would have sold your favors." It wasn't a question, but a statement of fact, and Susannah bowed her head as she silently acknowledged Aaron's acute summation of her position.

"I knew I was held in reserve. Should a powerful figure debate the wisdom of voting as John asked, he would have offered me as a bribe. I was threatened more than once, and finally I decided to take legal action to rid myself of his influence over my life."

She shuddered visibly, her fingers clasped tightly. "Have you any idea how difficult it is to retain a lawyer for the purpose of divorcing your husband? How the laws are bent in favor of a man?" She met his gaze, shame in her eyes as she spoke her disgrace aloud.

"The lawyer I sought out demanded proof of John's infidelity, as if I would fabricate such tales."

"And did you have proof?" Aaron's face was rigid, the muscles and bones forming a mask, as if he questioned a stranger about the sordid details of her life.

"I found letters in his desk, a diary of names and contacts, women he kept on the string. I took it to the lawyer and he agreed to represent me. That was the day before I went to Washington to challenge John. I'd made up my mind to rid myself of him, and I would have told John the details, had I been given the chance. But there was no time.

"He was with his latest mistress, and I wonder now if she wasn't used by the men he was involved with. I suppose I'll never know. I think I've already told you, Bettina was her name, and she sounded sincere, as if she really thought John would get rid of me in order to marry her." She laughed again and wondered at the harsh sound, fearful that she was losing control of herself.

"Little did that flock of women know," she whispered, her voice almost gone, her throat tight with anguish, "John was protected from them by my presence in his life. He was legally tied to me, thus he could not follow through on his promises to the other women in his life. He even had the wife of the French ambassador in our bed, Aaron. And bragged about it, as if he'd pulled a trick on our own government, let alone the people of France.

"I couldn't live with it any longer." Her voice broke, her head bent and hot tears fell to stain the bodice of her dress.

So desperate, so filled with despair, her plight, that of a woman rejected and scorned, touched his heartstrings as had little else in his life. Aaron went to her, lifted her against himself and held her close, his hands moving against her back in a comforting rhythm, as if he would take her pain to himself, share with her the agony she owned.

She was a woman to be cherished, a woman brave enough to face the horror that was her existence and attempt to escape the consequences of her youthful folly.

A woman who, one night in the early spring, when the miseries of her life had finally seemed insurmountable, had gone to the capital and the house where John Carvel had been entertaining his current mistress. The last in a long line of women he'd met and bedded, rather indiscriminately actually, not caring if his current bed mate was in society or from the gutter. A pretty face, the lure of the forbidden—who knew what had determined his criteria when it came to the women in his life.

Aaron's lip curled, the sound issuing from his throat almost a snarl as he thought of the brute who had so cruelly used his wife. The urge to deliver his own brand of justice to such a man ran riot in the part of him that was the very essence of the law. At that moment, had John Carvel been alive, he would have met with the dispassionate judgment delivered by a lawman's gun. Never in his career had Aaron felt such anger, such hatred toward another human being.

And in his arms was the woman who had dared

to fight a losing battle against the man. His jaw firmed, his arms held her with tenderness and he vowed that such filth would never again touch her.

CHAPTER TEN

THE NEXT MORNING FOUND their train speeding toward the Rocky Mountains, past the prairies, heading for Denver. Susannah relished the warmth of the man behind her, whose arms circled her as he woke slowly from his night's slumber, whose body was already prepared to properly begin their day. And so it was that they were almost late for the serving of breakfast.

Aaron, deeming it safe for them to attend the morning meal with other passengers, took her to the dining car, making a late entrance, as many of the passengers were ready to head back to their seats. Although the day had begun on a high note, she found herself without appetite, picking at her food, unable to eat the meal she'd ordered.

"I'm sorry, McBain," she told him. "I seem to have lost my appetite."

"You're getting thin," he said, his gaze sliding from her face, down the front of her gown and to the waistline, where the fabric hung in folds. "Try to eat just a little, sweetheart." He watched her for a moment, and then as if he would ask a large favor of her, one he feared she might not comply with, he haltingly presented the boon he desired of her.

"You called me Aaron last night. I liked it, Susannah. At first I kinda got a kick out of you using my last name, but now I've found I like hearing you speak the name my mother gave me. I have a yearning to hear you murmur the syllables beneath your breath and whisper it in my ear when I please you."

She blushed. The stain of her flush ran up from her breasts to color her cheeks, and she ducked her head. "I didn't know you felt that way," she said, lifting her head to meet his gaze. "You should have told me before. I'll do anything you ask, you know that. Aaron..." Her voice lingered on the sound and he thought she had a slight burr that touched on the second syllable.

"Are you Scotch, or Irish perhaps?" It was a guess, but one she had not expected, for she lifted her chin and blinked as if stunned by the query.

"My father was of Scottish descent, and my grandfather spoke with a distinct brogue. I well remember listening to him, and wishing I could say words the way he did."

"Whitfield. Wasn't that your maiden name?"

"Yes, but my grandmother was a McPherson, a Scots woman born and bred."

"I thought I detected just a touch of the burr in your speech. I noticed it once before, but didn't mention it."

"My grandmother had a long strip of fabric, woven in the plaid that bore her maiden name, and she was so proud of it. She always said it would one day be mine." Her smile was dreamy as she reflected on the warm memory. "I wonder what happened to it."

"Perhaps we can look up your family and find out, once we get things settled."

Her eyes filled with unbidden tears and she brushed them away with the hem of her napkin. "Do you think that day will ever come?"

As if he could not bear her sadness, Aaron stood and went to her, offering his hand to help her from her chair. He led her from the dining car and into the narrow passageway that led to their compartment. Without a word, he unlocked the door, leading her inside and snapping the lock in place behind himself.

He settled on the single chair and pulled her into his lap, a position he was rather fond of, one that found her tucked against him neatly, his arms folded around her, one hand against her back, the other holding her bottom, keeping her from sliding to the floor. He bent to touch his lips to her forehead, brushed the soft, clear lines of her brow with kisses that only comforted, asking nothing of her but the opportunity to give her what solace he could.

"WILL WE GO HOME to your house?" The train was slowing for their stop, the conductor having called the name of Ottawa Falls, and Aaron was gathering their belongings, making ready to depart the compartment.

Susannah reworded the query she'd spoken already, as if fearful of unknown men causing problems for them. "Will we be safe there?"

"We've taken all the precautions needed. It won't be long till we have company, and in the meantime, I've got an office to run, and you've got a house to take care of." His smile seemed almost light, as if their future were written in a joyous hand. "You don't mind being a housewife, do you?"

"You know better," she admonished him. "I just don't want to worry about you being hunted down because of me."

"Do you think I'm going to hide?" His eyes wore a chill patina, as if he anticipated a showdown and was ready for it.

"No, I just…" She'd yearned for the slow pace of Ottawa Falls, for the small house where she'd lived for so short a time with the sheriff of the town, where people like Hattie Cooper came to call. Perhaps one day... Perhaps all would be as she'd dreamed. Their life would be placid, uneventful. If wishing would make it so—

"You'll be safe in the house," Aaron told her quietly. "We'll have this whole thing straightened out in no time. Once our agent arrives, we'll have the protection for you we need."

She was Mrs. Aaron McBain now, and that fact alone gave her a sense of belonging, a knowledge of her importance to the man she'd married. No matter the outcome, she had shared the most precious time of her life with him during the past week, and nothing could ever take that from her.

"What are you thinking?" he asked, amusement tingeing his voice. "Whatever is on your mind right now, it must be a happy thought." He'd watched her, standing at the door of their compartment, bracing herself for the braking of the train, looking out upon the scattered houses lying on the out-skirts of Ottawa Falls.

Her lips were curved in a smile that he could not decipher, somehow sad, yet filled with a joy he had seen often over the past days.

His arms went around her waist as he stood behind her and his lips touched the soft bend of her neck and shoulder, a spot he'd found to be espe-cially sensitive to his lips. She shivered in his embrace, her head tilting back and her face turning to his. "I'm proud to be your wife, Aaron," she whispered. "I was just thinking that no matter what happens, no one can take that from me."

"No one will ever take you from me, sweetheart," he vowed. "We'll work things out." His hands clasped at her midriff and he tightened his hold, keeping her secure as the train jolted to a halt.

The sight of an empty wagon beside the platform seemed an omen of good luck, Aaron thought as he searched out the owner. As he had suspected, Ellis Monroe strode from the station master's office, heading for the baggage car.

"You looking for the mail, Ellis?" Aaron sought the blacksmith's attention and was not disappointed as Ellis turned to face him. "Suppose we could get a lift out to the house?" Aaron asked.

"Give me a couple of minutes and I'm all yours, Sheriff." With a grin and a small salute, Ellis waited as the mailbags were handed down to him. He turned, trudging back to his wagon and awaited Aaron's pleasure.

After lifting their small amount of luggage into the wagon bed, Aaron took Susannah's arm and led her to where the high seat awaited them. He lifted her easily, hoisting himself to sit beside her, and then smiled at the blacksmith. "That oughta do it," he said. "Sure beats walking."

"Any time, McBain. You're right on the way to the post office." The team of horses moved out slowly and within minutes, they were deposited at the front walk leading to Aaron's house.

The door was unlocked, as he'd known it would be, Hattie no doubt having made a daily trek to check on things. Aaron swung the portal wide, ushering Susannah over the doorstep and into the house.

"We've got the place to ourselves for today at least," he said, carrying their valise to the bedroom, speaking louder so that she might hear him. "I'm hoping the man they send from Washington will be one I know."

"I didn't realize you were familiar to so many people in the east," she said following him, her gaze touching on all the familiar objects in the house as she went.

"If our agent is who they've promised, I'll know him all right," Aaron told her, walking from the bedroom and into the kitchen. As if he'd known she would be plotting a meal, he stood in the doorway and watched her.

The stove was cold, but Susannah found kindling and started a fire, seeking out several short pieces of wood to add to the flame. "Who is he?" she asked, even as she lowered the lid on the top of the range. A small pan was put into service as a dipper and she splashed water from the reservoir into the basin in the sink.

With familiar movements, she washed her hands, sought out a towel in the pantry and turned again to find Aaron's eyes focused on her.

"I like to watch you in the kitchen. You're so graceful, putting things in order." His eyes warmed as he approached her. "I can't tell you how happy I am to be home with you, sweet."

"Well, at least we won't starve. It looks like Hattie left us a fresh loaf of bread and a nice pat of butter on the table. She must have been here today."

Aaron watched as she filled the coffeepot, measured a handful of grounds into it and sat it on the front burner to boil. "I'm not starving. Bread and butter is fine with me."

"I'll open some fruit from the pantry," she said, taking cups and plates from the cupboard. She placed dishes before him and he pulled her down onto his lap.

"Let me answer your question while the coffee boils. I want you to know about my agent friend Sam."

"Like what?" Her brow wrinkled, as if she'd forgotten the subject at hand.

Aaron grinned at her, squeezing her against himself. "He lived in Texas, we were friends growing up and then we went different ways, he to Washington, while I found my way to Colorado.

I've kept in touch with him over the past couple of years.

"A bit after I saw your picture on the poster mailed out by the federal government, I looked him up and sent a wire to his office. I suspect he'll be the one coming out here to work with us."

"He'll think I'm a criminal, won't he?" The thought made her shrink within herself, and Aaron would not let it be.

"He'll think you're my wife, and hopefully he'll give me credit for choosing a woman of quality. You don't look much like a criminal, sweet and, trust me, Sam will recognize that fact."

"Will he be here soon? Today, perhaps?"

Aaron shook his head. "No. Maybe tomorrow, hopefully, if we're lucky. For today we only need to hunker down and relax, spend the day together."

"You don't have to go into the office?"

"No one knows I'm here, except for Ellis, and I doubt he'll go around town telling everything he knows." He laughed, offering her a sly glimpse of his intentions. "We're all alone for now, sweetheart. I'll take a walk into the office later on this evening, let my deputy know I'm back if he hasn't heard from the station master by then."

"And in the meantime, we can eat our dinner?" she asked.

"Yeah. That, too."

She frowned at his cryptic reply, locating the
bread knife, slicing the tender loaf and locating the
promised quart of peaches for their repast.

Before long, the coffee was finished and the
food eaten and appreciated. A knock at the back
door revealed Hattie, her slight figure outlined by
the bright sunlight.

"Come in," Susannah said, opening the door
fully. "You must have seen us arrive."

"Sure did," Hattie said. "Brought you a nice
sweet roll, fresh baked this morning." She
bustled into the kitchen and deposited her
offering on the table.

"Pour yourself a cup of coffee," Susannah said,
unwrapping the package with care. The scent of
cinnamon and the sight of plump raisins and white
icing met her gaze and she offered a piece to
Aaron. "This is a real welcome home. I can't tell
you how good this looks."

"Well, for some reason or another, I had a suspicion you might be back home before long,"
Hattie told her, settling herself in a chair. She
sipped at the coffee cup she held and smiled with
pleasure as Aaron and Susannah took their first
bites of the tempting rolls.

"I appreciate you looking after the house,"
Aaron said.

"It wasn't any problem," Hattie assured him.

"I'm just glad you're home, Sheriff. It don't seem the same without you here to look after things."

If she was curious as to their journey, she offered no trace of it, only speaking of the activities at the general store, and offering the news that two men had fought in the saloon and were now in residence at the jailhouse. "Guess that's all the excitement hereabouts," she said finally, finishing her coffee and standing to take her leave.

"I'll be by with fresh bread tomorrow," she told Susannah. "Might even teach you how to put together a loaf or two, young lady."

"I'd like that." Having Hattie in her kitchen would be an honor and Susannah let the woman know her thoughts. "I need someone to give me a few pointers. I know the usual things about cooking, but we never baked bread at our house."

"Every housewife should have the know-how," Hattie announced, opening the back door. "I'll see you tomorrow. And you, too, Sheriff." With that the door closed behind her and they were left alone, Aaron lifting his cup in a gesture that invited its refilling.

"Doesn't look to me like you've got any dusting to do, does it? Seems like Hattie took care of everything for us. Maybe we could just take it easy for the afternoon. What do you think?" He offered an innocent look and a smile that spoke of not-so-

innocent plotting. His eyes were dark, his color
high and the seductive glance he shot in her direction made Susannah's flesh tingle.

"Are we talking about a nap?" Her tone was
coaxing and Aaron was not one to pass up an opportunity. For he picked her up in a quick
movement that had her clutching at his shoulders,
one arm reaching to circle his neck and her face
seeking the warmth of the smooth, sun-kissed skin
of his throat.

The muscles that stretched across his chest were
tight with expectation as he carried her to the bed,
his smile one that made her think of a conquering
hero in some saga she might have read. The man
had no qualms about handling her, his arms and
hands more than capable of bringing pleasure to
bear upon her body. Hands that were fit for meting
out justice, even pain to those who were outside the
law, now softened as they touched the slender
curves he cherished. He lowered her to the mattress
and stripped her of the multitude of garments
hiding her from his view, leaving her only in the
dainty chemise she wore next to her skin.

His aim was simple, his need apparent. He
offered her the abundance of joy his masculine
form was capable of supplying. The sweet touch
of his loving hands eased the throbbing ache of ex-
pectancy that reigned in the depths of her body.

Anticipation made her ready for him, so quickly did her feminine self respond to his embrace. She felt herself transformed from an independent female to a clinging creature who craved each loving whisper, coveted each kiss, yearned for every caress that blessed her soft curves and slender form.

Her need for him was so great, so urgent, she could barely whisper his name as she watched him drop his shirt on the floor. The scent of his arousal filled her, the masculine aroma he wore lured her into his web, and she grasped at him as if she feared he might leave her bereft, might walk from her and leave her wanting.

There was no chance of that. As urgent as her need, Aaron's was even more so, his arousal taking his attention, his trousers tight and binding, his masculine being filled with a desire so strong, so powerful, he could barely contain it. With swift movements he shed his the rest of his clothing, then bent to her, aware of the size and shape of his arousal, knowing he could hurt her should she not be totally accepting of him.

Her hand reached to touch him and she whispered soft words, indistinct, but welcome. She uttered a murmur that seemed to have been born in her very depths, a sound so ethereal, so filled with awe. He felt a new level of arousal, an immensely powerful demand, vibrating within her palm, pulsing with a resurgence of blood, hot with the rushing flood of his life's force that begged to be spilled within her.

The woman would be the death of him, he thought, unable to remove her fingers from their grip on him, yet knowing he would disgrace himself should she continue to hold him in such an intense embrace.

"Susannah." He spoke her name softly, then repeated it as a plea, yearning to own her now, with an immediacy he could not control. He rolled atop her, his hands splitting asunder the soft fabric that separated him from her body, his eyes feasting on the soft skin he exposed. Helpless to control his hunger, he spread her legs. With a groan, he found his place between her thighs, lifting her bottom in his hands, piercing her fragile opening with the force of a man who has been without his woman for longer than his body could bear.

And yet, it was not so, for only hours before he had taken her to himself. And now, he halted his movement, his body joined with hers, their hearts beating as one, his manhood buried deeply within her tender body. His words were a plea to the Supreme Power who had created him.

"God help me, Susannah. I feel as though it's

been years since I touched you, and I know better than to use you this way." He bent his head, burying his face in her throat, his voice a whisper. "Forgive me, sweetheart."

He rolled with her, catching her close to him, facing her, taking his greater weight from her, fearful of harming her slender form. She clung to him, her breasts flattening against his chest, her hands seeking purchase as she pressed her palms against his back. He began to move then, his body held in check, his thrusts deep but measured and she sang her siren's song in his ear, her whispers and cries of delight manna to his hungry soul.

"You give me such happiness." His mouth opened against her throat, his lips suckling the soft skin, knowing he would leave his mark, but unable to halt the need to own the very essence of his woman.

Susannah closed her eyes against the fever that ran through her veins, held fast to the man who offered joy to her heart, and knew a moment so perfect, so filled with bliss, she found tears flowing down her cheeks, silent streams of happiness she could not contain.

"Ah, love," he whispered, loosing his hold. "Am I hurting you?" Aware suddenly of the dampness against his chest, he stilled his movements.

"Susannah, don't cry. Please, sweetheart, I can't bear to make you cry."

"I can't help it, Aaron," she whispered, his name given the distinct burr she was so unaware of, but which delighted him immensely. "I'm so happy with you I can hardly bear it. It's as if I can't contain the pleasure you offer me." She opened her eyes, tilting her head back, the better to meet his gaze.

"No matter what happens next," she murmured, "I'll have this to remember, I'll have the joy you've given me to sustain me through the hard times." Her arms held him with a strength he wondered at, for she was a slender, slight woman, not given to great feats of endeavor. But in this moment, in this time of sharing their bodies and hearts and minds, she exhibited the strength of a woman fit for warfare. And unless he missed his guess, warfare was exactly what awaited them during the days to come.

THEY SLEPT. AS IF THE WORRIES that possessed them had vanished with the closing of their eyes, they slept, entwined in the wide bed, skin against skin, her slender warmth heating the passion that seemed to be his constant companion. The sun slanted across the early evening sky before they woke, Aaron rousing to find Susannah watching him, her gray eyes soft and cloudy with the remnants of passion shared.

Her fingers entwined in the line of curls beneath her face, the triangle of hair that grew in profusion, that offered a resting place for her cheek. "You're the most passionate human being I've ever known," she said. Her voice was hesitant. "I don't mean to sound pompous, but I need to tell you that it's not just the passion of your desire for me that lures me. It's your passion to recognize right from wrong and your willingness to live up to the creed you've made a part of your life."

"I'm honored," he said, his voice resounding against her ear as she nuzzled the wide planes of his chest, and she laughed softly.

"I've never known a man like you, McBain." Her voice was strong now, as if she must make a firm statement, as though she must let him hear the words she stored in her heart. "I've found more happiness and joy in the past week than I have a right to. I should be dreading each day, fearing the worst to happen and yet I find myself eager to open my eyes each morning, because I know your face will be the first thing I see, your voice the first thing I hear. I love the way you say my name, the kisses you offer and the thrill of knowing you seek my pleasure before your own."

His arms tightened, his body wrapped her in their warm shelter, and they slept.

IT WAS MORNING BEFORE they roused again, the sun casting its golden glow into their bedroom window, awakening them even as the rooster from next door crowed his song.

"You didn't go into the office," she said, feeling just a tinge of guilt that she had so occupied his thoughts that his job had been forgotten.

"No, I didn't, did I?" His words held a smile, a hint of laughter, and he wrapped her again in his embrace. "Now, sweetheart, if you don't make the first move toward getting up, I'll just keep you here and have breakfast in bed."

"I'm up," she said quickly, rolling from him and rising, searching out her clothing. "My chemise is ruined," she said, picking up the tattered bit of silk from the floor.

He did his best to look ashamed and subdued, and failed miserably. "Yeah. I tore it, didn't I?"

"You know you did," she said, crossing to the dresser to find clean underclothes. Looking back over her shoulder, she caught his eye, noting the satisfied look he wore. "And I don't even care, Sheriff. You can just buy me another one."

"I can do that. A couple of them." He rolled from his side of the bed and gathered up his clothing. "I'm going to wash up and then get dressed while you find the coffeepot, sweet. I'll help you with breakfast in ten minutes."

She nodded agreeably and quickly found the clothing she sought, buttoning her dress as she left the room.

AARON MADE HIS WAY TO TOWN after they ate, checked with his deputy and looked in on the two men in cells. Both sported bruises and blackened eyes and he shook his head as he surveyed the damage. "You're pitiful, the both of you," he said. "Now, get your lazy bones out of here and behave yourself. You could both do with a bath and a shave, and if you're not making tracks in the next minute, I'll haul you before the judge for disturbing the peace when he rides into town next week."

The two men hustled out the cell doors, once they were unlocked, and made haste to go out the back door of the jailhouse. Neither of them seemed willing to continue their brawl, both intent on locating the barbershop for some much needed care.

It was almost dinnertime when Aaron left for home, stopping to greet townsfolk as he walked down the wooden sidewalk. It seemed that most of the citizens were well aware of his wedding, for he found congratulations on every hand, and it seemed for a while that he would never reach the end of the parade of well-wishers.

Even the stationmaster greeted him, hastening toward him from the train station, waving a piece of paper in his hand.

"This came for your wife, Sheriff. Just got it off the wire. A message from Philadelphia. Looks like it might be considered good news," he said with a wide grin, admitting his own curiosity readily. In order to have written down the message, the man would have had to hear it for himself, and so Aaron could not find it in his heart to reprimand the man.

"Thank you. I'll take it to her. I'm just on my way home now." Without perusing the scrawled words, Aaron put the message in his pocket and hurried home.

"Sweetheart—I have something for you," he called out, walking across the threshold, searching out the parlor for her presence. She came from the kitchen, smiling, open-armed and headed directly for his embrace. He gave it gladly, then held her apart from himself and made his announcement.

"I have a wire for you. Just came in at the station."

"What does it say? Who could be sending me a message?"

"Find out for yourself," he said, pulling the long slip of paper from his pocket and pressing it into her hand. "I haven't read it, Susannah. It's your message, not mine."

"You could have," she murmured. "I wouldn't have cared." And then she seemed lost as she scanned the long message she'd received.

Aaron nudged her, impatient with her silence. "He said it was from Philadelphia."

"Yes." She raised wide eyes to look into his gaze. "My parents. They've been looking for me, Aaron. And I didn't let them know where I was. I should be ashamed not to have let them know…something, anything."

"How did they find you?"

"They contacted someone in Washington, I suspect. My father knows a multitude of important people. Anyway, he heard from the U.S. marshal's office that I was here in Ottawa Falls, safe and sound."

Aaron reached for her, holding her tightly. "I'm glad they know."

Her eyes were dazed, her expression bewildered as she looked up at him. "That's not all. They went to the house in Philadelphia and found insurance papers that yielded a large amount of money upon John's death. They took it upon themselves to sell the house. I think my mother knew how unhappy I had been living there. And then they went to Washington and got rid of that house, too. They have all my belongings. And they have a considerable amount of money for me. They want the name of the banker in town, so they can have it transferred here."

"We can take care of that right away, Susannah," he said, his mind boggled by the news of her inheritance. Susannah was a well-to-do woman, it seemed. No longer dependent on him for her day-to-day living. That thought struck him with a pang of foreboding.

"What will you do with it?" he asked.

"The money? Save it, probably." She leaned back in his embrace, her eyes thoughtful. "If I'd had it a few months ago, I wouldn't be here now, Aaron. I'd be a long way west of here, still hiding out, still wandering."

"I'm glad this news didn't make itself known until now. I've got you neatly tied up and married to me," he said with a chuckle.

She nodded slowly. "But it's good to know that I'm not without funds should the occasion ever arise."

What occasion? The silent query filtered through his mind and he banished it. There would never come a time when Susannah would need her funds to run away again. The occasion she spoke of was no doubt a thought for their future, perhaps a larger house.

They ate their noon meal and he took his leave, promising a stop at the bank to speak with the gentleman in charge there. "I'll be home for supper," he promised.

The afternoon went quickly and he made the promised stop at the bank and then walked home. The gate to his house stood ajar and he strode to the porch, his hat in one hand, the other reaching for the doorknob.

"Are you home, sweetheart?" he called out, entering the parlor.

"Where did you think I'd be?" Her appearance in the doorway was a sight to behold, he decided, her hair shining, her dress crisp and unwrinkled, as if she had just pressed it, readying herself for his arrival. She came to him without hesitation, opening her arms and welcoming him with the warmth of her embrace.

"Supper is about ready. I fried up a chicken for you. Hattie killed a couple this morning and brought one over to me." Susannah cringed visibly. "I don't know if I'll ever get used to the idea of killing and cleaning one. It kind of ruins the whole thing for me."

"You don't have to. The butcher has them in his store, all cleaned and ready to cook."

"But not as fresh as the ones from Hattie's chicken coop. And this one is just the way you like it, all crisp and brown."

"I'll eat it any way you fix it," he told her, releasing her from his arms and sniffing the air with appreciation. "Just let me get washed up."

He went to the kitchen sink and scrubbed his hands and arms, rolling his shirtsleeves to his elbows first. He bent his head and splashed water on his face, then ran his fingers through his hair, dampening it down, taming the waves.

"Come and sit down." Susannah pulled his chair from the table and then brought the platter of chicken from the warming oven. Bowls of vegetables, beans from the garden, carrots swimming in butter, fluffy potatoes and a pitcher of gravy completed the meal. They sat down and she bent her head, speaking words of thanksgiving for their safety and for the food they would share.

Then a knock sounded at the door, and Aaron bolted upright, rising in a movement that spilled his chair to the floor.

"Don't move," he said, the words sounding harsh, his voice carrying a note of command. With long strides, he crossed the room, found the gun he'd laid aside just minutes ago and spun the cylinder, seeking the sight of cartridges within. He held it at his side and turned his attention to his wife.

"Go into the bedroom and shut the door, Susannah," he said, his tone one she could not ignore. She did as he asked and he turned away, crossing into the parlor where the sound of a fist vibrated against the front door and a voice called his name in strident tones.

"McBain. Let me in."

CHAPTER ELEVEN

"WHO IS IT?" AARON'S TONE left no room for dispute, no space for dithering, and the man outside his door laughed, a harsh bit of amusement that McBain obviously had not expected.

And then he spoke, his voice resounding with authority. "Sam Peterson." There was silence for a few seconds, a silence broken abruptly as McBain turned the lock and swung the door to one side.

"I thought you'd be expecting me." The man who leaned against the doorjamb was big, broad chested and tall, almost a twin in height to the giant who faced him. He looked across the room, past the sofa and the armoire that graced one wall to where the bedroom door stood open.

"You've got company in here?" Sam asked, looking past Aaron.

"Yeah, but she's supposed to have the door shut." His lips tightened. "Susannah. Come on out here.

"My wife," Aaron said, casting a look of ownership in Susannah's direction as she passed through the bedroom doorway. She exuded curiosity, glistening gray eyes on the visitor, the glow of her countenance seeming to stun Sam where he stood.

Aaron allowed his eyes to feast on her, proud of the loveliness she possessed, knowing that the look of happiness she wore like a second skin was of his doing. "Say hello to Sam, Susannah."

"Hello, Sam," she said obediently, a flush rising to color her cheeks with a hue resembling a ripe peach, even as she eyed the two men with a measuring gaze, as if she compared them and found them to be like two halves of a pair of bookends. And then her gaze flew to encompass Aaron. Her smile was secretive and a thing of delight, her eyes sparkling as if she sent him a silent message.

"Susannah." As though speaking her name was address enough, Sam Peterson removed his hat, a wide-brimmed piece of apparel that closely matched that favored by her husband, and held it at his side. "Would you like me to go away and come back in fifteen minutes?" he asked. "I hope I didn't interrupt anything."

Susannah shook her head. "We were just preparing to eat our dinner. If you'll just step into the kitchen, I'll put out a plate for you, and fill a cup with coffee. I knew someone would be showing up today, but I'd forgotten the time. I must have missed hearing the afternoon train. I fear I wasn't prepared for company."

"This isn't company," Aaron said mildly. "This is Sam."

"He's company to me," she told him smartly. "And I'll bet he's hungry if he just got off the train."

With a smile of pure masculine appreciation, Sam nudged Aaron toward the open kitchen door, then eyed him with a critical glance. "Are you certain I wasn't interrupting anything? You look a bit put out with me, my friend."

"No such thing," Susannah said, interrupting as Aaron opened his mouth to speak and sending him a telling glance. She had Sam settled at the table in moments, silverware and dishes in place.

"This looks like heaven," Sam said, spooning gravy over his helping of potatoes. "You fell into a bed of roses this time, my friend. A lovely wife and a good cook, to boot. I suspect you're one terrific lady, Mrs. McBain," Sam Peterson said, his eyes cruising with appreciation over the slender female across the table from him.

"Aaron always had an eye for a beautiful female. I'm glad he hasn't lost his touch," Sam continued, dishing up vegetables onto his plate, then adding a chicken leg.

"It sounds to me as if you know him even better than I," Susannah said blandly. "But out of all the females he's met, I'm the one he ended up marrying, Sam. And that's the best part of it."

His face sobered as she spoke. "I've known McBain for a long time, and I'd trust him with my life. I'm just joshing you ma'am. He's one in a million, and his concerns right now are all wrapped up in your well-being, I'll guarantee. We haven't had a chance to talk about it yet, but when McBain asks for my help, he has it. When he wants someone to guard his back, he has only to look my way. When he asked for an agent out here to check into things, I asked for the job."

"I had a notion you'd be the one getting off that train," Aaron said, picking up his piece of chicken, then biting into the crisp coating and shooting a glance of approval in Susannah's direction.

Sam made inroads on his potatoes and gravy, ate most of his green beans and then settled back in his chair, as if getting his second wind. "Well, this is an unexpected treat," he told them. "I know I'm here on government business, McBain, but I hope your bride will see me as a friend, instead of just a U.S. marshal."

"Yes, a marshal friend. How nice that will be," Susannah said, swallowing the lump that formed in her throat. The man had authority beyond that of Aaron, she thought, and obviously bore a lot of influence in Washington.

"No less." Sam grinned. "Makes me sound important, doesn't it?" He sobered a bit and directed
his attention solely to Susannah. "The fact that
I've known McBain for a lot of years was on my
side, and when the bureau found our connection,
they jumped at the chance to have us working
together on this. I'm here in an official capacity."

He broke off and his gaze softened as if
Susannah's stricken expression had hit a somber
note. "I didn't mean to upset you, Susannah," he
said quietly. "I'll grant you I'm a U.S. marshal,
but first and foremost, I'm Aaron's friend, and
I'll do whatever I can to get this whole mess
straightened out."

"Yes. All right." She floundered, suddenly
aware that the long journey she'd been traveling
had come to an end and the ordeal of investigating
John Carvel's death was about to begin.

IT SEEMED THAT THEY would live their usual day-
to-day existence for a while, waiting, as Sam said,
for the fun to begin. Susannah cooked and cleaned,
learning the role of a housewife, enjoying the
everyday circumstances of small-town life. She
was not allowed to go alone from the house, even
her shopping at the general store having to be in
the company of one of the men.

The scrutiny of the townsfolk when she

appeared with Sam at her side was enough to dampen her enthusiasm for the day, and she silently vowed to stay at home unless Aaron was able to accompany her.

Sam was the topic of discussion in town and the object of intense interest among the ladies, those who were still searching out a proper husband. Even the women who had families of their own and husbands at hand managed to give Sam the once-over, smiling and indulging in behavior that ventured on the edge of flirtation.

It was heady stuff indeed, this business of having two men at her beck and call, but Susannah was wise enough to realize that there was a deeper reason for their vigilance. The stationmaster had been notified that the presence of a stranger descending from a train would be immediately reported to the sheriff's office and he had offered his help should it be required.

Aaron's deputy was put on full-time alert and advised of the circumstances, and his presence at the jailhouse on a regular basis gave Aaron some much needed breathing space. Their evenings were free of official duties, with Walt Turner doing the late-night patrol of businesses in town.

A wire sent to Sam was cause for concern early in the second week of his sojourn. The stationmaster's appearance at the door brought Sam from the kitchen, with orders to Susannah to wait until he should check into things before she made an appearance. Sam's utter silence in the parlor once the door was closed behind the messenger brought Susannah into the kitchen doorway.

"What is it, Sam?" Her eyes were pinned on the paper he held and she felt a shaft of disquiet pierce her as he turned to meet her gaze.

"News I'd rather not have heard. Not that it affects you directly, Susannah, but it isn't a good sign."

"Aaron will be home for dinner in a few minutes. Do you want to wait till he gets here before you talk about it?" She made the offer, hoping he'd refuse it and instead give her whatever news he'd received.

It was not to be, for Sam grasped at the straw she'd tossed in his direction and folded the message quickly, placing it in his shirt pocket. "Might be a good idea. Aaron won't want you upset, and in the mood you're in—" He shrugged and smiled, a strained gesture that gave her no comfort.

"I'm not a child, Sam," she said abruptly. "I can handle most anything that comes down the pike. After my years in Washington, nothing would surprise me."

The sound of the door opening made the discussion redundant as Aaron stepped over the threshold and joined them.

"I hope I'm not too late for dinner. Had to do some last-minute cleaning up at the saloon before I headed for home."

"Cleaning up?" Sam's words held a tinge of laughter and he grinned as he met Aaron's gaze.

"The usual, just a couple of cowhands who decided to fight over one of the girls there. They managed to break up a couple of chairs and bashed in a table. They'll lose their pay for the next couple of weeks to pay for it."

"And in the meantime they'll sit in a cell."

Aaron nodded. "We'll set up court before we let them go. Otherwise, they'll likely collect their wages and be out of the county before old Nate over at the saloon gets his money."

"Sam just received a wire from—" Susannah halted her words and looked blankly at Sam. "You didn't say who it was from, did you?"

"No, but I'm sure you've got a good idea," he told her. He turned to Aaron. "We need to take her testimony right away, McBain. A man is coming in tomorrow to get it all down in black and white, and he'll wire it on to Washington. We want everything legal and aboveboard in this."

"The stationmaster will be reading the wire?" Susannah's words were stunned, her active mind already whirling with the possibilities inherent in allowing another person to be privy to her past.

"It'll be all over town by Friday," she said. "Nothing is private to a small-town citizen."

Sam's face took on a hard cast that was guaranteed to strike fear to the heart of anyone who dared cross him. "I don't think so, Susannah. This isn't so unimportant a matter as the wire you got from your parents. When you deal with the United States government, you don't pass around gossip. And should the words you speak get into circulation, the person who caused the ruckus will be out of a job, and spending his time in a federal prison. We don't play games with people who don't abide by the rules."

"It's that important?" She knew her voice wavered, but couldn't seem to put a halt to the trembling that had overtaken her body. "What do you want of me, Sam?"

"When our man arrives, he'll take your statement. Probably down at the sheriff's office. And then it goes to Washington. And we wait."

She nodded, shrinking within herself, knowing that the very marrow of her bones would be exposed in the words she must speak. Her private self would be opened to inspection by the men who sought her out. *Will Aaron still want me, once he knows how the filth of politics has stained my soul?*

As if he knew her unspoken thoughts, Aaron rose from his chair and rounded the table. "Don't look so stricken, sweetheart. Sam and I will be there, and you only have to tell Sam what you've already told me."

"Tomorrow?" she asked, her voice tight, her throat closing with the fear she could not repel. No matter that Aaron and Sam were here to protect her, her words might set loose the very demons of the underworld, with the intent of negating her ability to speak against their members.

Sam's jaw clenched as he shot a look at Aaron, a glance that seemed to be part apology, part a seeking for permission. And without words, Aaron gave what he asked, his head moving in an almost imperceptible nod.

"Yes." Sam spoke the single word that brought terror to Susannah's heart. "Tomorrow."

TOMORROW ARRIVED SOONER than Aaron was ready for the time to come. Once inside his office, he offered Susannah the most comfortable chair of the three surrounding his desk and met the young man sent from Washington.

"Susannah, this is Phil Hogan," Sam told her quietly, nodding at the dapper form of the secretary, a tall, dark-haired man, open-faced and seemingly mild-mannered. "He's the best at what he does. Namely, taking your statement and then helping to keep you safe."

"I'd like to say I'm pleased to meet you," she murmured, "but my mama taught me not to lie."

The smile she received in reply was genuine, and Aaron breathed freely for the first time in this whole live-long morning. He'd dreaded this ordeal for Susannah's sake, and his pride in her expanded as he watched the woman settle in for the interrogation that was ahead, almost as if she were playing hostess at an afternoon tea. She was a lady, from stem to stern, and that fact was brought home to him as she folded her hands in her lap and gave her attention to Sam.

Only someone who knew her well would recognize the difficulty she was having, holding all ten fingers in a graceful position instead of being wrapped like tentacles around each other. Her jaw was taut, but her expression was contained, and the glow in her eyes spoke of integrity.

Pride filled him as Aaron watched her. Pride of possession that this woman belonged to him, that she had agreed to spend her life with him, the self-respect she exuded as an intrinsic part of her very being, and the upright tilt of her head that exposed her fully. She was not fearful of the truth, indeed she gloried in it, and today would mark the end of the turmoil she had carried with her for so long.

"Are you ready to begin, my dear?" Sam used the term so easily, Aaron thought. *My dear, indeed.*

And yet, he had said the words as a tribute, and Phil Hogan showed every sign of hearing and appreciating the depth of Sam Peterson's respect for the woman. His own eyes appeared to touch her with a new dawning of admiration, and he readied his pen and paper to take her statement.

"Mrs. Carvel," he began, and Susannah held up a hand to halt his address.

"I'm now Susannah McBain," she said firmly. "I will never again answer to the name I took upon my first marriage."

"Yes, ma'am," Phil said, his lips curving just a bit. "I apologize, ma'am." He cleared his throat. "Will you begin with your marriage to the senator?" he asked. "What was the state of your relationship with him?"

Susannah's cheeks colored as her head bowed for a moment, and then she spoke, words that touched Aaron's heart with her pain.

"My husband was a womanizer of the first degree. He had numerous women as his companions, his mistresses, if you like. We had not occupied the same bed for several months before his death. I was living in Philadelphia, at the family home, while he moved back and forth to the capital, depending on his work.

"I went to Washington as needed, to hostess parties, or to appear with him at balls and formal occasions in the social structure of Washington."

"Did you stay with him at those times?" Phillip had become merely a voice in the background, it seemed, for Susannah simply answered his query without moving her gaze from the wall before her.

"I stayed at the Washington house, eating meals with his political acquaintances, filling the place prescribed for me as his wife."

"And did you hear of his doings at any time? Any demands that might have been made on him by his contacts in the mining industry?"

She paused, her long fingers entwining in a nervous fashion, and Aaron ached to reach out to her, his own hands yearning to close over those trembling fingers. But it would not do. She must face this alone.

"Not much," Susannah answered. "I knew he was in contact with the men who owned the mines, and I knew they were fearful of the workers going on strike. There was legislation in the works that would prevent such a thing from happening, and the coal magnates were prepared to pay dearly for protection from the union organizers. There were numerous politicians in our home, at meals and parties, but the meetings he had with the mine owners and the men who were prepared to sell their votes to him were always conducted late at night. I was not privy to them, and I have no idea which senators or representatives were in that group."

Her eyes flitted to McBain and found him seemingly relaxed, leaning back in his chair, one foot propped on the other knee, his gleaming western-style boots at home here. There was a comfort in his placid acceptance of this, she thought. As though he feared but little for the outcome.

Sam spoke then. "I'll ask you some leading questions and you can answer or not, as you please, Susannah. I'd advise you, however, to give us as much information as you can about the night of the senator's death."

She nodded, felt the trembling of her mouth and then the touch of Aaron's hand on her shoulder, as though he had known of her fear. As if she were transparent before him, all of her anxieties exposed and visible.

The next hour was long, the tension almost unbearable as she spoke aloud the memories that haunted her days and nights.

She'd reached almost the end of her story, reluctant as she revealed the shock she'd felt upon entering her bedroom in the Washington house. "He called her Bettina, but I have no idea what her last name was. She was blond, pretty, his usual sort of girlfriend." She smiled grimly and lifted a hand from her lap, brushing it over her dark hair and then returning it to its resting place. "As you can see before you, I did not meet his criteria."

Her hair gleamed in the light from the window, her eyes filling with tears as she described the cruel destruction of her marriage. And Aaron thought he would like to kill the man who had so betrayed her, had he not already met his fate at the hand of another.

"Bettina." Sam repeated the name and glanced at the man who had joined them for this occasion. "Sound familiar, Phillip?"

The man nodded, rose from his seat and opened his briefcase, left conveniently on the floor by the desk. Withdrawing a sheaf of papers in his hand, he gave them to Sam and took his seat, careful to steer clear of the area where Susannah sat, as if re- alizing she was the personal possession of the lawman just behind her.

"That's what I thought," Sam said, the papers in his hand rustling as he scanned them. "I was certain I remembered the woman, and surely it is not a com- monplace name. Bettina Crawford. According to our reports, she was a party girl, part-time mistress to a number of politicians and full-time floozy."

"Was?" Aaron asked quietly.

Sam looked up, nodded and handed Aaron the first sheet of those he was perusing. "*Was* is the de- finitive word. She was found floating in the Potomac three weeks ago. It seems that the lady lost her popularity with someone. And I think it would behoove us to find out just who that someone is. It may answer a lot of questions for us."

"She was murdered?" Susannah asked, the memory of the blue-eyed blonde still alive in her mind.

"Sure looks that way," Sam said. "Drowned, but probably not of her own choice. I doubt the woman dove in for a swim. More likely she was tossed in, perhaps already unconscious, if the large bump on the back of her skull was any indication."

"No clues?" Aaron asked briefly.

"Nothing so far," Sam said, acknowledging the current state of the investigation.

"We've been questioning people who knew her, but no one wants to admit to anything," Phil offered. "She was an enigma, it seems. A friend to many, enemy to a scattered few and available for hire to men who needed information."

"Any idea who hired her in this case?" Aaron had straightened in his chair at Phillip's statement. "Was she looking for something more important than a relationship with the senator? Perhaps delving into his private affairs?"

Sam threw an apologetic look in Susannah's direction as he divulged his opinion. "The easiest way to find out about a man, they tell me, is to sleep in his bed. Personally, I wouldn't know, having limited my bed partner to the woman I married, since the day I spoke my vows."

"A man after my own heart," Susannah said softly, her voice barely audible, yet obviously at a level that brushed Aaron's ears, for he reached to touch her, a simple laying of his hand over her forearm, but a touch that brought her attention to him in the form of a small smile, one he seemed to understand.

Phillip continued, with an inquiring look at Sam. "At any rate, Bettina had made a pretty lucrative business from her pursuit of information. Obviously she made someone very unhappy with her a few weeks ago. She vanished from her room at the hotel, and was not seen again until they pulled her from the river."

Sam spread his hands in a gesture expressing his frustration. "The department is working on it now, according to this report." He indicated the papers he held. "They're tracing her whereabouts, the men she was seen with, the places she visited."

"With no luck?" Aaron asked.

"Oh, we know she was a good friend to the gentlemen who lobby for the coal mine owners, a close friend of the French ambassador, the gentleman whose wife had a torrid affair with an unnamed member of Congress. The senator himself had close ties to people who hung around in the shadows, supporting the coal industry, but negotiating their own little deals. In fact, Carvel had made some political promises to the big shots about introducing bills that would make it illegal for the coal workers to go on strike." He looked at Susannah.

"I fear they thought you were privy to that information, Susannah. And they don't want you talking to the authorities about their plans."

"John told me nothing. He sent me from the room when his visitors arrived, late at night sometimes. They were not men who appealed to me in any way. Brawny, bold, with poor language and no manners to speak of. I never minded not spending time with them."

Sam listened carefully to her words and then spoke knowingly. "Those were no doubt the men who own the mines. They were very unhappy with the senator over the promises he failed to keep. He had the ability to either make millions for them or bring them to the brink of disaster. The organizers were uniting the workers and making threats and if they were to go on strike, it would mean millions of dollars from someone's pockets."

Sam leaned back in his chair, his fingers touching, forming peaks that seemed to hold his interest, so totally did he concentrate on them. "That's the one lead that intrigues me, and will probably split this case wide open. Carvel had enemies in high places, and those people aren't above sending out a hired gun when they need to issue a general warning."

"You think he might have been the victim of such a person, a hired gun?" Aaron asked.

Sam shrugged, his attitude clearly one of ignorance as it applied to the problem at hand. "Anything is possible, McBain," he said. "It would certainly make sense to turn the finger of suspicion on the senator's wife, make her look like the bad guy in this whole mess. Right now we have a whole laundry list of people who were out for the senator's blood. He wasn't very good at keeping his friends and enemies separated. I'm told the French ambassador was out to get him, and when it gets to a point where he's hated on an international level, a man needs to be watching his back. I think our friend got careless, and lost his life. Could be he trusted the wrong person."

"His mistress? Bettina?" Susannah spoke the words almost under her breath, but Sam's hearing was astute and he nodded.

"Did Bettina kill him?" For the first time, Susannah put words to the solution she'd hoped for. "Did they know for certain that he was shot in the back?"

"Oh, yeah. The bullet that killed him came from behind. What we don't know is who was on the bed with him. No one else was there but you, your husband and his mistress, according to your story."

"And you don't believe me." She spoke it as a statement of fact, and Sam shook his head.

"I didn't say that. I only said that your version of the story leaves you in the clear. The problem is that there are those who won't believe it. You're the likely target, Susannah. If Senator Carvel was shot by a hired gun, the men who wrote out the contract would likely be very pleased to see you on trial for the murder. They might even offer proof that you were in cahoots with them."

"You think she's in danger?" Aaron asked quietly, his gaze direct as he faced Sam.

"Again, I'll have to say I don't know. I wouldn't take any chances if I were you. Keep a close eye on anyone who seems to be approaching her, watch for problems."

"Do they know where I am?" Susannah's fear was apparent to all three of the men, Aaron probably the most aware of her trembling, sitting behind her, watching the movement of her gown as shivers moved over her body.

"I wouldn't be surprised. By now, they've no doubt traced you to Denver at least, and maybe even to Ottawa Falls. Did you use your legal name at the hospital here when you were working as a nurse?"

"No. I'm Anna Whitfield on the records there."

"Whitfield is on your birth certificate." Sam spoke the words slowly, as if aware that her maiden name was of public record. He directed a look of intent at Aaron. "We'll need to take precautions, McBain. Don't let her out of our sight, until this thing is finished."

"Do I have to go back to Washington? Will there be a trial?" Susannah asked the questions that had preyed on her mind all morning, indeed for the past weeks.

"Not if we can prove the involvement of the mine owners."

"Don't worry, sweet." Aaron's words came from directly behind her and he rose, lifting her from her chair, his arm encircling her waist. "We'll look after you. Between Sam, Phil and myself, you'll be as safe as a baby in its cradle."

THE WALK BACK TO HIS HOME was quick, Susannah surrounded by the three men who seemed prepared to guard her with their very lives. Phillip had spent long minutes at the train station, preparing his report and sending it off to Washington, then returned to join them as they made the jaunt to Aaron's home.

"I'll fix something to eat," Susannah offered as they entered the parlor. "It'll only be a half hour or so."

"No such thing." A new voice entered the flow

of conversation as Hattie Cooper poked her head through the kitchen doorway. "I've got soup and corn bread all ready for you to eat. Made a big pitcher of lemonade, too. Come on in the kitchen."

Susannah's smile was genuine as she approached Hattie and hugged her impulsively. "I'm so glad I found you, Hattie. You've proved to be a good friend."

"I'll help look after you, Susannah," the older woman told her. "I spoke to your friend here, Mr. Peterson, and he told me a little about the problems you've had. You know I'll do anything in the world for Aaron McBain, and that automatically includes you."

Susannah felt tears approaching and she steered Hattie back to the kitchen. "I'll introduce you to our other visitor later," she said. "Let me help you put this meal on, first."

"That's the lady who shot the bank robber, isn't it?" Sam asked Aaron.

"I suspect you already know that," Aaron replied. "She seems to be acquainted with you already. When did you have time to speak with her?"

"I met her on the street the day I arrived in town. We already had a report on the robbery she interrupted. Banks are protected under the government, you know, and Hattie Cooper is a heroine, so far as I'm concerned."

"She certainly knows how to use that little derringer she carries," Aaron said quickly. "And I'm mighty thankful for that."

The meal was eaten and well appreciated by Susannah and the three men, Hattie serving them, with Susannah doing more watching than eating. Aaron tossed several looks in her direction and she knew she was in for a scolding when they had a moment of privacy. He didn't approve of her lack of appetite lately, and had been vocal about his concern for her loss of weight.

Accordingly, she bent over her bowl and ate what she could of Hattie's soup, relishing the flavors of fresh vegetables and the underlying hint of beef. Aaron's smile lent encouragement to her efforts, and the men pushed back their chairs and prepared to retire to the parlor.

"I need to go to the general store, Aaron," Susannah said as he would have walked past her. "We need a few things in the kitchen, and I want to get a roast for supper."

"I'll go with her, Sheriff," Hattie offered. "We'll keep a good eye out."

"I doubt there's been time enough for anyone to arrive in town set on giving your wife any trouble," Sam said in an undertone. "And Miss Hattie will no doubt have her trusty derringer handy if need be."

His smile lent a bit of humor to his words, but Susannah knew he was deadly serious about her welfare. She felt safe with Hattie, knowing that the townspeople would be surrounding her in the store and she'd be more than visible walking to and from the center of town.

SHE WAS HERE, NEARBY, he could feel it. The woman he'd come here to locate, to speak with. The woman who held the fate of influential men in her palm, did she but know it. The man looked up and down the sidewalk, searching out the female he'd been told to find, with no success, for no woman met his gaze who might be Susannah Carvel.

He was patient. Leaning against a post before the saloon, he kept an eye on the townspeople who walked the boardwalk. He could wait. She was here, somewhere. He could feel it and his intuition was seldom at fault. It was why he was so good at his job.

CHAPTER TWELVE

SUSANNAH WAS JUST leaving the livery stable when a tall man appeared before her, a smile on his face. He was unknown to her and she froze, a sense of foreboding touching her spine, a shudder gripping her body. She'd felt safe with Hattie by her side for the shopping trip, but Hattie was waiting for her at the Emporium. The man reached for her as he stepped closer to where she stood and gripped her forearm roughly. She was stunned to face him, a man she'd never seen before, yet one who filled her with a sense of dread, his face wide and cruel-seeming—his hands harsh against her skin.

"Susannah Carvel. Just the lady I've been looking for." His voice was smooth, cultured, but his eyes held a danger she feared. Hatred spewed from dark eyes, chilling her body like a cold flood of river water.

"Let loose of me," she said, struggling to free herself from his hold, not wanting to draw attention to herself in public, yet fearful of the danger he represented.

"Not till we talk for a minute." He was planted firmly before her and his hand was strong, his fingers clutching her, allowing her no recourse but to stand where she was, under his control for the moment. Built in a stocky fashion, he resembled a man of the docks, or perhaps a fighter in the ring.

With a shout, she could have roused attention, but the row of old men who frequented the bench before the Emporium were unlikely to be of much use as rescuers. She did not take well to the idea of putting them in peril. The man before her was no doubt in possession of a weapon and she would not place others in jeopardy if she could help it.

"You've got a lot of secrets stored in that pretty head of yours, Miss Susannah," the brute said quietly, his smile a travesty as he spoke, lest he appear to be the ruffian he really was. "I'm here to tell you that it would be to your advantage if you keep what you know private, and keep your mouth shut. Sam Peterson is a smart man, but he can't do josh without your word as a witness, and there are those who are determined to rid this world of his sort."

"I don't know what you're talking about," she said, her arm feeling numb as his fingers clutched at her more tightly.

"You know damn well what I'm speaking of, and you'd better know that the wrong word out of your mouth will mean your husband's life. We don't care who gets in the way of our guns, and if we weren't in the middle of town right now I'd be tempted to pull my own weapon and use it on you. Kind of leave a lesson behind.

"The men who run things in Washington don't want any hassle from you, Mrs. Carvel. Don't think you'll get away with spilling what you know to the sheriff or his friend. In fact, you'd be wise to head out of here, take a train west and stay away from the sheriff and the U.S. marshal. They'll be safer without you around. This is a warning. You won't get another."

His grip loosened on her and he stepped down into the street, watched for a moment as a buggy neared and then climbed to the high seat as the driver snapped the reins and spurred the horse into a swift trot.

"Susannah!" Aaron's voice was harsh, his movements quick as he approached, his eyes intent on her arm where the man's fingers had been so recently fastened. "If I'd been just a minute sooner, this wouldn't have happened," he told her, searching her face, visibly shaken by the sight. After spotting the man talking to her, he'd run the last few steps to reach her. His words were breathless, his voice trembling.

"What did he say to you?" Aaron's voice was toneless now, as if he'd gathered his self-control and held it firmly, his words soft, spoken next to Susannah's ear as he stood beside her. "Did he hurt you?" His gaze touched the long sleeve of her dress, as if he would peer beneath the fabric that covered her skin and examine the flesh that had been contaminated by the man's hand.

"No, I may have a bruise, but I'm not hurt," Susannah said quietly. "I have no idea who he was, but he told me I'd do well not to talk to anyone about anything, and get myself on a train out of here."

"Did he threaten you specifically? Was he wearing a gun?" And if he had, Aaron would track the monster down if it took him forever. To his relief, she shook her head.

"He said he had a gun, but I didn't see it."

"Stay close to me. We won't take any more chances with you being alone. That fella must have been watching for a chance to have you to himself, and when you appeared out here in front of the Mercantile, it was no doubt an answer to his prayer.

"Now, let's get you home." Aaron looked up as his name was called, and Ellis Monroe pulled his wagon to a halt before the store.

"Hey there, McBain," Ellis said. "Got a message for you, but I didn't expect to see you here. I came by to pick up your wife and take her home with her shopping. Walt Turner over at the train station said there was a fella got off the morning train from the east. He thought you'd want to heed the warning."

"Thanks, Ellis. We've seen him already."

Behind them, the door opened and Hattie stepped out onto the sidewalk, the proprietor behind her, his arms full of parcels that Susannah had selected earlier. He obeyed Susannah's silent nod and deposited them in the back of Ellis's wagon. Hattie followed and added her contribution to the pile, then turned back to where Aaron stood, his arm circling Susannah's waist.

"Y'all gonna ride on the wagon with me?" she asked and then shook her head knowingly. "Just as I thought. The walk home will do Susannah good, get her a little exercise, Sheriff. I'll get this stuff put to rights in the kitchen by the time you get there."

With a strong arm, Ellis tucked Miss Hattie on the seat beside him and picked up his reins, bending to hand a folded bit of paper to Aaron. Tipping his hat at the couple watching him, he set off down the road, and Aaron turned Susannah toward home.

"Did you recognize him?" he asked as they strolled along. His eyes scanned the sidewalk ahead, the passing buggies and wagons on the road and the people who walked hither and yon, both on the road and the sidewalk.

Susannah shook her head. "I don't have any idea who he was, but he had the general appearance of the men who used to visit the house in Washington. He was big and even though his clothing was of first quality, he didn't fit it well." She looked up at him. "Does that sound foolish? Not that it was too large or small for him, but somehow not what he was accustomed to wearing. I suspect he's long gone now. A man in a buggy picked him up and they drove off out of town."

"He looked like a scoundrel to me," Aaron said sharply. "A man being used as a weapon by his boss. I probably should have gone after him, but I wanted to get to you." He turned her in at the gate before his house and they stepped up onto the porch.

"I'm frightened," Susannah admitted, turning to him just inside their door. He raised his hand, halting her words and motioned with his palm that she should remain where she was, holding a finger to his lips in a gesture of silence. Quickly, he made a tour of the rooms, both the bedroom and his study, checking the closets and looking behind the draperies, finally returning to where she waited.

"Everything seems to be in order. I can hear Hattie in the kitchen, and it doesn't look like anyone has been here. Sam and Phillip have gone to my office. I was on my way there when I saw you in front of the Emporium with that stranger.

I'm glad I took a quick look around before I went inside. I'd have missed you otherwise."

"I've never lived in fear like this," she said softly. "Oddly, even when I was married to John, I felt safe, protected from many of the world's cares. Now, suddenly, I feel adrift, and no one is to be trusted."

He gripped her shoulders and turned her to face him. "You told me once that you trusted me with your life, Susannah. Has that changed?"

She looked up into eyes that seemed to hold the answers to all her problems. "Oh, no, Aaron. You're the one part of all this that gives me courage to walk the next step into the future. I know Sam is on the up and up, but I don't have the same faith in him that I have in you. I love you, Aaron McBain." She leaned up on her tiptoes and sought his mouth, pressing her lips against his in a gesture that he thought rather telling.

The woman was no longer shy with him, but able to demand what she wanted of him. And right now, that demand was for comfort, for arms that would hold and protect her, giving her a small oasis of safety against the rest of the world. She curled against him, and he went to the sofa, holding her tightly as he pulled her into his lap.

From the kitchen, Hattie's voice called her name, and in moments the lady appeared, obviously noting the high color that rode Susannah's cheeks.

"Sit right where you are, missy. That man wants to take care of you, you just let him. I've got the roast ready to put in the oven, and when you get done with your shenanigans, you can help me put together a batch of bread."

With a conspirator's grin aimed at Aaron, she turned and swept back into the kitchen, leaving a gaping Susannah behind, Aaron laughing as he held her immobile on his lap.

"*Shenanigans,* is it? Is that what you're plotting?" Susannah asked, embarrassed to be found in such an indecorous position.

"No," Aaron said softly, "just a man who wants to make certain his wife is all in one piece, with no harm done to her. I want you come in the bedroom with me, sweetheart. This room isn't private enough for what I have in mind."

"None of that," Susannah told him firmly. "It's the middle of the day and I've got things to do, and a friend waiting in the kitchen. I'll be teased enough as it is."

He lifted her from his lap and towed her behind himself to the bedroom, closing the door silently and then reaching for her again. His arms enclosed her and she felt his big body tremble against hers.

"I was scared to death, sweet," he managed to mutter, and Susannah didn't have the heart to break from his hold. She fit there, as if the space had been designed for her to fill. His hands traveled across her back, down her ribs and then to the buttons that lined her dress. They were no barrier to the body beneath, for he swiftly opened and spread the bodice wide, feasting on the vision of lace and silk beneath.

"You own the most delicious assortment of undergarments any woman has ever had in her possession," he told her. "I'll need to find your supplier and keep you well covered with his products."

"How many women have shown you their undergarments?" she asked pertly, and then her eyes widened as if she'd stepped beyond the barrier to his past he'd set up. "I'm sorry, Aaron. I had no right to ask you that."

"You have every right," he said, denying her words. "You're my wife, and I owe you my allegiance. Anything you want to know about me or my past is an open book, as far as you're concerned."

"I really don't want to know," she whispered, hiding her face against his throat, denying her own curiosity, the questions that burned to be answered.

He tilted her back and looked directly into her eyes. "I'm not going to list any names or give you any numbers. But, I've known other women in my life, Susannah. I'm sure you're not surprised to hear that. I'm thirty-six years old, and I haven't been a virgin for a very long time."

"I figured that out, right off," she said, "and I didn't expect you to be. In fact, I'd have thought there was something wrong with you if you hadn't known other women."

"Well, know this, sweetheart." His hands cupped her face and he forced her to meet his gaze, those dark blue eyes that seemed to see all of her secrets and then some. "I may have known other women in my past, but from now on, my life is yours. I'll never look at a female who doesn't bear your name. Susannah McBain is my wife, my sweetheart."

He kissed her then, a soft, passionless blending of their lips that told her he had just made a vow he intended to keep, that he was pledging himself and all that he was, that his loyalty was owed to no other but his wife.

"My underwear is from the Emporium," she confessed. "I left most everything I owned in Washington when I fled there, and you'd be surprised at the selection your storekeeper here has on hand."

"I'll have to give him my thanks." Aaron grinned as he beheld the soft silken garments that covered her. And then he sobered.

"I brought you in here because I want to see your arm, sweetheart," he said, pulling the dress down over her shoulders, freeing her arm from the fabric and lifting her hand in his, his gaze washing over the red bruising that had formed on her pale skin. The definite line of the man's fingers was there, and as Aaron turned her hand in his, a bruise came to light beneath her arm, on the delicate, fragile area where her veins flowed so near the surface.

He lifted it to his lips, blessing her flesh with soft kisses, words breathed against her skin that were barely audible to her ears. And she blushed, torn between pleasure at his whispers of caring and anger at the damage left behind by her assailant, and the other emotion Aaron's actions brought into being.

"I like you kissing me," she whispered, "but I'd like it better if we were on the bed and you could do a more thorough job of it. And then we'll take this up after dark, right where we leave off now."

As if he had only awaited an invitation, and so quickly she knew he had yearned for just that very thing, he lifted her and carried her to the bed.

"We've got just ten minutes to cuddle, McBain. And then I've got work to do."

His eyes darkened and his mouth took possession of hers as he spoke his reply, his chuckle a sound of intent.

"That's long enough."

THE POT ROAST WAS A rousing success, the men declaring it more than stood up against the finest restaurants in Washington. At the end of the meal, they got down to what Sam called *brass tacks*. "They're closing in," he said firmly, "and that means you can't go out alone again, Susannah."

"I had Hattie with me," she said, defending herself.

And to no use, for Sam shook his head. "And you walked right out of the livery stable, big as you please, all by yourself. How was Hattie supposed to be of any use when you left her behind?"

Susannah's face fell, her eyes widening as she recognized her foolishness. "I only was looking for a ride back to the house from someone I might know out there," she said.

"And found yourself being attacked by a man who threatened your life," Sam told her bluntly. "I'm still amazed that he didn't shoot you while he had the chance."

"Too many people around," Aaron put in quickly. "The sidewalk was crowded and he was in plain view. That sort would rather wait for a private moment, with no watchers."

"Well, he made an impression anyway," Susannah said glumly. "He said you couldn't make a case, Sam, without my testimony. Those were his general words anyway. And he told me to keep my mouth shut."

"He apparently doesn't know that her statement has already been sent to Washington," Sam told Aaron.

"What do we do now?" Aaron asked, his gaze not leaving his wife.

"Sit and wait, just like I told you. Keep Susannah out of trouble and hope that my bosses will be able to make some arrests."

"I'm to be a prisoner in my own home?" Susannah asked, her voice shrill, as if she were halfway to having a fit of anger.

"Better than being dead in the cemetery," Sam said bluntly. "Right now, you hold the key to this whole thing. If the coal-mine owners could persuade you to give a statement absolving them of any shady dealings, it would be to their benefit, and that may be their next move."

"I can't tell what I don't know," she said sharply. "I can't seem to persuade anyone that I'm as much in the dark as anyone else. It's too bad Bettina isn't still around. She apparently knew more than I did."

"And look where it got her." Sam's voice was hard and forceful as he spoke. "She was a hired gun, Susannah, not a wife pledged to honor her husband's doings, and keep his secrets. John Carvel was the example the magnates set out for the rest of the politicians to see. Do as he did and you'll end up the same way. A simple message, one they made obvious.

"Now you may be standing in their way." He shot a look of warning at Aaron, as if knowing that the other lawman would recognize the danger and take whatever steps he must.

PLAYING CHECKERS GOT OLD in a hurry, Susannah decided later that evening when she had been roundly beaten for the third time by Phillip Hogan.

"At the risk of sounding like a poor loser, I think you cheat, Mr. Hogan," she said politely, rising and casually tilting the board into his lap.

He sat amid the rain of checkers and laughed, the sound a hearty tribute to her final words. "Wouldn't think of it, ma'am. Now, would anyone else like to take me on?" He looked around the gathering and was met by sour looks.

"Poker's more my game," Sam said. "Got any cards available, McBain?"

"Cards a'plenty," Aaron answered, opening a buffet drawer and taking out a new pack. "You in for some five-card stud, Phil?"

They gathered around the kitchen table, Susannah watching wistfully from the doorway. "I've never played poker. Do you suppose I could learn?"

"You ever hear of beginner's luck?" Sam asked

the other two men. "I'm willing to take the risk if you are."

Aaron shrugged. "Why not. Come on over here, sweetheart, and sit by me. I'll show you the ropes."

"I'll look over her shoulder and give her a hand," Hattie offered from her place by the sink. "The kitchen's all cleaned up and the cinnamon rolls are rising on top of the stove for breakfast. I'll warrant I could give missy a few pointers."

"You a card shark?" Sam asked, narrowing his eyes as the older woman drew up a chair and settled down behind Susannah.

"What's that?" Eyes wide, Hattie shrugged. "Don't know what you're talking about, young man."

She deftly gave instructions to Susannah over the next two hours, and in short order, her words were hardly necessary, so quickly did Susannah pick up on the game. They laughed quietly as they conferred, the three men watching them closely, but finding no trace of either of the women looking askance at the gentlemen's cards or switching their own to their own better interest.

"Pure luck," Sam said, watching as Susannah swept another pot to rest in a pile before her chair. "I told you, McBain. You can't trust a woman with a deck of cards, especially one who says she doesn't know the game."

"I resent that," Susannah said sharply, lifting her chin and shooting a grin at Hattie. "We just played the cards you gentlemen dealt us. Didn't we, Hattie?"

"Sure did," that lady replied, her eyes intent on the pile of coins in front of Susannah. "Gonna split with me?" she asked.

"You'd better believe it." With a laugh, Susannah swiftly counted out the money while the three men watched with wary eyes.

"I still don't know how you did it," Phil said. "I would have sworn you didn't have a thing in that last hand and then you laid down four kings, just as sweet as you please."

He watched as his money was swept up with that of the other two men, finding its way into Susannah's pocket and Hattie's reticule. "Tomorrow, we play some seven-card stud, men only," he said firmly. And earned the nods of agreement Sam and Aaron both spent on his statement.

HATTIE'S BISCUITS WERE a rousing success with the three men, and Susannah's sausage gravy was welcomed with waiting forks. A crock of scrambled eggs was added to the feast and cheese sprinkled over the top made it a tasty dish.

"Never put cheese on my eggs before," Hattie said in an undertone as she took her seat next to Susannah.

"Our cook back in Philadelphia did it all the time. My mama liked eggs that way."

"Learn something new every day, don't you?" Hattie helped herself to a biscuit and put one on Susannah's plate. "Better get one while the gettin's good," she announced bluntly. "These look like hungry men."

The men ate well, complimented the ladies as they watched white icing drip down the sides of cinnamon rolls and took their share as the pan went by.

"Want to move in with us, Hattie?" Aaron asked, licking the tip of his index finger, cleaning it of icing.

"I live close enough to run by when your wife needs me," she answered quickly. "You two need some privacy. Being newlyweds and all."

"Well, they're having to put up with me for a few more days," Sam said easily. "I'm not straying too far from Susannah until things are settled."

"And I'm stuck in the hotel," Phil said sadly. "I get to miss all the fun."

"You'll be heading back before you know it," Sam told him. "And in the meantime, I'll warrant that Miss Hattie and Susannah will feed you on occasion."

Susannah spoke up readily. "Three times a day if you like, Phil."

SUSANNAH STOOD BY THE RAIL fence that outlined the property Ottawa Falls had set aside for its children's education, and listened to the shouts of boys playing catch, the laughter of little girls who jumped rope and took turns with the swings that hung from a tall oak tree. Just as her own children might one day laugh and play in this schoolyard, she thought wistfully. Belonging in such a place held a multitude of joys. Recalling her own childhood, she yearned passionately to give a child of her own the pleasures of a happy home, friends and family to share their lives.

And if her calculations were correct, she might, in eight months or so, begin just such a family. She'd recognized the absence of her monthly time, realized that it was not on schedule, and this morning had felt a twinge of uneasiness hit her stomach.

Even the dreaded pangs of what the women called "morning sickness" did not dim her quiet happiness. For Aaron McBain, she would live through any amount of discomfort, including the months of waiting entailed in the beginning of a family.

Though he hadn't spoken of children, she knew, with a woman's intuition, that Aaron wanted the same sort of life as she, that he would welcome the thought of a child of his own gladly. She'd wait, she decided, watching as two little girls leaned against a tree and whispered secrets. Time enough and plenty in which to tell Aaron of her suspicions.

Hattie had cast her a long look of inquiry this morning at the breakfast table when Susannah had refused coffee, saying she had a yen for tea. The woman had smiled, bringing the teacup to her, her eyes twinkling as she placed it on the table, and in a low tone had suggested a plain biscuit for starters.

She *knew*. With a flash of memory, Susannah recalled the very moment when Hattie had begun to suspect that a secret was in the making, that Susannah quite likely carried the tiny mite of Aaron's making within her body.

CHAPTER THIRTEEN

"WELL, IF IT ISN'T Mrs. McBain, the sheriff's lady."
The voice from behind her struck Susannah with
its chill menace, and she turned her head from the
schoolyard in front of her to catch a glimpse of the
man who had manhandled her in town and who
now had managed to approach mere inches from
her back without her sensing his presence. In fact,
if the buggy pulled to the side of the road was any
indication, she had been deaf to all else but the
happy children before her.

"What do you want?" she asked, already
knowing his intent.

"I want you to get your pretty little self on a train
and head out of here," he told her. "I'd like to see
you in a grave, but we'll settle for a few hundred
miles from here."

"I don't understand," Susannah said, her heart
suddenly pounding at a rapid rate. "Why are you
so intent on chasing me from here?"

"You've made a big mistake, marrying a

lawman," the voice behind her said sharply. "He's got a vivid imagination, and his curiosity might be the death of him yet. Poking into things he's got no business investigating…it may be a fatal mistake."

"Aaron has nothing to do with any of this. I don't know anything about Senator Carvel's business," Susannah told him. "He was my husband, but he didn't confide in me, and I didn't know the men he pandered to."

"Wives always know what their husbands are up to. And that's a fact. We don't think you were any different than any other wives in Washington. You heard and saw plenty, probably more than was healthy for you. The gentlemen I represent can't take a chance on you carrying tales to the wrong people."

"I can't tell what I don't know. John Carvel was my husband, but there were other women who knew much more about his business than I. Try the French ambassador's wife, why don't you?"

The man's voice was amused now. "You sound like a woman betrayed."

"I *was* a woman betrayed. In more ways than one. John Carvel used me, used my money, used my talents as a hostess and my…"

She'd almost said the unthinkable, had almost admitted that John had come to her bed, treating her as he might have a woman bought cheaply by the side of the road. And to that she would not admit to other than Aaron, no matter the truth in it. She'd been a convenience to the senator, a source of ready cash. Indeed, he'd about emptied out her bank account, but had held on to her for the promise of her inheritance, should her parents lose their lives.

In fact he'd threatened that very thing, should Susannah not cooperate with him. It would have been easy for a man of John's caliber to find a way in which two people might die unexpectedly. And that threat had kept Susannah quiet, had given her a reason to obey her husband's dictates.

Until the night she'd had enough, until the lawyer in Philadelphia had assured her that she could find justice in the courts and finally rid herself of the man she'd married.

Now John was gone, but the ghosts of his lurid past still haunted her. And the knowledge she was suspected of possessing was hanging over her head like the sharp side of an ax. It was too much.

"I don't know anything that would do any damage to the Washington scene," she said in a low voice. "John didn't confide in me. I was not present when he entertained his gentlemen friends, and I have no knowledge of his doings."

"Your husband tried to double-cross the men on

top," the voice behind her said, his tone vicious. "He was paid an enormous amount of money to gain favor with certain politicians, and he failed to live up to the contract. Now, those same men stand next door to ruin, should their involvement with the good senator be made public knowledge."

Susannah trembled, her hands visibly shaking as she turned to face the same man who had bruised her arm just days since. "I can't do you any good. I've told what I know to the government men who came here. My statement has already been wired to Washington, and my value as a witness is practically nil."

"You shouldn't have done that, ma'am. The next thing you know they'll be after you to go to the capital to testify against the men who wanted your husband dead."

"I'm out of it. I've done what the government asked of me. Now I only want to live in peace, here in Ottawa Falls." She felt the strings of self-control slip through her fingers as she spoke. It seemed that the nightmare would never be over, that her past would not remain just that. And unless she was totally blind to the situation, she feared that she might know, somewhere deep in her subconscious, some bit of information that would nail the coffin lid shut on the men who haunted her.

"We can't have you trotting off to Washington to testify under oath, ma'am."

"I'm not running off anywhere. I have no intention of further contact with government agents, and I'm certainly not valuable to anyone outside of Ottawa Falls."

A hard hand gripped her wrist and Susannah knew she had no chance of twisting free of his hold, until he decided to turn her loose. "If you've already given your statement, then your husband, the good sheriff, has been made privy to more knowledge than is good for him."

"Leave him out of this." Susannah's voice rose in intensity. "What happened to me in Washington has nothing to do with Aaron McBain."

"We'll see." Her arm was set free of the painful grip he'd inflicted and the man turned away, climbing into a buggy and lifting the reins. Susannah watched as he drove the horse toward the livery stable, and felt a chill slide the length of her spine. A threat to her own life was one thing. The thought of Aaron being in danger because of her, another.

Yet, her own life being in jeopardy included Aaron in a way he would not tolerate. Should she be harmed, his child would be in peril, might even die, should her own life be forfeit.

Perhaps running might be the only solution to the tangled web. If she were not here, Aaron would no longer be at risk. And keeping him safe seemed to be uppermost in her mind right now.

Susannah turned from the schoolyard, where the children had obeyed the summons of their teacher to return to class. Silence reigned behind her, the shrill voices stilled, the playground empty. As empty as the future appeared to her heartsick eyes.

To no longer be wife to Aaron would be a tragedy she might not survive. Yet to be his widow was even more daunting. For Aaron's sake she would make the sacrifice if need be, would leave Ottawa Falls for another place where she might make a life for herself.

Yet, would that keep her lawman safe? Were the powerful men who sought to cover their tracks fearful of what a small-town sheriff knew about them? Sam would surely protect Aaron. She was certain that his presence here had more to do with keeping his friend safe, keeping his wife alive and cleaning up the mess he'd been assigned to deal with than he'd let on.

Susannah turned toward home, to the small house that held her hopes for the future. She was safe for now, perhaps the men who sought her would recognize that she bore no threat to them. The white picket fences lining the well-trod path to her home were familiar, comforting, a symbol of what she had chosen.

Marrying Aaron had seemed such a blessing, he

with his stubborn insistence on making her his wife, she with her insecurities and failures finally finding a haven where she might be safe and secure. And the bonus of living with a man of honor had been the greatest blessing of all.

The thought that she might not spend her life with Aaron was not to be considered, yet his welfare was her first concern.

No, her first concern was the tiny life she held secure within her body.

Tears slid from her eyes, staining her cheeks, almost blinding her to the path she followed. Aaron's voice shocked her, brought her from her thoughts with a jolt of pure joy and she turned her head to find him pacing toward her.

"Susannah. Wait up." He was tall, handsome, dressed in dark garb, with a gun on his hip, a silver badge on his shirt, and she felt an overwhelming love for him swell within her breast.

"I didn't know you were coming home so early," she said. "I just walked toward town, and got stalled at the schoolyard, watching the children play."

"Hattie didn't know where you'd gone." His voice held a stern note and she ventured a pleading look in his direction.

"I just took a walk. I thought about going to the Emporium, but I didn't want to go so far from home alone."

"You shouldn't have left the house by yourself."
Aaron's words left no room for her excuses. His
eyes pinned her without mercy, his jaw hard with
anger. "What happened? You look like something
has frightened you to death."

"The same man who approached me at the
livery stable found me watching the children at
the schoolyard. He's determined I know more than
I do. I can't seem to convince him that I was as
much in the dark as to John's doings as anyone
else."

"Makes sense that a man's wife would be the
one to have an open line to his affairs."

"Oh, I knew all about his affairs. He didn't try
to hide his women from me."

"That's not what I'm talking about, and you
know it, Susannah."

She halted where she stood and looked up into
blue eyes that burned with fury. "You don't believe
me, do you? That I was in the dark about John's association with the men who own the coal mines?"

"I think you know more than you've admitted
to. You may not realize how important some of the
conversations you overheard were. There's a lot of
money involved in what John Carvel was doing,
Susannah. It stands to reason that you were privy
to inside information, whether you know it or not."

She felt a shaft of agony settle in her chest, a

pain so deep she might not be able to contain it. "I can't believe that you think I've lied about this, Aaron. I told Sam everything I know."

"Then why do you suppose your life is being threatened?"

She could not speak. The one sure quality in her marriage she had so cherished was no longer viable. Aaron did not trust her. Her chin tilted upward and her mouth formed a thin line, sealing within the pain she would have spewed upon him.

"Come on home, Susannah. I don't want you wandering around by yourself. I thought I'd already made that clear."

She felt like a truant, a child not to be trusted alone, and her heart pounded in her chest in time with the hasty footsteps she took. "You've made much clear to me, McBain. I'm beginning to see more clearly just what our relationship is. You're the jailer, I'm the prisoner."

"Not true." His voice was sharp, his tone deep, his attitude that of a man unjustly accused. "You're my wife, Susannah. I'm doing my level best to protect you and you aren't cooperating too well."

"You wouldn't have a need to protect me if you hadn't married me."

"Ah, but I did, didn't I? And even if you were only my nurse, as it was in the beginning, I'd be honor bound to guard your safety."

They'd reached the gate in front of his house, and Susannah opened the latch and swept toward the porch. Behind the screened door, Hattie watched them approach, her gaze accusing.

"You ran off and didn't let me know where you were going," she said curtly. "Made me feel like a dunce when McBain here came in looking for you. I thought we had decided you weren't goin' anywhere alone?"

"I only walked to the schoolhouse," Susannah said defensively.

"And met up with the man who's been stalking her," Aaron said bluntly.

"*Stalking* is an evil word," Susannah said quickly.

"*Evil* is the best word I can come up with to describe the man who put bruises on you the other day," Aaron replied. "Did he leave his mark today?"

Susannah refused to answer, stomping her way across the porch and into the house. Stubbornly, she turned to the bedroom, closing the door behind her as she entered, seeking a privacy she had not before sought from Aaron's presence.

Her wrist throbbed from the fingers that had clamped around it earlier, and she unbuttoned the cuff of her dress, looking beneath it, the obvious marks of fingertips bruising her flesh. Behind her the door was flung open and an angry man appeared on the threshold.

"Don't close the door on me," Aaron said tightly. "You might know I'd come in anyway."

"Everyone deserves a little privacy sometimes," Susannah said, hiding her unbuttoned cuff in the folds of her skirt.

"You won't hide from me, Susannah." He reached for her and her hand tangled, catching in her skirt as she would have escaped his hold. A wince she could not conceal, a slight whimper that was involuntary and the closing of her eyes all spoke of pain to the man who watched her.

"Let me see what he did to hurt you this time." Aaron's hands were gentle as he lifted her fingers to his mouth, and as her unbuttoned cuff fell open, he caught sight of the reddened places she had thought to hide. Aaron felt a rush of hatred so deep, it was almost frightening. That he could despise so thoroughly a man he'd never laid eyes on was almost unbelievable, yet it was so.

He held her hand tenderly in his, lifting the fabric from her skin, turning her hand to see the underside of her wrist, and finally raising it to his lips once again, to press his lips against the damage done.

"I'm not a wilting violet, Aaron," she said, her voice soft, yet positive. "I've been bruised before, and probably will again. You're making too much of nothing."

"You're my wife, Susannah, and any man that

hurts you in any way, shape or form will answer for it. Some way, he'll pay for your bruises with scars of his own."

"You frighten me sometimes, Aaron," she said quickly, reaching to touch his cheek with her fingertips. "Not for myself, but for the hurt you are capable of dealing out to others who offer you harm. I suppose I'm a peacemaker, but I don't like the idea of revenge, even though I was tempted to mete out my own brand one night a few months ago."

"You couldn't have physically harmed that man, sweetheart. I don't believe you have a violent bone in your body."

"And you, on the other hand, possess a skeleton full of them."

He bent quickly to press a warm kiss on her lips. "But never will I hurt you, love. For you I feel only the deepest sort of caring. Call it *love* if you like, but whatever it is that draws me into your presence, I plan to keep it alive and growing for the rest of my life."

She bent her head, her cheek pressing against his chest. "You're my safe place, Aaron, my haven, my home."

From the kitchen came a call that brought their heads up, their lips curving in identical smiles. "If y'all want your dinner, you'd better high-tail it in here right now." Hattie's voice sang out the invitation, but an underlying tone told them to make haste if they planned on eating a warm meal.

"We're coming, Hattie," Susannah called, loudly enough to penetrate the closed bedroom door.

"I need to wash up," Aaron said, "and you need to comb your hair. I'm afraid I messed it up a bit. But I sure do like the feel of it, sweetheart. It's like raw silk in my hands."

She lifted an eyebrow and stepped away from him. "You're exaggerating just a bit, don't you think?"

He shook his head. "I love you, Susannah. You should know that by now. I love everything about you," he said, the words distinct and clear, as if he would make her aware that his every action, his every decision would be wrapped in this knowledge. The admission that he craved her welfare above all else, that he would die to protect her, that his masculine form would stand against the world to keep her safe, should the need arise.

"I know," she whispered. "And I love you, Aaron. With all that I am. I love your body, your heart and your soul. You are the man I sought in the midst of my wildest dreams. The lover I craved even before I knew what it meant to have a lover, a man who would treat me in just this way, as a wife, a woman who is loved."

She felt hot tears rush to her eyes and blinked rapidly lest they fall. "I feel humbled, McBain. I'm not worthy of so much caring, I fear."

He dragged a clean handkerchief from his back pocket and pressed it into her palm. "Here. Wipe your eyes, or Hattie will think I've been harsh with you. And pin that curl in place." His index finger touched the stray lock that had fallen over her forehead. "It makes me want to kiss you when I see it there."

She turned to the commode, where the mirror revealed what he had so well described. With a well-aimed touch, she fit the strands of hair back into place, brushing back the sides and replacing two pins that had slipped from the crown of her head. She dried her eyes quickly with his handkerchief and was ready for dinner.

Together they entered the kitchen, where Hattie was dishing up hot chicken soup from a big kettle. The scent filled the room, and Aaron sniffed with appreciation. "You sure do cook a dandy meal, Miss Hattie."

"Sit yourself down and pick up your spoon, Sheriff," Hattie said, her eyes twinkling as she reveled in his praise.

"Soon as I wash my hands." Aaron stepped to the sink and made quick work of using the soap he found there. A single surge of water from the red pitcher pump rinsed his hands and he turned to the table, finding his chair and settling in for the meal. From the front of the house, the sound of the front door opening caught their attention, and then Sam strolled into the kitchen.

"Anything new happening?" Aaron asked.

Sam shook his head. "Just a wait-and-see situation." He looked over at Hattie.

"Time to eat?" he asked, grinning as he inspected the kettle of soup simmering on the stove.

"Usually is this time of the day," Hattie told him, slapping his hand as he would have picked up the big spoon. "You can have a whole bowlful. Just sit yourself down and I'll dish it up. I don't allow no man to be messin' around with my cooking utensils."

"Yes, ma'am." Sam's tone was respectful, but his grin in Aaron's direction told of his amusement at the woman's words. Within seconds, he had a bowl in front of him and nodded his thanks at Hattie.

Aaron leaned toward Sam, peering into his soup and inhaling deeply. "Sure looks good, and smells even better."

"You have the knack of making a cook feel downright appreciated," Hattie told him, placing his own helping before him. A platter of corn bread followed and the meal was ready to be consumed, Hattie in her usual seat.

She looked up at Aaron after her first spate of hunger had been satisfied. "Did you scold her real good?" she asked.

Aaron nodded and cast an admonishing glance at Susannah. "I surely did. I let her know that she doesn't go anywhere, even to see the children in the schoolyard, without you right behind her."

"She snuck out on me," Hattie told him.

"Will the pair of you quit discussing me like I'm invisible?" Susannah sounded a bit put out, Aaron thought, and well she might. "I'm a full-grown woman and if I want to walk to the general store, I shouldn't have to worry about a nasty man creeping up behind me. I think our local sheriff and his Washington friend need to scout up the fellow and toss him in jail."

Aaron's jaw clenched and his eyes shot fire. "That's exactly what I intend to do. I'm going to the hotel as soon as we've eaten and find out if he's there. If not, Sam and I will scour the town till we come up with his rotten hide."

Susannah smiled sweetly. "Don't lose your temper, Sheriff. Just do your duty."

He blithely ignored her, scraping the bottom of his bowl in an unspoken bid for more soup. Hattie obliged quickly, refilling it from the big kettle on the stove and placing it before him again.

"This sure hit the spot, ma'am," he told her. "Think we'll just keep you around."

"If I didn't have my chickens and cow to tend to, I'd think about taking you up on your offer, Sheriff." She sat down across the table from him and drew her own bowl before her. "I manage to find my way to your kitchen often enough, I think."

She cast a long look at Susannah. "You feeling up to snuff, missy? That soup agreeing with you all right?"

Susannah felt a flush creep up her cheeks. "Your cooking is always good, Hattie. In fact, you make me look like an amateur." And then with a look that begged an end to the subject, she said quietly, "And I feel just fine."

Ignoring the hint, Hattie pushed a bit further. "Just wondered. You've been looking kinda peaked lately."

Sam grinned and lifted a hand in Susannah's direction. "Personally, I think she looks right pretty these days. Kinda got a glow about her."

Aaron seemed to consider that thought for a moment and then his head turned to Susannah quickly. "Is Hattie right? Have you been feeling badly?"

She refused to meet his gaze, her own eyes concentrating on the spoon she lifted to her mouth. "No. I'm sure you'd have noticed if I had."

"Hattie?" His voice held a multitude of questions as he spoke her name, and Hattie shrugged her shoulders. Aaron looked back at Susannah, his eyes alight with curiosity. "Are you sure you're not coming down with something? I haven't heard you coughing. Is there something I need to know about?"

Sam cleared his throat and tossed an appraising look at Susannah before she could drum up a reply. "Maybe she's not getting enough sleep."

With an exasperated look in his direction, Susannah assured Aaron of her good health. "There's not a thing wrong with me, and I get plenty of sleep. I'm fine. Just feeling a bit tired lately, and Hattie is a fussbudget."

"Maybe with good reason," Aaron said bluntly. "Maybe you need to see the doctor."

"Oh for heaven's sake." Susannah rose from her chair and stomped from the kitchen, leaving Aaron's mouth open and Hattie grinning like a Cheshire cat, while Sam merely looked down at his bowl of soup and smiled.

"I can't see that either of you have anything to smile about," Aaron said dourly. "And if the woman is sick, you'd better not try to keep it from me."

Hattie shrugged blithely. "She'll tell you before long. I'll guarantee it."

BEDTIME LURED SUSANNAH like a beacon. She'd hardly been able to conceal the yawns that would not be put to rest after supper, and when it was full dark, she quietly rose from the sofa and gathered her mending. "I think I'll go to bed."

Sam looked up in surprise from his spot on the sofa, and Aaron's eyes narrowed as he watched her cross the parlor. "It's barely dark, Susannah. I thought maybe we'd play some checkers or something."

She looked back at him from the doorway. "Sam loves the game. Ask him. Or see if Hattie is interested."

From the kitchen, the woman in question answered bluntly. "Hattie's goin' home. And if a woman needs a little extra rest once in a while, it ain't nuthin' for anybody to be worrying about. I'll see you in the morning."

They heard the back door close as she went out, and Sam grinned from his place on the easy chair. "I know when my wife started taking naps and going to bed early I caught on right quick that things were not going along as usual."

"And what does that mean?" Aaron asked. He slanted a glance at Susannah and she simply shrugged and went on into the bedroom, pulling the door closed behind her.

"I can't believe you haven't been asking questions before this, McBain." Sam's words bore a touch of amusement, and Aaron felt totally out of sorts. There seemed to be some sort of a conspiracy going on in his house and he was about to get to the bottom of it.

With a muttered curse, he followed Susannah's path to the bedroom door, opened it and entered. His boots clattered loudly against the bare wooden floor and not until he reached the oval braided rug near the bed did the sound of his approach lessen.

"Susannah." It was but a single word, a simple calling of her name, but it struck fear to her heart. Aaron had never sounded so frustrated, so angry with her, so full of fury that she feared he might... Might what? He'd never hit her, she knew that without even thinking. His hands would never deal with her in cruelty; his body would never overpower her with the pent-up strength of his muscular bulk. He was a big man, but his anger had never been loosed upon her. Yet, she dreaded the thought of his scorn or harsh words being dealt out in her direction.

"I'm sorry, Aaron," she said quickly, with no hesitation. She lifted her gaze to his face, watching as his lips thinned, and the darkness burning in his eyes was turned in her direction. "I need to talk to you, and I should have done so earlier today, but there didn't seem to be a chance. And then tonight, between you and Sam and Hattie, I got upset and acted—"

"That's enough," he said firmly, crossing to

where she stood and taking hold of her shoulders. His grip was firm, but his fingers did not cause pain. His body overwhelmed her, as it had on other occasions, but even his sheer size was not threatening. For his fingertips moved to her cheeks, his palms encircling her face, his head lowering to touch her lips with his.

"What's wrong?" He searched her face, his gaze filled with concern, and she felt hot tears fill her eyes and overflow to stain her cheeks.

"I need to tell you something, Aaron, and I didn't want it to be this way."

"How did you want it to be done?" he asked, a small smile curving his mouth. "I'm open to anything you suggest, love. And I'll listen to anything you have to say. I never want you to fear me, and your eyes were filled with dread when I approached you a few minutes ago."

She lifted her arms, wrapping them around his neck, burying her face against his throat. "I love you so much, Aaron. And I only just realized that our love has come to fruition. I should have run to you as soon as it occurred to me, but I didn't, and I'm so sorry. Hattie suspected for the past couple of days, and I—"

"You're talking in circles, sweetheart," Aaron said, chuckling beneath his breath, holding her firmly against himself. "Slow down and tell me that we're going to have a child. Unless I'm mighty mistaken, that's what all the yattering at the supper table was all about. Between Sam and Hattie, I thought they were gonna make you fightin' mad."

She looked up at his wide grin, her mouth agape, her eyes wide and her cheeks turning pink. "You knew? You already knew? And here I've been trying to plan how to tell you. I was afraid you might not be ready to begin a family, and unless I'm totally wrong, I think we already have."

"Nothing would make me happier," he told her gently, his eyes intent on hers. "I've wished for years that I might have a wife and children of my own, but the right woman never came along until I woke up in the hospital and saw an angel standing over me. And so far as you having a surprise for me, did you think I wouldn't notice that your…ah… *schedule,* let's say, has been a bit off the mark?"

"Well that's one way of putting it. And as far as my being an angel, I fear I'm not much of a heavenly being," Susannah said ruefully. "I'm impulsive and I'm only now beginning to learn how to keep a house the way I should and how to be a good wife."

"You're already the best woman in the world," Aaron told her, shushing her words with a finger held to her lips. "You don't need to learn one single thing to make me happy, love. You're kind and loving and your biscuits are wonderful. What more could a man ask? Unless it's to have a baby join the family and make us complete."

"I'm so glad you feel that way. I've been so plinzy in the mornings and my stomach doesn't seem to be able to handle food the way it used to, and I get tired so quickly in the afternoons and—"

"Shush," he said, shaking his head at the declarations of her symptoms. "I want you to go to see Doc Hansen tomorrow. Better yet, I'll take you over to his office in the morning and we'll see if he thinks everything is going the way it should. After all, a first baby is a brand new experience for you and we—"

"Aaron, stop right there." Susannah's eyes met his and he was silent at the bleak look of despair he encountered there.

"What is it, sweetheart? You're not worried about having a baby, are you? You'll be just fine. Women do this all the time you know, and you'll be a wonderful mother."

She only shook her head, unable to speak for a moment, and Aaron held her closely against himself. "What is it, Susannah? What has you so upset?"

"I haven't told you everything there is to know about my past," she began. "I was going to one day, but all I managed to do was get weepy and I just couldn't, Aaron."

She buried her face in his shirtfront and allowed the sobs to hold full sway for a moment, while Aaron's hands swept over her back and his kisses fell unhampered on her head.

"Don't cry, sweet. Whatever it is you need to tell me isn't important enough to merit all these tears. You're with me now and nothing can hurt you."

She shuddered in his arms and lifted a teary countenance to him. "This is important, Aaron. I know I told you about the child I lost several years ago, and I can't help the fear I live with now. I was only twenty-three, and six months into a normal pregnancy when I lost the baby and…" Her voice trailed off as if the words she sought were too painful to be uttered aloud.

"What he did to you will never happen in this marriage, Susannah. I can pledge you that, but it's up to you to trust me and my promise to you." Aaron spoke quietly, almost dreading to prompt her into an answer not to his liking. She allowed her gaze to rest on him, her eyes wary as if she had no trust to offer, as if she could not speak of her pain.

"He was unkind, brutal and not worthy to be called your husband," Aaron said bitterly. One finger beneath her chin tilted Susannah's face up to his. He winced at the drawn lines of pain she wore, and his head bent, his lips touching each line, each evidence of her loss.

"I told you, Aaron. He was angry with me, said I wasn't fit to have out in company, being so fat and out of shape as I was. And he said he'd never wanted a child, and I'd tricked him by becoming pregnant."

"Was that when he forced you into his bed, Susannah?" The question fell between them and she gritted her teeth, as if she would not pick up the gauntlet he'd thrown down. And yet, he deserved to know. He'd healed her wounds without thought of himself up until now, and if he demanded an answer, she was almost obliged to give it.

"He…was cruel, Aaron, and when I wouldn't give in easily, he punched me and kicked my belly. The doctors at the hospital seemed to suspect that I'd been beaten, but I couldn't press charges. It would have been a scandal too horrible to imagine. John came to me in the hospital. He said he was sorry and hadn't known what he was doing. But I lost my son, Aaron. He was too small to live. They let me see him, so tiny but so perfect. And then a minister I knew made arrangements for his burial."

She looked up at him with swimming eyes, her face pale and wan, and he felt crushed by the agony in her eyes. "He never breathed, Aaron. I labored for a long night and part of the next day, and the doctors were afraid that I'd die, and even worse, they said I might never be able to carry another child." She shook her head and took a deep breath.

"I wouldn't have cared right then if I had died. When they told me my child was stillborn, I felt as though my life was over."

Her voice faltered again on the words and she bent her head, allowing the hot tears to fall where they would.

Aaron felt he couldn't bear it, the sobs, the agony in her voice, the sadness that caused her shoulders to bow, and the tears that would not cease their flow.

"Ah, Susannah…please love. Please look at me." His own eyes were welling over and as he lifted her face to his once again, she melted, one hand reaching for his face, her fingertips brushing away the evidence of his pain.

"I don't want you to cry for me, Aaron."

"How can I help it, love? You're my wife, the very center of my life. When you hurt, I hurt. When you feel pain, so do I. And when you ache from a great loss, one that has so changed your life, it makes me want to go out and fight demons for you. I have the need to do something to change it so that you will never cry these tears again. And I know that cannot be. That you'll always bear the loss of that child. But don't fear that it will happen again. The babe you carry will be healthy and all that any parent could desire."

"And loved by both of us, Aaron," she said, wiping her own tears now, as if she would set them aside lest she pain him any longer by her grief. "With you as a father, the child will be most fortunate."

"I'll do my best, and you know I'll take care of you, Susannah. I'll love our child and try to be a good father."

She straightened, her shoulders firming, her chin lifting as if she would face the perils of the world so long as she had his support. "I'll stop all this weeping now, and concentrate on the baby I'm carrying and try to put my first child into the past. I can't let the pain of that night put a damper on the joy I feel now," she told him, as if she made a vow she would cherish.

"After all, women have babies all the time, and I've never heard of one of them feeling so weepy as I do," she said. "And I hate to wake up in the morning, lest I have to throw up in the slop pail before you leave the bedroom. But, I think the worst of all that is about through. From now on, it will be better."

Aaron narrowed his eyes and sought assurance. "What does Hattie say about it?"

Susannah blinked, puzzled by the notion that Hattie might have suggestions for her. "I didn't think to ask her. I just thought I was being foolish and I hated to think that I was too immature to have a child of my own. I wanted a baby, one who would have a father to love him, but I can't help but worry that something might happen again."

"Well, I think you need some expert advice, sweet. Let's ask Hattie. I'll bet she's a fountain of wisdom. She's not had children of her own, but maybe she knows more about it than we suspect. She's lived for a long time."

"I'll talk to her tomorrow," Susannah said, not wanting an audience when she bared her soul and expressed her shortcomings to her friend.

"You'll see," Aaron told her. "Hattie will set it all to rights. Just ask her the questions you need to have answered."

CHAPTER FOURTEEN

AND SO SHE DID. AARON LEFT for the sheriff's office right after breakfast with a reminder that he would return in a hour or so to take Susannah for a walk into town. She only nodded her compliance and followed him to the front door, kissing him with a new appreciation of the man she had married. Anyone would think he knew all the ins and outs of this baby business, and she appreciated his confidence in her, but he was still as new at the job of parenthood as she.

"What's going on?" Hattie was blunt and forthright, and not for the first time, Susannah was happy that it was so. It made it easier to plunge right in when the woman fully expected her to confide in her.

"I think I'm going to have a baby," Susannah said, feeling the words to the depths of her soul, as if by speaking them aloud, she had made a permanent commitment to this project she'd undertaken, all unknowing, but willingly.

"Land sakes, I could have told you that a week ago," Hattie said with a laugh. "You've been moping around in the mornings, making a face when you smelled breakfast cooking and barely tasting your coffee. And by noontime you're dragging like a goose on his way to the dinner table."

Susannah felt a surge of indignation swelling in her chest. "Why didn't you say anything? I didn't remember that my feeling so nauseated and tired was a sign of something so wonderful as being in the family way. I had begun to think I was sickening with some dreaded disease. And then I realized that my monthly hadn't been on time. In fact I haven't had it for several weeks, more than two months. I usually keep pretty good track of it, but things have been so hectic lately, that I—"

"Just simmer down, young'un. A woman doesn't always catch on right quick the first time she gets in the family way. You've had a lot on your plate in the past few weeks. I think you can be excused this time. Next time around the track, you'll be catching it right off."

"Next time? I haven't gotten used to this time," Susannah said, torn between laughter and impending tears. "And that's another thing. I need to talk to you about something else, Hattie. Besides feeling like a watering can all the time lately, I've been worried that this baby might not make it. I've shed more tears than anyone has a right to. And Aaron just hugs me and loves me and..."

"And aren't you the lucky girl?" Hattie laughed aloud. "I told you he was a good man, didn't I? He'll make a wonderful father to your baby, you just wait and see." She pulled a kitchen chair and sat down at the table, motioning to Susannah to do the same. "Now, let's talk about this. What on earth makes you think the baby won't make it? You're a healthy girl, and made to bear children."

And so over the next half hour, Susannah opened her heart, allowing the sad tale to flow to Hattie's ears, the whole episode ending with the two of them clinging helplessly to each other as they cried out their anger and pain.

"I'd like to hang that fella up by his—" Hattie halted her diatribe midway and pursed her lips. "Well, never mind. Just as well he's already dead. I'd go after him with my derringer. And you'd better believe that, girlie."

Susannah had to laugh at the look on her friend's face. So angry and dark with vengeance on her mind, she could hardly sit still, Hattie stormed around the kitchen, as if she felt helpless in the face of impotent fury.

And then they settled down over matching cups of tea and shared the joys of motherhood as Hattie had seen it experienced throughout her life. Susannah felt a new confidence at Hattie's words of wisdom, for the woman had served many times in cases of childbirth, and was full of advice for the preparations they would make before the babe arrived.

By the time Aaron came home, Susannah had heard the details of each one of Hattie's experiences with pregnant women, and the factual accounts of labor and delivery. "Nothing to be afraid of girl," Hattie had said. "I told you that you were made to have babies, and every bit of the process is as natural as the sun rising in the eastern sky in the morning."

Together they had put together a meal, and with Aaron's arrival, they sat down to eat roast-beef pot pie, made with the leftovers from the previous night's supper.

"You've sure turned into a good cook, sweetheart," Aaron said, sopping up the last bits of gravy with a piece of bread.

"Hattie did most of it," Susannah admitted. "I just watched and tried to remember everything she did. I think I could pretty well duplicate it another time."

"Well, if we can keep Hattie happy with us, maybe she'll give you a hand over the next months till the baby comes. I don't mind one little bit, hiring you some help in the house, and Hattie is the best there is for the job."

"I won't argue with that." Susannah looked toward her friend who was dishing up bowls of apple cobbler for dessert and was pleased to see a quick nod and a smile that flashed approval in her direction.

"Maybe Hattie will tend to the dishes while you and I take a hike to see the doctor, sweetheart," Aaron said as he finished his meal. "Sam's gonna keep an eye on things in town this afternoon. He's following a couple of leads we picked up on, and I told Doc Hansen we'd stop by a little later on. We'll get you checked out."

THE DOCTOR MET THEM at the door of his office and ushered Susannah into a small examining room, Aaron hot on her heels. After deftly unbuttoning her dress, with Aaron's sharp eyes on his every move, the doctor slid the bell of his stethoscope inside her bodice to listen intently through his earpieces as her heart thumped in a rapid beat. "Things have changed considerably since you worked in the hospital," Doc Hansen said.

With a small smile no doubt meant to soothe her anxiety. "Glad to see you again, and for such a happy occasion. If the sheriff here is right, and he usually is," he added in an afterthought, "then you're only stricken by a familiar female complaint, one that has a limited lifespan. In fact, you'll probably be feeling just like your old self in seven or eight months."

Susannah was silent until the instrument he'd used on her chest was withdrawn, then, surprised by the calm tone of her voice, she expressed her sentiments regarding the doctor's diagnosis. "If what I suspect is true, I won't be inclined to call my condition a *complaint,* Doctor. More like a miracle, or perhaps a gift from heaven."

Obviously taken aback, the medical man sat upright on the stool he'd drawn close to the examining area and grinned widely. "Now that's a refreshing thought."

"Don't most women find it pleasing to be carrying their husband's child?"

He pursed his lips. "I suspect that depends on how often they're put to bed with the same complaint. We'll see on the day you deliver this baby just how happy you are with the sheriff here."

Aaron cleared his throat. "Are you so certain then that Mrs. McBain is definitely in the family way?"

"Well, she sure has the look," the doctor said blithely, pulling down one of Susannah's bottom eyelids to peer at the membrane exposed. "See that? Unless a woman is pregnant or anemic, that oughta be nice and red. Your wife's membranes look a bit white, which is a mighty suspicious sign. But this sort of thing requires a more thorough examination than that." He turned to peer at Susannah more closely. "I suspect you already knew that, didn't you?"

She only nodded, feeling her confidence rise as Aaron clasped her hand.

"Why don't you just lie down here for a minute, little lady," the doctor said, one hand on her shoulder as he guided her back to the pillow provided. A handy ledge was brought to table level on which her legs were propped, and then Dr. Hansen placed a broad palm on her belly.

She flinched with an involuntary movement, Aaron's hand tightening on hers. The doctor's fingers probed gently, forming a shield over the place where the tiny form was protected by Susannah's body, and as she watched, the doctor's face lit from within. It was as if some superior power had gifted him with a magic unknown to ordinary humans, one that allowed him to sense the muscle, tissue and bone beneath the surface of feminine skin.

His eyes brightened when he turned them on Susannah. "We'll have to do a little more involved examination here, but I think I can safely say that you're about three months into a healthy pregnancy here."

Susannah felt happy tears fill her eyes, and then dampen the hair at her temples as she heard the words that decreed her future for the next six months. "I thought that might be the case, but I wasn't sure," she said softly, as if the moment were too precious to merit ordinary voices, suited more to whispered words.

With an uplifted brow, the doctor looked Aaron's way, and at the lawman's nod, he merely shrugged and continued his examination. It was not pleasant, but Susannah felt the comfort of Aaron's hand in hers, and kept her eyes tightly shut while her clothing was adjusted and the kindly doctor made a quick survey of her condition.

"There you go, Mrs. McBain," he said heartily, helping her to her feet a few minutes later. "I'll expect to hear from you when it's time to take our first look at this baby, and if you have any problems, or think there's trouble of any kind, I'll expect a visit from our friend here, should the occasion warrant a call." He nodded in Aaron's direction as he spoke and then reached to shake his hand.

"Congratulations, Sheriff. I'd say you're well on your way to becoming a family man. Don't hesitate to let me know if your wife has more than the ordinary amount of nausea or any bleeding at all."

They walked home, surrounded by a cloud of happiness, Aaron clasping her hand tightly, his smile a mute testimony to the joy that filled his being. He'd never felt so rich, so full of happiness as at this moment. A beautiful wife by his side, a baby on the way and a future that promised to be beyond his wildest expectations.

And then the thought of the danger implicit in their situation dampened his mood. "It's more important than ever that you watch yourself, Susannah," he said solemnly. "Don't take any chances, sweetheart." He couldn't be with her twenty-four hours a day, and the thought of some mishap, some bit of mischief as yet unknown to them, made him cringe. She was his life, his love, and yet he feared that he couldn't protect her to the extent he wanted. If something should happen to her, he would never forgive himself, and would feel an abject failure at this business of being a husband and prospective father.

With a shake of his head, he set aside his morbid thoughts and concentrated instead on the woman who walked beside him, who had pledged to share his life, and who was even now harboring his babe in her belly. The fear he lived with was real, but his every thought was for her and her safety.

She lifted sparkling eyes to his, her contentment alive in her gaze, her lips curved in a smile that held secrets. "I won't take any chances, Aaron. I'll be so careful, you won't even believe it's me. No more solitary walks, and definitely no talking to strangers or going outside without Hattie or you along with me."

He felt relief fill him at her statement, knew it to be a valid promise, and walked proudly by her side as they greeted townsfolk as they made their way home.

Hattie was unsurprised by the news, her usual placid demeanor well in place as she made plans for Susannah's future. Yet she left no room for argument as she set a schedule of regular naps in the afternoons, three solid meals a day and a regime that included no climbing or reaching up into cupboards in the kitchen.

"We're not taking a chance on this baby, no way, no how," she said firmly, her edict backed immediately by Aaron's firm nod.

And with the two of them so firmly in charge, Susannah was left to sit for an hour in the parlor, feet on a stool while Aaron went back to work and Hattie busily fussed over supper preparations. Being pampered had its benefits, she decided, leaning her head back on the high sofa. Being the wife of a man well able to hire help for her was more than a benefit, it was a blessing. And having Hattie as a friend would prove to be a comfort in the days to come.

The scent of Hattie's cooking was appealing, she thought, her eyes closing as she thought of the future, imagining the sight of a child at the table, sharing the meal with doting parents. They'd have to buy a high chair, or perhaps have one made, one that would fit beneath the table edge, yet bring the baby up to a comfortable level to eat. And a bed, a crib of sorts, although a basket would do at first. A list began to take form in her mind, and visions of tiny kimonos and gowns, lines of diapers flapping in the breeze, and soft knitted blankets folded on a shelf, filled her thoughts.

She woke with a start as Aaron bent over her, kissing her tenderly, taking her hands in his as he lifted her to her feet. "We're about ready to have dinner, sweetheart, and I'd say you've already taken your afternoon nap for the day." His voice was teasing, and Susannah stood before him with a sure knowledge of being loved and cared for.

"Do I have your permission to work in the garden this afternoon then, sir?" she asked pertly. "I've got tomatoes ready to put up in Mason jars, and the beans are still hanging on the vines."

"So long as Hattie keeps an eye on you, and you don't overdo," Aaron said, pulling her into his embrace. His whisper was low, the words meant only for her own hearing as he bent his head. "Do you have any idea how much I love you, sweetheart?"

A leap of pure happiness within her was almost enough to merit Susannah's first thought of towing Aaron into the bedroom for a quiet time of loving.

But the quick realization of Hattie setting the table and dishing up food in the kitchen squelched that idea in the bud, and she settled for a squeeze and a kiss that made her blush, so readily did Aaron fall into her mood.

It seemed that life held more promise, that each day was painted in a brighter hue, and even the thought of danger faded as Susannah went about her everyday duties. The garden required several hours of work during the next week, canning jars were filled with tomatoes and beans and the first harvest of potatoes was set aside to be carried to the fruit cellar beneath the house.

Aaron and Sam did that chore, piling the results of Susannah's digging potatoes in one corner of the cellar, making another pile of carrots closer to the steps, and hanging long strings of onions from the low rafters in the small room. Making pickled beets was a chore lasting more than a week; changing the brine on the pickles they'd begun was a daily chore, and Susannah felt for the first time the satisfaction of preparing her house for winter.

There would be food aplenty for the cold days to come, and when a local farmer brought a side of beef to Aaron, she only gulped as she considered the carcass, then plunged into the chore of cutting it into pieces fit for the canning jars. It would provide for many a meal of stew or some such thing during the long months ahead, Hattie told her. When the cold weather arrived in earnest, they would purchase hams and sausage from the same farmer and hang them in the shed out back, enclosed and unavailable to animals who might seek out the scent of hanging meat.

Susannah's vigilance had been tempered by the mundane chores that filled her days, and she had no fears of what might come to pass. Perhaps the storm of political struggle in Washington was a thing of the past. Probably she was as safe as a woman could be, since there had been no more sightings of the man who had approached her weeks ago, perhaps due to the constant watchfulness of the man who guarded her.

And so the sight of Phil at her door brought about no qualms of any sort. He'd stayed in town to help with surveillance, and occupied a chair at their table on an almost daily basis. His smile this morning was welcome as Susannah opened the door to him and invited him inside. "What brings you out so early in the day?" she asked.

"It's not that early," he said, pulling his pocket watch out and flipping open the lid. "Almost eleven o'clock already, and I've got plans for you."

Susannah grinned at his cocky attitude. "You have? What sort of plans?"

"First off, where's Hattie? She out in the kitchen?"

"No. I made a list and she went to the Emporium to pick up a few things. She'll be back shortly though."

"I'm surprised she left you alone. But it makes this a whole lot easier to handle." Phil's easygoing mood seemed to darken as he looked about the parlor, then settled on Susannah's boots on a mat near the door. "Get your boots on, Susannah."

"I'm not planning on going anywhere anyway," she said, frowning at his words.

"Ah, but you are going somewhere," Phil told her. "We're going to take a ride together."

A pang of foreboding struck her suddenly and she looked up into eyes that were no longer soft and friendly but had assumed a look of cold calculation. "I don't think I understand." Even to her own ears, her voice sounded shaky and she cleared her throat, hoping that her imagination was running away with her.

It was not to be, for Phil took her arm and pushed her into a chair near the front door, handing her the boots she'd left there after her last outing. "Here. Put these on, Susannah. There's no taking no for an answer, ma'am. You're coming with me."

A cold dread filled her soul as she looked at the man who had said he was their friend, a man hired by the government to help protect her. "Who are you?" she asked, not willing to be kept in the dark, aware suddenly that this was a face she did not know, a man she feared.

"I think you can figure things out, Susannah. You're a smart lady. And you'll soon find out all about it. Just get those boots on." He watched as she tugged them into place and then took her elbow, lifting her to her feet easily.

"Don't do this, Phil. You know that Aaron will kill you if I'm hurt, not to mention Sam putting in his two-cents worth. I don't know who's hired you, but I'm not going to do anything to cause Aaron to worry about me. I'll not go with you."

She planted her feet, her back to the wall. And Phil only smiled, a flash of impatience lighting his eyes with anger as he approached her. "You're coming with me, like it or not. And don't start planning on escaping from me. I've got a friend on the front porch who's only too willing to put you to sleep if you don't cooperate."

"Put me to sleep?" She felt the blood leave her face as she considered the implications in those words. "Permanently?"

Phil laughed. "Depend on a woman to get dramatic. Hell, no. We're only taking you on a little ride. There's some men who want to talk to you, and they're mighty interested in getting in touch with Sam and your husband. We figure it won't take long for the two of them to follow our trail and fall into a nice trap we've prepared."

"He'll kill you." From the depths of her heart, she knew it to be true. Should harm come to her, McBain would not hesitate. He'd draw his gun and fight till his dying breath for her well-being.

"Not if he's as smart as I think he is," Phil said. He looked around the parlor, snatching up a warm scarf from the coat rack and tossing it in her direction. "Here. You may need this."

She caught it with an automatic gesture and wrapped it around her neck. "I can't believe you're doing this. I can't see what good it will do anyone."

Her thoughts were in a frenzy, one part of her hoping against hope that Hattie would not return any time soon, another part wishing for Aaron to make a surprise jaunt home, and yet hoping he would stay away from the danger that faced her.

Phil hustled her from the house, one arm around her waist, the other holding her hands in a tight grip as he led her to the wagon that awaited them near the front gate. From the porch, another man appeared, then paced by her side down the path to the road. A quick glance at him revealed the face of evil, the man who had left bruises on her on two different occasions, and Susannah's heart shuddered within her breast.

The full impact of her situation became real as

she was lifted into the bed of the wagon, the second man holding her down on the floor so she could not be seen by any passersby. With harsh hands, he tied her wrists together behind her back, then covered her with a rough blanket, hiding her from sight.

"One peep out of you and I'll put a gag in your mouth. Or maybe worse," he said in a gruff voice.

Never doubting for a second but that he would do as he said, Susannah only nodded, moving her head a bit, as if searching out a softer place to rest it.

"Sorry the accommodations aren't more to your liking, lady," the man said, his sneer erasing the meaning of his words. "You just lay down there and don't make a fuss. Any noise out of you and I'll crack your skull." He brandished a length of lumber before her face, and Susannah closed her eyes, unwilling to view the means of her own pain so closely.

The wagon rumbled on the rutted road, the conversation between Phil and the man beside her limited to single words of inquiry and directions as to the destination they sought. "Will Harmon be there by now?" Phil asked.

"Yeah, he came in on the late train yesterday. I saw him leave town early on this morning."

What their plans for her entailed was beyond Susannah's imagination, but she knew with a sick dread that her life might be forfeit should the men who had sought her out assume she possessed more knowledge about Carvel's doings than she had admitted to.

Questions filled her mind, but fear of reprisals from the man beside her kept her silent and she closed her eyes beneath the covering of the rough blanket that hid her from view. It might have been an hour, perhaps longer when the wagon drew to a halt, then she felt it jolt sharply as it turned and continued on up a rougher road.

"That the place?" Phil asked, and the man beside her muttered a single word of agreement. Within a few minutes, the vehicle drew to a halt and she was unceremoniously dragged from the wagon and grasped by one arm by her captor.

"Walk, lady," he said, dragging her along as if she had filed a protest. She had no such intentions, willing to do as she was told, lest she invite the harm she knew would be done by the length of board he held in his other hand.

There were two steps up onto the porch of the ramshackle house they'd chosen, and she hoped there were enough furnishings within to guarantee a warm spot for her to sit on. Perhaps they'd built a fire, should there be a cookstove or a fireplace in the house.

Her spirits were lifted a bit as warmth met them at the open door. At least she wouldn't freeze to death, although death by another means might be her ultimate destiny. She was pushed roughly into a second room. Outdoors, the weather had deteriorated, rain falling steadily, the wind blowing against the aged walls and whining through the cracks in the siding.

She shivered at the desolate place surrounding her, fearing that Aaron would not reach her before her captors decided their next move. Already they were speaking to a third man at the kitchen table, leaving her alone in the parlor. Not even tempted to rise from the sofa where she'd been placed so abruptly, she instead drew her legs up beneath her skirts, warming herself as much as possible under the blanket they'd left with her.

Raised voices from the other room caught her attention, and she heard a voice speaking with authority. "If McBain knows anything at all about this whole mess, and I'll guarantee he's learned a snootful from our friend in the parlor, then he's a dead man. Along with Sam Peterson."

"What are you gonna do with her? Get rid of her tonight?"

"No, we'll keep her alive long enough to make certain McBain follows us. He'll be on our trail before you know it, him and Sam Peterson, too. She's just the bait in this trap."

"The bigwigs back east are certain she knows

too much to be left alive," said another voice, one she recognized as Phil's. "Personally, I think she's just a bystander, but I'm not gonna argue with the men holding the money."

"You know yourself that a woman can coax a man into spilling the beans real easy like." The remark was followed by laughter, and Susannah shivered at the cruel intent of these men who held her captive.

"I hadn't thought of it that way. But considering the lady's charms and the senator's having the inside track with her, so to speak, I'll have to agree with you that maybe she does know exactly what Carvel was up to," Phil said. "She's no dummy, that's for sure. It didn't take long for him to find himself a sweetie on the side, but most married men have a hard time keeping secrets when they're sleeping with a woman. And there wasn't a one of his birdies could hold a candle to our Mrs. Carvel in there."

"McBain. McBain." Susannah shivered as she whispered the name to herself. The hated title of Mrs. John Carvel was a thing of the past and even the thought of being known as the man's wife was anathema to her now. She yearned for Aaron's presence with her, yet at the same time wished him miles away, lest he fall into the same danger that faced her.

"Is Howie keeping a good eye out for visitors?"

Phil asked, and Susannah heard a chair scrape across the floor in the kitchen as he spoke. He'd apparently risen and walked across the room, his footsteps on the bare wooden floor barely audible to her.

"He's watching from the barn, and if anyone comes up the lane from the road, he'll let us know." It was the second man's voice who announced the lookout's position, and Susannah upped the odds a bit in her mind. Four men here, and possibly only Aaron and Sam looking for her. She trembled in fear. Not only for herself but for the men who would even now be on her trail.

CHAPTER FIFTEEN

"SUSANNAH? WHERE ARE YOU?" The house was empty, of that there was no doubt, and Hattie's call went unanswered. A chill went through her as she searched from room to room, knowing as she did that the woman she sought was gone, and if her instincts were right, it had not been by her own volition.

It took only fifteen minutes to locate Aaron at the hotel, his office being empty. The sight of Sam Peterson in front of the hotel alerted Hattie, and she hurried to speak to him. Together they went into the lobby and when Aaron saw them, he felt his face go pale, so anguished were Hattie's features.

"Sheriff," she began haltingly, her voice trembling. "She's gone. She's gone."

"Slow down, Miss Hattie," he said quietly, turning from the desk and the curious man who stood behind it. "What happened?"

"I went to the Emporium and when I got back, Susannah was gone. Not hide nor hair of her to be seen. Her boots are gone. It's like she just disappeared into thin air." Close to tears, Hattie looked older than her years, and Aaron's heart felt compassion for her, even as his anger was fired with the news that the dreaded happening he'd feared had come to pass.

Sam spoke quietly from behind Hattie. "I think we need to check the livery stable, see if Ellis has rented out a horse or wagon or whatever to anyone. They must have had transportation of some sort to haul her away in."

"You do that," Aaron said. "And I'll see if I can round up a couple of men to ride with us. Tell Ellis to get my horse ready to ride, and get one for yourself."

"I want a buggy," Hattie said firmly. "I'm going along."

Aaron looked at her mutinous expression and only shrugged. There'd be no arguing with the woman, that was for sure, and in a buggy, she'd be riding in their dust anyway. Probably wouldn't be able to keep up for long. Yet, knowing Hattie as well as he did, he knew of her determination and the intelligence she possessed.

Within minutes, Aaron had located his deputy and two men from town who were willing to form a small posse. Together they hastened to Ellis Monroe's livery stable, where horses were being saddled and a mare being harnessed to a buggy. Hattie had made a quick detour to her house, carrying a blanket with her, waiting for her vehicle to be ready.

They set out quickly, the five men riding at a measured pace, not knowing how far they would travel, and not wanting to tire their horses quickly. When they reached Aaron's house, the tracks of a wagon were readily visible in front of the gate. Aaron wished fervently that he'd done something different this morning.

Perhaps he should have stayed home with Susannah, kept a better eye on her. Maybe he'd been sloppy in his vigilance over her, becoming relaxed as the days had passed with no more signs of danger.

His mind spun to thoughts of her inheritance. Surely the funds had been transferred by now. And should Susannah have wanted to access them, it would have been a simple matter for her to appear at the bank and thence to the train station, where the noon train was even now on its way west.

He shook his head impatiently. She wouldn't do that. Susannah was happy with him, delighted with the fact of her pregnancy. Yet, if she feared for him, worried that he might be in danger because of her... He clamped down tightly on such thoughts. But wasn't the chance of her escaping town and the peril she'd been forced to anticipate here more than possible? Possible, yes. Probable, no.

She'd been lured away somehow, by someone who had a need for her silence. Someone who would not believe her story of innocence regarding the doings of the senator and the men who owned the coal mines. He knew that determined men could find a way to overcome a helpless woman and snatch her up should they be so inclined.

"I'll guarantee she was taken by the joker that's been hanging around. I should have done more to find him, put him in jail. This is my fault." He was heartsick, berating himself on her account, and then a thought possessed him, striking terror into his heart.

"Do you think they'll kill her?" he asked Sam, his voice cold and harsh. He knew that should Susannah's life be taken the world he lived in would be empty without her presence.

Sam shot him a quick look. "I think they'll try to find out what she knows first. They'll be more interested to know who she's talked to, and that includes you, McBain. You're at risk as much as she. I think you've already figured that one out. They're probably after me, as well. And Phil, too, for that matter. We've all been privy to her statement."

"Sure wish I knew where Phil was," Aaron

said thoughtfully. "I thought he'd be at the hotel, but the desk clerk said he'd left early on this morning. I wonder where he went? He say anything to you?"

Sam shook his head. "No idea. I know he was planning on packing up and heading east in a day or so. He got a wire yesterday. I saw the stationmaster go into the hotel, and Phil said last evening that he'd been called back to Washington.

"Wish we had him along. He's a good shot, I hear," Sam continued.

But Aaron was stewing and barely heard the words. There was something wrong with Phil's actions. Some reason for worry, and he couldn't put his finger on it. "You don't think—"

"No. Not a chance," Sam said, interrupting his words, as if he'd read Aaron's thoughts. "Phil's got top clearance in Washington. He's well known."

"Well, someone got to her, and when I find him, he's a dead man," Aaron said beneath his breath.

They followed the tracks of the lone wagon for an hour, Hattie not far behind them, her buggy visible on the road less than a half mile back. When the tracks turned into the lane of an abandoned farm, they halted, the four men sighting down the long lane to the unpainted house that squatted in the middle of the field before them. A few scattered structures lay behind it, a dilapidated barn and several smaller buildings.

"I'll warrant that's where they've got her," Aaron said harshly, drawing his gelding to a stop, the other men close beside him. "Sam?" His unspoken query brought a nod from his friend, and he pushed his hat back with one finger, peering through the falling rain to where a light gleamed from a side window of the house.

"Looks likely," Sam said. "But there's no point in getting ourselves shot right off the bat, Aaron. I'll guarantee they've got a lookout somewhere, just waiting for us to ride up, big as life."

"Let's think about this a minute." Even though every instinct he owned cried out for speed, for a quick finish to this task, Aaron slowed his responses, his control on a fine edge as he thought of what might have already taken place in that house ahead.

"We'll do better to wait till dark before we make our move," Sam said quietly. "I know that's a good four hours away, and we'll do better under cover of darkness. There's no point in setting ourselves up for failure."

"I hate it when you're so logical," Aaron said, tossing his friend a look of aggravation. "I'm having a hard time sitting here on this horse, when I should be bursting into that place with my gun in my hand."

"Yeah, and you know damn well what will happen if you do that," Sam told him bluntly. "They kill her before you get within twelve feet."

Aaron's heart stuttered in his breast as he heard those words, and he lowered his head, fearful of the anguish on his face being revealed to the other four men. "I know, Sam. What do you think we should do?"

A small grove of trees lay to their right, and it was in that direction that Sam turned his horse, the other men following quickly. He came to a halt within the shelter of the trees and looked at the house behind them. "I think we're pretty well out of sight. And our best bet is to wait for twilight."

"I don't see Hattie. She should have been right behind us," Aaron said thoughtfully. "She's disappeared."

"She'll show up, no doubt," Sam told him. "She may have already taken cover back up the road aways."

The men dismounted, tying their horses to handy tree limbs, then squatted in a circle as Sam drew a diagram in the dirt before him. "This is what we'll do."

HATTIE HAD INDEED taken cover, pulling her buggy from the road into a patch of brush as the five mounted men rode up the lane toward the abandoned house. They seemed certain that this was the place they'd sought, and she knew an urgency that prodded her into action. The men might be willing to wait for a better chance to attack and rescue Susannah, but Hattie had no great amount of patience.

She tied her horse and sought out a small bundle she'd brought along. A bit of bread and a piece of leftover beef were enough to stifle the hunger pangs that caused her stomach to growl, and she needed the time for thinking anyway. So she chewed and swallowed slowly, her ever-vigilant eyes roaming across the house and outbuildings.

A movement from the largest of the scattered structures caught her eye, and she watched as a man ran from the wide barn doors toward the house. Leaping onto the porch, he disappeared from sight, and she felt apprehension cover her.

Perhaps the five men had been spotted. And if so, they would be the object of scrutiny, even now. It might be that she had the only chance of approaching unseen, should she be able to travel on foot through the sparse wooded areas surrounding the house and approach by a more westerly direction.

What she would do when she attained her goal was up for grabs, but at least she'd be doing something, and anything was better than sitting on her hands back in Ottawa Falls, while the young woman who'd become such a good friend was in trouble.

Her reticule hanging from one wrist, her skirts held from the muddy ground with the other hand, she picked her way silently and cautiously through the wooded area that circled the house.

"DAMN, I WISH HATTIE WERE in sight." Aaron whispered the words, and Sam nodded his agreement. "I'd feel better if she were where we could see her. She's a feisty old lady, and I don't trust her not to get herself shot."

"Maybe she's coming through the woods now, trying to reach us," Sam said with a grin. "Isn't she the one who shot the bank robber and saved your life a few months ago? If so, I'd say I'm glad she's on our side."

"The very one. And, bless her heart, she's been a tower of strength for Susannah over the last couple of weeks. Almost like having a second mother."

THE AFTERNOON TRAIN from St. Louis arrived on time, and the conductor helped two middle-aged people from its steps, complete with a pile of luggage.

"You folks visiting someone in town?" he asked, noting the number of suitcases and boxes.

"Our daughter is married to the sheriff," Olivia

Whitfield said, as if it were a great honor to be related to a lawman. She was a tall and vivacious woman, still youthful-looking despite her white hair.

"We haven't met him, yet," her husband, Bert added. "They haven't made it to Philadelphia and we decided to take matters into our own hands and come for a visit." He adjusted his tie, a handsome man, well-groomed and seeming fit for his age.

"I'm afraid you came at a bad time," the station-master said, approaching the couple. "They're in the middle of a mess, and the sheriff took a few men to follow after his wife. Seems she got carted off by a fella from out of town."

Bert's eyes darkened and narrowed. "Would he be a government man?"

"Could be, I reckon. Anyway, I heard from the man at the hotel that the sheriff was mighty upset and took off like a bolt of lightning when he found out his wife was gone."

"Which way did they go?" Bert picked up two of the bags and waited impatiently for an answer. Then added a request. "How do I locate a buggy or wagon for hire?"

"You goin' after them?" The stationmaster lifted his eyebrows at Bert's words. "The livery stable is down the main street aways, and he hires out his vehicles. You don't want to be getting in the middle of a gunfight."

Olivia sniffed elegantly. "If our daughter is in peril, we'll do whatever it takes to help with her rescue. It's a known fact in Washington that she's being sought by men who aren't particular about their methods."

"Washington?" The stationmaster sounded properly impressed. "Well, I reckon I can help tote your bags down to Ellis Monroe's place and help you get a buggy."

"If you don't mind, we'll leave them here, under your care, until we return. No sense in dragging all our belongings across the country." Bert did not offer it as a request, but as a given, and the stationmaster nodded agreeably, lifting two other bags and carrying them into his office.

"I'll look after them for you, sure enough," he said. "And as soon as we get your belongings all settled, we'll walk down to see Ellis about a wagon or buggy for you."

TWILIGHT HAD FALLEN by the time the older couple headed out of town, a quick visit to the bank having been in order. Ellis told them the direction the sheriff had taken and they set forth.

"Bert, do you think she's all right? Who do you suppose has kidnapped her?" Olivia's words were low, her voice trembling as she spoke of her beloved daughter and the fate that might even now be hers.

"Now, Mother, don't get all upset until we know for certain what's happened," Bert said, his demeanor as cheerful as he could make it. "Our girl is smart and well able to handle herself. We just need to have faith that her husband is on top of matters, and will know what to do to effect her rescue."

"I hope he has men along with him," Olivia said fearfully. "I don't know that we'll do him much good."

"I have a gun and I know how to use it." His voice grew rough as if he recognized the peril his daughter was in. "We'll find her, and one way or another, we'll get her back, safe and sound."

The horse-drawn buggy traveled slowly, the driver careful of the unseen road. Darkness surrounded them and had it not been for the moon above, they'd have been without any light to guide them. And yet, Bert seemed impelled to continue on the road they followed, and after several miles of traveling with the rain falling around them quietly, he nudged his wife.

"Look. Up ahead. There where the lane turns off to the right. See that place under the trees?"

Olivia nodded, leaning closer to him, the better to see where he pointed. "It's a house and a barn out back. There's smoke coming from the chimney, Bert. I hope she's warm if she's inside there." Her voice faltered. "I'm so scared."

"YOU SUPPOSE THAT FELLA of yours has followed us?" Phil asked tauntingly.

Susannah glared at him, unwilling to give him the satisfaction of a reply, but he would not stand for it.

"He's gonna be a nice target if he tries sneaking up on the house. We've got two men out there keeping an eye on the road. Maybe he'll have enough sense to go on back home and leave you here."

"I wouldn't count on that if I were you." Susannah could not allow his taunt to go without reply, and then rued the words she spoke, knowing it would please the man if she gave him an argument.

"Well, are you ready to talk to us about the mess in Washington yet?" Phil slid the query in smoothly, catching her off guard. "I don't relish the thought of shooting you, Susannah, but unless you can find it in you to be honest about this whole thing, I'd say you're heading for an early grave. The men who set this thing up aren't about to let you free to talk."

"I don't know anything to tell you," she said quietly. "I've already given you chapter and verse of everything I know about the senator. I was smart enough to stay as far away as possible from his doings. He kept me in the dark, and I was glad to stay there."

"The men out in the kitchen don't believe you,"

Phil said slowly. "They think I might be able to get you to talk more readily than they can. And I'm hoping you'll tell me the truth."

"I already have," Susannah said, feeling hopeless in the face of such stubbornness on his part. "You know what my statement consisted of, Phil. It was all there." She pulled the rough blanket over her shoulders and curled up to conserve the warmth beneath it.

"They're not willing to wait much longer, Susannah," he said. "They'll try other methods of making you tell us what went wrong in the senator's plans, if you don't spill the beans on your own, and give us the names of the men John was working with. It's important to the men in the know that they find what went wrong with the deal they had set up. At this point, they don't even know who's on their side in the Senate or the House. They need names of men they can contact, men they can trust to do the job that John Carvel didn't take care of."

Susannah covered her eyes with one hand. "I won't be of any use to you, Phil. They can't force me to give information that's unknown to me. I know men who came and went from our house in Washington, but I was only in their presence as a hostess, a woman at the dinner table."

"A lovely woman, Susannah," he said with a look

that smacked of evil intent, Susannah decided. "A woman I wouldn't mind taking good care of myself."

She sat up straight and cast him a look of horror. "I'm not certain what you're saying, Phil, but I don't think I like the implications."

He walked to the sofa and sat down beside her, one arm reaching to pull her against himself. "You might like them better than you think. I'd be nicer to you than the sheriff. I probably know a whole lot more about what makes the world go around than he does."

She shook her head, unable to speak aloud as his head lowered and his lips touched hers, his mouth opening over hers. His arms held her in an embrace that felt like a vise, giving her no room to shift about, her lungs expanding like the bellows at the blacksmith's forge.

She gagged and pushed at him frantically. "Phil. Stop this. Please." Her words were raw and rasping against her throat, but he only laughed aloud.

"Why don't you begin searching your memory, Susannah? What were the names of the senators who came to visit at your house? Those men who had dinner at your table and visited with John in his office?" As he spoke, his hands roamed over her back, one sliding to rest against her ribs, bare inches from her breast. His fingers tightened their hold and he slid them upward, his aim obvious to Susannah. And allowing this lowlife to touch her so intimately brought about a wave of nausea. She retched and Phil lifted his mouth from hers. Again his hand moved and her breast was clasped in the hollow of his palm.

Aaron, please help me. I can't bear this. The plea rang in her head and she tore at Phil's hand. "Phil. Please don't do this." She knew she was begging, knew that her dignity was shattered, but the image of what Phil might do to her body made her shudder with an aching pain she could not contain. She stiffened against him, one hand rising to strike at his face, wriggling against his hold and fighting to escape his embrace.

"I like it when you challenge me, Susannah," he said, laughing softly at her struggles. "It's always more fun when a woman struggles and plays coy."

Susannah's hands found the center of his chest and she shoved him a bit off balance. The sound of her dress tearing was loud in her ears as his hold on it tightened. She drew in a deep breath, releasing it on a moan. "I'm not playing games with you," she murmured. "You're making me sick."

"Go ahead and scream, why don't you?" he taunted her. "My friends out in the kitchen will enjoy knowing that I'm succeeding in frightening you."

"You're not frightening me," she said, the words

coming out in a whisper, as though her voice had deserted her. "I'm not afraid of you, Phil. I just can't bear to have you touch me."

"I'll do more than that, my dear," he said, his voice smooth and cunning. "I'm planning on having a good time with you. I almost wish you'd give us a hard time and give me a chance to persuade you. You sure are a tidy little armful, Susannah." His eyes were sharp and cruel and his cheeks were flushed as Susannah played her trump card, hoping for a miracle.

"Phil." She spoke his name softly, carefully, as she stiffened again, holding herself as far from him as she could. "I'm going to have a child. Don't do anything to harm my baby. Please."

He glanced down at her quickly. "That won't work, Susannah. I don't think I believe you. Since when did you decide you were going to have a child? You didn't say anything before."

"I only just found out. I lost my first chance for a baby, Phil, when my husband, the honorable senator, beat me one night and put me in the hospital. If this baby doesn't make it, I don't think I will, either."

He sat up straight, tugging her by one hand until she lost her balance, so intent was she on holding her dress together over her breasts. His lip curled and his eyes narrowed, seeming to pierce her very being as he gazed down into her face. "Then make it easier on all of us, Susannah. Tell me what these men want to know. I wouldn't wish harm to you or your child, but I can only do so much."

Fear of what was to come struck her with the force of lightning. She allowed the tears to flow, shaking her head helplessly. "I can't tell you what I don't know." The blood seemed to rush from her head and she heard a buzzing radiate through her ears. The sound was terrifying and she felt dizziness overtake her, until she closed her eyes against the firelight that blurred her vision. That this man could make threats such as he had, that he would speak so boldly about her, was more than she could fathom. Surely Aaron would find her, certainly he would come through that back door and rescue her.

And at what cost? She winced and lifted her hands, hiding her face behind her palms. Should Aaron be shot, should he be killed by one of these men—it was more than she could take in, more than her mind could consider.

"Are you worried about him, Susannah?" Phil's voice sounded with mockery, and she shuddered, forsaking hiding behind her hands to clench the blanket closer, attempting to cover her breasts with the rough fabric.

Her eyes were burning, the tears held in abeyance

as she looked up at his mocking face. "What do you think? If there were anything I could tell you to make you believe me, I would. And if you hurt McBain, you'll never hide from me. I'll kill you myself, Phil."

He laughed mockingly. "A little thing like you?" With cruel hands, he shoved her back down to the sofa and settled beside her, one arm circling her shoulders.

From the doorway across the room, a faint whisper drew their attention, and when Susannah looked through the dim light to where the door opened a bit, she gasped with surprise.

Hattie stood in the shadows. Clenched in her right hand was the derringer she always carried in her reticule. "You're right in my sights, mister," she said in a low tone. "Get your hands off that girl and scoot away from her. One wrong move out of you and you're a dead man."

"Well, if it isn't Miss Hattie Cooper. The lady with the gun who saved the sheriff's life," Phil said with a grin. "Also the lady who taught the sheriff's wife how to play poker and won every last cent I had on me one night." The look he aimed in her direction was derisive. "Tell me, Hattie. Is it true that you shot that bank robber or did someone make up the tale?"

"You'd better believe it, mister. And I never miss my target."

"How did you get in?" Susannah was astounded

at the woman's presence in the house, frightened that she might become another victim in this whole mess.

"Climbed through a window in the bedroom," Hattie said quickly. "Went through the woods till I saw a likely window to use."

"There's three men with guns here, Miss Hattie," Phil told her. "How long do you think you'll last against the three of them?"

"No matter to you, sonny. You'll be dead right off the bat," she said. And then she came through the doorway into the parlor, skirting the fireplace until she reached a chair near the window.

From the kitchen a raised voice got their attention. "Phil. I hope you can hear me in there. We're running out of time. That woman needs some persuading, it sounds like to me. Thought you told us you could handle her."

With a long look at Hattie and the small gun she held, Phil answered carefully. "We're discussing it now."

"Well, she'd better decide to cooperate right quick," the man called back. "I'm about out of patience. Did you let her know she either talks or we get rid of her?"

"Yeah, I told her that." Phil lied without hesitation, wincing as Hattie's gun lifted, the small barrel aimed at him.

"Ten minutes is all she's got left," the voice from

the kitchen said ominously. "We've got to be making tracks out of here. The late train will be leaving the station at midnight and we need to be on it."

"Should we take her along with us?" Phil asked, his eyes narrowing as if he considered an alternate plan.

"I'm not toting a woman along," the harsh voice answered. "She can stay here and rot for all I care, so long as she gives us the names we need."

"That's your deal, Susannah," he told her mildly. "You talk, and you talk now, or it'll go bad for you."

Susannah slumped against the back of the sofa. "When you leave, I'm bound to be lying here dead, so tell me why I should keep saying the same thing over and over, Phil. Don't you think I'd cooperate if I could, if it would keep McBain from getting hurt?"

He stood and jerked her from the sofa. "Come on, Susannah. Let's go into the bedroom and have a little talk."

Hattie bristled, taking a step forward and holding her gun at the ready. "Not another word, young man. This little girl's not going anywhere with you. Just keep your hands to yourself."

Susannah shuddered as Phil's arm tightened around her back. "Hattie, don't you know that I'll never leave this place alive? Those men plan to kill me, and with you here..." She halted, her voice breaking. "We're not going to live to see another day, Hattie."

"That's up to you," Phil said smoothly. "You know I'd give a whole lot to turn you loose, Susannah. But you'll have to come up with what we need. I'm not planning on running with a price on my head, and neither are the others. The coal people need the votes of the men John was in contact with. They aren't playing games."

"TAKE A LOOK AT THAT, will you?" Sam pointed at the house, where dim light showed through windows at the front. "There's someone in that room, there just to the right of the window. And I'll be doggoned if that doesn't look like a woman with a gun in her hand."

Silhouetted against the window was the figure of a small woman, and something about her size and shape jogged Aaron's memory. "I'll be damned. That's Hattie Cooper," he said quietly. "How do you suppose she got in the house?"

"A better question is what does she think she's doing in there?" Sam asked fiercely. "She's gonna get herself killed."

"She's tougher than you think," Aaron said. "And if she's got her gun, someone is about half a heart-beat from being shot. That lady is a cool character.

"I'm going to go in that window. I'm sick of

waiting and worrying." He checked his own weapon again, then drew his hat lower on his head.

"I suspect you're right, Aaron. Chances are that's the room they've got Susannah in," Sam said. "I doubt we should wait any longer. We'll find a way around without being seen from the barn. They've got at least one man out there."

The five men bent low and ran across the field, keeping a watchful eye on the barn as they crossed the open area, heading for the long front porch that fronted the old farmhouse.

Through the window they caught sight of Susannah curled in one corner of the sofa, wrapped in a blanket, Phil by her side, with one arm clutching her close to him. Across the room, Hattie Cooper stood, her gun held firmly in a two-handed grip, her shoe-button eyes fixed on the man next to Susannah.

"Damn Phil, anyway," Sam said, his low voice holding an abundance of menace. "I'm gonna throttle that bastard once I get my hands on him. He had high clearance, according to the bureau in Washington. Just goes to show you how our government works, doesn't it? No wonder things are in a mess in Washington. We can't even spot a traitor in the midst of things."

"Well, if he harms my wife, I'll put him six feet under myself," McBain said, his own voice harsh, even as he subdued the volume. "She looks to be all right though, don't you think?"

"She's tough," Sam said, his words hopeful. "It'll take more than that idiot in there to beat her. You've got a woman who's one in a million, McBain."

"Don't I know it." His lips tightened as he watched the silent movements of the three people in the room before him. "Do we dare break the window?" he asked after a moment.

"So long as they don't hear from the other room, I'd think it would be the best way of getting in there," Sam told him. "Here, wrap my scarf around your hand, so you don't cut yourself." He took it from his neck and offered it to McBain, then watched as the lawman wrapped his fist in it and broke the window at the lowest edge of the top sash. It took only a moment to reach in the hole and lift the window, allowing the men room to climb inside.

At their appearance, Phil jumped up from the sofa and swore, an oath that drew a muttered sound from Hattie. Her gun held steady, she aimed it low and, from what McBain could tell, she was about to pull the trigger.

"About time you got here," Hattie said shortly. "I could use a little help."

With that, Phil dug a gun out of his pocket and took quick aim in Hattie's direction, a move she had obviously not expected, for her reflexes, slowed by age, were not up to the move and she froze. With a muttered oath, McBain lifted his own weapon and shot in a reflex action, the gun in Phil's hand hit by the bullet, rendering it worthless. Phil yowled in pain, his hand clutched against his chest, and sent a series of curses in McBain's direction.

"Looks like you settled his hash, sure enough, Sheriff." Hattie, none the worse for wear, tucked her trusty derringer into her reticule and sat down promptly on the chair behind her. "I suspect I'm getting too old for this sort of thing," she murmured beneath her breath.

"You all right, Hattie?' Aaron asked urgently, and was answered by a nod from the elderly woman who now looked her age and more. "You won't be needing that gun anymore today," Aaron continued quietly. "We'll take over from here."

Hattie nodded, obviously pale and shaken. "Be my guest, McBain. I'm ready to park myself right here for a while. This wild and woolly life ain't for me. I'm too old."

Aaron laughed softly, so fervent were her words. "Not so, Hattie. But for now, I'd say we were about even."

Hoping futilely that the noise they'd made was not readily audible in the next room, Aaron crossed to the sofa and bent over Susannah. "Are you all right, sweetheart?"

She looked up at him and attempted a smile. "I am now." It was meager assurance, but the best she could offer, and McBain seemed to be content with it for now.

Apparently alerted by the shot fired at Phil and the sound of men rattling around the parlor, the men in the kitchen took alarm. From the noise they made, as chairs were pushed across the floor and the stomping of feet against the floorboards, company was about to descend on those in the parlor. When the door burst open, the last of the makeshift posse was climbing through the window. With guns drawn and eyes alert to the men coming through the doorway, they took their stance and waited.

The deputy, Walt, lifted his weapon, shooting once, the bullet burying itself in the wall beside the door, a warning that halted the kidnappers in their tracks.

"Just leave your guns where they are, gentlemen," Sam said, his voice a threat in itself. "You're all under arrest."

The men looked at each other and then at Phil, who only shook his head in silent admission of defeat. Their weapons were quickly taken by one of the men from town.

"Got any rope around here?" one of them asked, and when no reply was forthcoming, Sam went into the kitchen and returned with a dirty coil of clothesline from the pantry. "This oughta do," he announced, cutting lengths of it with his pocket knife. Within moments, the captives were tied and pushed to the floor.

"There's still one more in the barn, if I'm not mistaken," Sam said. "I'll bet he'll be here in no time, trying to find out what's going on."

At that, the back door swung open, banging on the wall as a man rushed inside. "I heard a shot," he called out. "Did you fellas shoot that gal?"

"If one of them had, he wouldn't still be alive," McBain said, standing in front of Susannah.

"Come on in and join the party," Sam told the man from the barn, taking aim as the fellow came through the parlor door. Without a word, the last of the ruffians pulled his gun, offering it to Joe Hodges, the newspaper man from town who'd managed to collect all four pistols now.

"I didn't know how exciting it was to be a posse member, Sheriff," he said, grinning widely.

"Sometimes it's downright dangerous," Aaron told him. "We were lucky this time."

Susannah watched from the sofa as McBain turned to face her, bending low to touch her cheek, as though he feared she might disappear if he didn't keep hold of her. "When can we go home?" she asked in a low voice.

He bent to her. "In just a few minutes, sweetheart. As soon as we get these crooks into the wagon bed and settle them down for a trip to town."

A knock on the door interrupted them, and Hattie turned to open the latch, swinging the door wide. The two people who stood on the porch had eyes for no one but the woman on the sofa, and with a cry of relief, Olivia ran to her daughter.

"Susannah, are you all right? I was so frightened for you."

As if she could not believe her own eyes, Susannah shook her head, reaching for the woman who held her. "Oh, Mama, I'm so happy to see you. How did you get here?"

"Followed these men," her father said gruffly. "The stationmaster told us what was going on and we made it our business to tag along."

McBain rolled his eyes as Sam laughed quietly. "Now we're havin' a damn reunion," he said sharply. "Of all the ways to meet my in-laws, this isn't how I'd planned it."

"This is my husband, Mama. Aaron McBain." Susannah's voice was proud, her look loving as she spoke Aaron's name, and her mother shot him a look of disdain.

"Seems like you're not taking very good care of

my girl," she said sharply. "I didn't plan on having
to look for her out in the middle of nowhere, surrounded by gunmen and in fear of her life."

"Not what I'd planned, either," Aaron said
curtly. "I'm just thankful we got here in time to
keep her in one piece. I'd have hated to have to
shoot a whole roomful of these poor excuses for
men."

"Better them than your wife, Sheriff," Sam said
quietly. "I don't think they planned on her leaving
here alive."

Phil blustered at that and squared his shoulders. "Not true," he said. "I'd have made sure she
came out of this in one piece. I never intended for
her to get hurt."

Sam lifted an eyebrow and shot a dark look at
the man. "Now, why don't I believe you, Phil?
You're in this up to your neck."

Phil shook his head. "Believe it or not as you
please, I'd have gotten her out of here alive. I never
intended that Susannah get hurt."

CHAPTER SIXTEEN

"THOUGHT I WAS GONNA BREATHE my last in that old shack." Hattie grimaced as she stirred a kettle of soup in the McBain kitchen the next morning.

From a chair at the table, a seat she'd been told to maintain by the sheriff himself, Susannah tried to chuckle, turning it suddenly into a sad vestige of a laugh. She looked up at her friend and tears gathered in her eyes.

"Hattie, I thought the same. But the thing that made me so angry was that you were in that mess because of me."

Hattie shook her head forcefully. "No such thing, missy. It was the fault of those big shots from Washington and you well know it."

"The point is that I was the one they were after. I still don't understand why they didn't just shoot me to start with, without all the messing around, issuing threats in my direction. Phil had to know that I couldn't tell them any more than I'd already told him. At least I hoped that was the way of it.

The fact is that while I sat there, wondering if we would live or die, my mind was flooded with names and numbers I'd apparently forgotten I ever knew. I'll be able to be a bit more help now. Perhaps we should write down the things that I remember before they're gone again." She looked up at Hattie. "It made me feel so foolish, to think that I'd forgotten things, that my memory played me so badly. I signed that confession in front of Phil before he sent it off to Washington. Maybe he was right not to believe me in the long run. But I swear, I told the truth as I remembered it."

From the doorway, Aaron's voice joined the conversation. "Don't think so badly of yourself, sweetheart, the mind can play strange tricks on us sometimes. And as far as Phil is concerned, I suspect it was his doing that you weren't shot right off. From what Sam gathered, Phil was sure he might get some names out of you, names you hadn't divulged to us before, hoping to insure us that you were in the clear."

Susannah snorted, a sound of pure disbelief. "From what I heard, out at that ramshackle house, Sam was sure that Phil was in it. Up to his neck, was the way Sam put it, if I remember right."

Aaron nodded. "I tended to agree with you, and I was halfway to shooting the whole bunch of them. Sam held me back, told me they had to face the federal courts. Then he interviewed all of them separately before he made arrangements to have an escort sent from back east.

"The other three made disparaging remarks and accusations against Phil, and called him soft in the head. Said he hadn't held up his end of the bargain. Seems he was assigned the task of drawing you out, or even forcing you to come up with what they wanted to know, before they even arrived in town. The names of the men who were in cahoots with the mine owners would have made it easier for them to succeed. When your statement didn't give them any answers, they decided to take matters in their own hands.

"But at least this whole disaster has a bright side. It looks like the vote in Washington is going to support the coal miners, contrary to what Carvel had tried to bring about. They'll be allowed to organize, and as a result, the men who own the mines will have to pay them a decent wage. It seems that Senator Carvel's plans to support the mine owners failed."

Susannah didn't seem so willing to exonerate Phil without an argument. "Getting back to Phil, I don't understand how he could fool all three men right up to the end."

Aaron looked at her with a sad smile. "You haven't figured that out yet, have you? He had reasons of his own that the others didn't know about. The man was besotted with you, love. When he recognized that you were going to be sacrificed on the altar of greed, he couldn't handle it. He had hopes, apparently, of wooing you into his arms, then taking you out of here. He told Sam he'd have taken you out the bedroom window if things had worked out the way he wanted."

Susannah smiled grimly. "Well, it didn't work, McBain. I wasn't about to let him maul me any more than he had, and I wouldn't have been a very cooperative prisoner." Her words trembled and she looked down at the table, as if she could not face the man who watched her, as if she feared his reaction to her ordeal. "I think I'd rather have died than let him—"

"Well, you're right on one count," Hattie said quickly. "He wanted to take her into the bedroom, he did. He'd already been huggin' and kissin' on her, and I knew what he had in mind for the next little while. If I'd let him haul her into that bedroom—well, I didn't anyway. I put a stop to that. I think the idiot knew I'd pull the trigger on him rather than let him get Susannah alone anywhere near a bed. He did his doggone best to charm her, but he didn't know what he was up against. And if he thinks he can pull the wool over my eyes with his story, he's got another think coming."

Susannah shot her a warning glance, intercepted neatly by Aaron, who left the doorway and approached the table. He looked down at Susannah's hands, fingers twisting together in front of her, her head bowed.

"Susannah." His voice was harsh now and she dared only a quick look in his direction before she began to rise.

"I think I'll go lie down for a while. I'm still not feeling as well as I should."

Aaron took her arm and turned her to face him. "Why didn't you tell me what that scum had done? You didn't say a thing about his planning to—" Before the words could leave his throat, Susannah cut in.

"Would you have felt better about things if I had?" As Aaron's mouth opened to answer, she put her fingers against his lips.

"Hattie gave you the facts. That man had his mouth on me." She shuddered. "I know you saw him with his arm around my shoulders, but I'd rather have died than allow him more liberties than that. I don't want anyone else ever to touch me, Aaron. Only you."

"You should have told me." He looked helpless and his forehead furrowed thoughtfully before he spoke. "Maybe it was better that I didn't know how close you'd come to disaster. I might have started shooting, and poor Sam would have had to step in."

Susannah spoke her agreement. "You're a lawman, Aaron. It's not in you to shoot a man who isn't holding a gun. I know you better than that." She paused, as if thinking further on the subject.

"You know, on one point, Sam may be right. I don't think Phil wanted to shoot me, nor did he want the others to kill me. He was nasty and mean, but maybe the man we knew over the past weeks was hidden beneath that harsh exterior. He wasn't acting like a killer. At least I didn't think so. I don't know if he was serious about the bedroom thing, but I know Hattie would have shot him dead if he'd tried to haul me in there."

Hattie uttered a disbelieving sound that sounded near to a snarl. Her opinion was short and silent then, but the look of fury on her face gave her away, and she muttered beneath her breath, uttering her wish to send Phil to a place of eternal punishment, in no uncertain terms.

Aaron took three long steps to the stove and bent low, his lips touching the older woman's cheek. His voice was strained, as if he were choking, but his words were firm, as if he spoke a vow of recompense. "I owe you, Hattie."

Hattie took charge, red-cheeked and flustered at the kiss he'd offered and the words that had followed. "Well, the bottom line is that we're both alive, those useless pieces of trash are in the jail, waiting to meet whoever is gonna take them back to where they came from, and everything seems to be falling into place. I'll bet they'll be sorry for the day they tried this stunt. And we still got good reason to be satisfied with everything."

"How do you figure that?" Aaron smiled down at her, willing to let her call the shots for now.

"We still got us a baby to look forward to." She paused as if she would offer some words of wisdom, finally choosing to speak with care. "This house ain't gonna be big enough for all three of you, Sheriff. And I'll warrant that that baby ain't gonna be the only one this girl will ever bear. You'll be shoved in a corner of that bedroom all by yourself if those little ones don't have a place of their own once they're old enough to get out of a cradle."

Aaron grinned. "You think we oughta add on to this house?"

Susannah put in her two cents worth. "I think we ought to buy a bigger place. We've got enough money to get a bigger house and some land. You'll want your sons to have a dog, maybe even ponies. There isn't any room for them here. And I think I'd like the idea of a house with rooms upstairs and a big front porch. Maybe some honeysuckle growing on a trellis at one end."

"Got it all planned?" Aaron walked over to where she sat, hauling her up from the chair, then clasping his arms loosely around her waist. "I hate to disillusion you, sweetheart, but selling this place isn't going to give us enough profit to do all that right now. I've got an account at the bank, but it's not healthy enough for what you're talking about."

She reached up, her hands framed his face and she hesitated but a moment. Then spoke her heart, almost fearful of Aaron's reaction. "I have lots of money, Aaron. The house in Philadelphia was sold and my father took care of the details. He brought the profits with him and made sure they were deposited in the bank here. All you have to do is find a place for us, and we'll use some of it."

His jaw tightened and his eyes flashed fire. "I won't let my wife support me."

"I don't plan on it," she said. "I only want to loan you the money. I'll give you a lifetime to pay it back, with no interest."

"Sounds like a deal to me," Hattie chimed in.

"It's not a deal." Aaron's voice was vehement. "When we buy a place to raise our children, I'll be the one footing the bill. Your money will stay right where it is. You can spend it on froufrou if you like, or save it for those children you're talking about."

Her heart seemed to still in her breast for long seconds, as if it had sustained a felling wound, and her face grew pale. "They'll be your children, too." Her forehead touched his chest then, and she took a deep breath. His arms tightened around her and he bent his head to peer into her face.

"Don't go fainting on me, either. You look like a goose just walked over your grave," Aaron said, even as he eyed her with a sense of fear. "I wouldn't hurt you for the world, Susannah, but I'm a man, and I was raised in a house where the man took care of his family. I wouldn't have any pride left if I let you pay for our home. No matter if that money rots in the bank, it's there because John Carvel lived and died. It's a part of that past and I don't want it to taint our future."

"All right." Her chin rose a bit and her arms folded around her waist for a moment. But the hands that pressed against his chest a moment later were firm, and her eyes filled with tears that cascaded over her bodice. She allowed them full rein. Indeed she could not have stopped the flow had she wanted to.

"I'm not looking for you to give in, Aaron. I just can't help feeling like I've tried to give you a gift and you've tossed it back in my face. And so far as the money tainting our future, it'll only do that if we allow it to."

Hattie's lips pursed and she murmured soft words. "Think I'll go home now."

Aaron held up a hand. "Stay here, Hattie. You made the soup. You can just pull up a chair with us and have some. This fuss can wait till later."

"Well, I sure hope you can use your breathing space to smarten up, Sheriff," she mumbled as she gave him a cutting look.

Susannah halted her own escape, one she'd just moments ago contemplated putting into action. Already halfway to the door, she turned back toward the table. "I'll get out bowls and cut some bread for the both of you. But I'm not very hungry."

Hattie waved her stirring spoon in Susannah's direction, scattering drops of vegetable soup on the floor. "You'll eat, missy, or I'll know the reason why. That baby needs nourishment and he ain't gonna get it by you pouting in the bedroom."

"She's not pouting, Hattie." Defending her with calm words, Aaron took Susannah's hand. "Come on, sweetheart. Just have a little soup and then you can take a nap."

"You sound like I'm about three years old, and I'm a grown woman," she reminded him.

"All that's true, but you're in the family way and you've been through the mill over the past day or so."

Susannah planted herself firmly. "I only need to get off my feet for a bit."

"Then put them under that table." And so

saying, he pulled out the closest chair and reached for his wife. In moments she was settled again at the table, and Aaron was sorting out soup bowls from the kitchen cupboard. He found the loaf of bread Hattie had baked early on in the morning and fished in the drawer until he came up with the bread knife. Then, bread board in the other hand, he approached Susannah.

Placing all three items before her, he spoke carefully, as if he feared upsetting her more. "Will you slice the bread while I set the table? The butter is out and I'll get some jam from the pantry."

Hattie placed a folded towel in the center of the table and lifted the kettle to rest there. She held the ladle in her hand and eyed Susannah's confusion with a tender gaze. "How's about just one ladle full of this? Enough to give that child something to grow on."

Outnumbered, Susannah agreed with a shrug, holding her bowl just inches from the kettle. Hattie filled it half-full and then filled Aaron's bowl with a generous portion, before she nodded with satisfaction. The aroma of beef and vegetables rose from the soup, and Susannah discovered that the appetite she'd thought was but a memory became of utmost importance.

"This is wonderful." She sniffed again with appreciation and watched as Hattie dished up her own portion. With a quick movement, the bread knife was lifted from the table and Hattie sliced expertly, thick slabs of white bread falling to the board in a familiar rhythm.

"Thanks, Hattie." Whether he thanked the woman for the meal or for her influence over Susannah, Aaron seated himself, offering his gratitude. He glanced up at Hattie as she banged her spoon sharply on the table.

"I'd think we all have a lot to be thankful for, Sheriff. You might want to start with the food and go on from there when you ask the blessing."

"Haven't done that since I was a kid, at home on the farm," he said, one corner of his mouth twisting in a grin.

"Well, it's about time you remembered how," she told him, her eyes snapping.

He felt properly chastised. "Yes, ma'am. I suspect it'll come back to me, and I'm more aware than you know how much I have to be thankful for." So saying he bowed his head and in brief words told of his heartfelt joy that Susannah and Hattie were back home where they belonged. Though far from eloquent, the words nevertheless touched the women who shared the meal, and Hattie cleared her throat, while Susannah wiped at her eyes with the hankie from her pocket.

THE NEXT MORNING FOUND Bert and Olivia ensconced in the parlor, sharing the sofa while Susannah sat in the depths of Aaron's big chair listening to their talk of the journey and the money they'd brought to her. Both her parents were obviously tickled to death at the news of her marriage, Susannah thought, once Aaron had told them a grandchild was on the way. Even though Olivia's eyes held a mist of tears, Susannah knew they were but a sign of her pleasure at the news Aaron had just given them.

Bert cleared his throat, reaching to take Olivia's hand, as if he shared her joy and wanted to make the fact clear. "Why don't you think about coming east to have your little one?" he asked. "Your mother and I would be more than happy to find you a place nearby and set you up. Having you and your family that close would make our lives a whole lot happier."

"This is my home now, Father." The statement falling from Susannah's lips left no room for doubt as to where her primary loyalties lay.

Bert rose and approached her chair. "We'll welcome your husband. You know that. But your mother and I are too old to be running back and forth across the country in order to keep track of our daughter and her children."

"My wife will stay here with me." Aaron took a stand, as if unwilling to allow Susannah to be the recipient of her parents' plotting. No matter if they missed their daughter, he would not allow them to persuade Susannah into something she didn't want to do, no matter how much disappointment they might have to bear.

"Aaron's right." Her simple words were welcome to Aaron as she spoke her mind. "I love him, I married him and I'll stay with him, wherever he might be, as long as he wants me."

Aaron's eyes held more than a generous portion of his love and commitment as he turned them on her face. "Then you'd better plan on having me around for the rest of our lives. I'll never want you anywhere else, but by my side."

Olivia's misty tears overflowed with that, but the smile she offered Aaron was sincere. The words she spoke were aimed at the man beside her. "I think you'll have to be happy with a long train ride every year, Bert. And as far as being too old to travel across the country to see my daughter and her family, I'll never reach that exalted age. The day comes when I can't step up onto a train headed for Ottawa Falls will be a cold day indeed. I'm willing to head for home now that I've seen our girl settled and happy."

SUSANNAH WAVED WISTFULLY as the afternoon train for the east departed a week later. Her parents peered from a window and she knew tears were present in their eyes, but her own face was wreathed in a smile. A deep sense of gratitude and love combined surged within her, the man at her side the recipient of all her devotion.

"Aaron, I've made a decision," she said haltingly as they climbed into the buggy that would take them home.

"And what is that? You've changed your mind about living here?" Even though he knew the words were foolish, he spoke them, as if he needed to hear a rebuttal, one that would soothe his heart.

As he lifted the reins, she grasped his arm, halting its movement. "Don't you know better than that by now? I only meant that if you refuse to allow the use of my insurance money Daddy brought with him, and the results of my parents selling the Philadelphia house for me, I'll sign it over to them. I won't let it come between us. There is no way on God's green earth that I would make you think I don't depend on you. I lived with a man I couldn't trust, and he was clear at the other end of the scale from you. I've found that I can give you my trust and lean on your strength, and on top of that I'd do anything in the world for you. And if that includes giving up the idea of a house and property for now, so be it. We'll make do where we are until you think we can afford something else."

His mouth thinned and she watched as color

rose high on his cheeks. "I feel liked I've kicked a puppy," he told her. "You're not signing any money over to anyone, unless it's to someone who has a home you want for your own. I've been thinking about this, too, Susannah, and I've decided it takes more of a man to accept a gift of love, than to sit and stew in his stubbornness, while his wife makes all the sacrifices and soothes his pride.

"If you really want to use the money for a home, I'll not stop you, and I promise to move there without a murmur. You're my whole life, Susannah. For the first time, I'm ready to acknowledge that I can cope with anything that comes down the pike. I'll take care of you and keep you safe. You and our children will always be at the top of my list of priorities. And besides that, a dog or two, maybe a barn cat and some horses sound like a good idea."

"Can I have a cow to milk?" she asked. "And will you teach me how to milk her?"

Aaron laughed. "I can just see you squatted down on a milk stool, aiming at the cat once in a while with a stream of warm milk. I'll show you how to do it, sweetheart, but for the most part it'll be my job. You'll have enough to do churning butter, feeding chickens and gathering the eggs."

"What chickens?"

He snapped the reins over the mare's hindquarters and the buggy moved toward home. "The chickens we'll have to get right off, as soon as we find a place we both like. I'm partial to eggs for breakfast and fried chicken for Sunday dinner."

Susannah could not hide her smiles. "Well, I'll consider the chickens if you'll plow up ground for me to have a kitchen garden."

Aaron's eyes rolled upward. "Now she wants me to buy a plow."

Susannah hastened to reassure him. "It's all right. I can use a shovel, and if we have a rake to smooth things out, I'll be fine. We'll just have to get seeds first thing, early on in the spring. I just hoped we might find a place with tools already there."

"Sweetheart, I was just joking. I know I'll have to have a plow. Probably a scythe to keep the grass down and shovels and hoes. All that sort of stuff. Maybe we can even get a goat to keep the grass at a decent height."

She darted him an inquiring look. "You're kidding, aren't you? I've never heard of such a thing, and besides, I'm not real fond of goats."

"Well, now that I think about it, a goat or two might not be a bad idea. And I'll bet if we started out with young ones, you'd figure out how make pets out of them. They're cute little things, kinda mischievous, but all kidding aside, they're used a lot to keep a yard looking good."

"Hmm…we'll see," she answered. "But don't count on me liking them overmuch. That's too much to hope for."

His laugh was telltale, revealing the excitement he felt as the knowledge of a larger house and land to call their own became real to him. "I'll make a deal with you, sweet. If you like, we'll use your money for a good-sized amount. I think they call it a deposit or earnest money. Anyway, we can see the bank and get a mortgage. I'll bet we could pay it off in five or ten years." He looked at her searchingly. "Will that solve our problem?"

"Only if you'll agree to go to the bank for the payments if we get in a bind. I won't have you worrying over paying a mortgage when we have money sitting there doing nothing."

"It'll be gathering interest," he said, and then relented. "All right, love. We'll do it just the way you want. For once, I'll let you rule the roost. Just don't get any ideas about me turning into a meek, worn-out lawman. I fear I'll be putting my foot in my mouth more than once by the time we finish this."

"Aaron McBain, do you know that I love you?" Her eyes glowed, her love a shining entity as she vowed her pledge to him. "I know I've told you that before, rather a lot, as a matter of fact. But this time, it's for posterity. I'll always love you, Aaron."

He ducked his head for a moment, clearing his throat. "You don't know how proud that makes me, Susannah. I honestly never thought I'd find a woman I wanted to spend my entire life with. And no one will ever convince me that your coming to me that day in the hospital was any less than a gift meant for me, directly from heaven."

EPILOGUE

SUSANNAH'S TIME WAS NEAR, Hattie said; almost in the same breath she uttered a novel idea, one Susannah had never heard, but the words tickled Aaron. *I figure it's got to be soon. The girl is nesting.*

So his patience was endless as Susannah had him beating the carpets from the parlor and helping her stretch the lacy curtains for the parlor and bedrooms. The curtain stretcher was an odd sight to Aaron, but Hattie was more than familiar with it, and Susannah said she had put many a pin in many a curtain as a girl. Hattie joined him in that chore, neither of them wanting the expectant mother to be bending and reaching. Hattie said it wasn't good for the baby and told a dire tale that involved an umbilical cord tangled around a baby's neck. Privately, Susannah doubted that pinning curtains to a frame or cleaning out the topmost cupboards in the pantry would do her child any harm. But for Hattie and Aaron's sake, she was willing to forego any exertion they banned.

Hattie had taken over the small bedroom at the

top of the stairs once the first snow had fallen, stating in plain language that Susannah needed her and she'd be a star boarder until the wee one was born. Between them, the two women churned butter, gathered eggs, fed the huge shepherd that had adopted them, and vice versa, a dog that wasn't any good for herding animals, the next-door neighbor had said with disgust as he'd tied a rope to the dog's neck and sent him home with Aaron. Susannah had adored the creature on sight and had promptly named him Sport, in honor of a long-gone collie, a remnant from her childhood memories.

In spite of Aaron and Hattie's concerns, Susannah was peeling potatoes for dinner when she felt a nagging pain in her back. "Are you all right, girl?" Hattie frowned, watching her closely.

"Fine. Just a twinge."

"Well, you get any more of those twinges, you sing out, hear? That baby looks to me like he's wanting to make an entrance."

Susannah laughed and bent to her work. "I will. But tell me how you know it's time for the big day?"

"Your baby has dropped. It's lower in your belly. Haven't you noticed that it's easier to sit, less of an effort to take a deep breath lately? That child has moved down, getting ready for the big push."

Susannah felt the pressure of another twinge. It

was less than five minutes since the last, and she winced as it grew, gaining power by the second. "Promise me you'll be here, no matter what." Susannah thought her voice sounded like that of a little girl, much as she had when as a ten-year-old she'd asked her mother for a baby brother. Her wish had never come true, for Olivia could not bear another live child and after burying three babies, she stopped trying.

"Where else would I be? Heaven knows I've fretted my way through this pregnancy with you. And unless I miss my guess, those twinges you've been having are gonna turn into labor pains. Can't wait to get my hands on that baby." Hattie sounded as if she were staking a claim on the unborn child, and Susannah was pleased at the woman's concern. She would have risen from the ground and gone to her, wanting to hug her, needing to let her friend know that she was more than appreciated. She was loved.

But her body would not cooperate. She bent to hoist herself into a crouch and felt another twinge. More like a pain, she decided. And this one was just beneath her belly, the strength of it taking her breath.

"Another one?" Hattie lifted an eyebrow knowingly as Susannah nodded agreement.

"I suspect we better let this child's daddy know

that things are popping." She looked out toward the barn. "I'm thinking I'd better go take a look-see, maybe I can find him. I doubt if I can lift you to your feet, but—" Her words broke off as Aaron came through the barn door. "Hey there, Sheriff," Hattie called out.

As if he knew. As though his instincts told him that he needed to hurry, Aaron went to the watering trough and washed his hands quickly, then headed toward the house and Susannah, speaking to her as he came in.

"What is it, sweetheart? The baby? Are you in pain?" Then with a look cut in Hattie's direction, he spoke again. "Should I go for the doctor?"

"I reckon I would, if I was you. She's starting off with her *twinges* pretty close together. I doubt we've got more than a couple of hours or so."

"Did this just begin?" Aaron asked, his face flushed as he knelt before Susannah.

She blushed and shook her head. "I've been having a few aches all morning long. I think it started in the middle of the night, but I wasn't sure what it was."

"Why didn't you wake me? And why did you let me go trotting out to the barn after breakfast? I should have been here." His flushed cheeks had turned ashen by the time he finished his queries.

"Quit frettin', Sheriff," Hattie told him shortly.

"Just get yourself on your horse and head for town.
Tell that doctor to hurry."

"Right away." With a quick movement, he
leaned toward Susannah, dropping kisses across
her cheek, then paused when his mouth touched
her lips. He lingered but a moment, but Susannah
felt the beginning of another pain and spoke his
name, freeing herself from his embrace.

"Aaron, you'd better go."

He stood quickly, then reached down and picked
her up, his strength not seeming tested by her
weight. Her dress pulled up, exposing her knees,
and she found that it didn't matter. Getting to her
bed was the order of the hour, and she wasn't disappointed, for Aaron carried her through to the
hallway and up the stairs.

At the door of their room, he nudged the door
wide open, Susannah having left it ajar, and took
her to the bed. Hattie was fast behind and waved
her hands in Aaron's direction, hastening him on
his way. Then it was time to ready Susannah for the
big event. She watched uneasily as Aaron left, and
was comforted by Hattie's everyday manner, stripping Susannah and sliding a nightgown over her
head.

FOUR HOURS LATER, DOC HANSEN announced that
the baby would make an appearance soon.

Susannah sincerely hoped the man was right in his guesswork, for she felt as though each pain was about as much as she could bear without complaint.

Aaron sat beside her on the bed, rolling her to one side, rubbing her back and whispering his love and pride for her into her ear. She shifted again to her back and suppressed the groan that would hardly be denied.

"You can let us know how you're hurting. Go ahead and groan if you feel like it," the doctor said, his hands cool against her skin. "You may want to scream your head off before this is over," he predicted, "and that's all right, too."

But, much to her own relief, and obviously to Aaron's, she kept her breathing shallow when the doctor told her what to do and managed to concentrate on the power of her child's birth, enough so that only a groan escaped.

Even that was too much for Aaron and he turned to the doctor. "Can't you do something to help?"

"Just watch now," the medical man told him. And as he spoke, a tiny form appeared, bringing immediate relief to Susannah, and she tried to lift her shoulders and peer at the proceedings that were taking place.

With that, Doc Hansen lifted the squirming child by the feet and delivered a slap to the tiny bottom. A cry that would forever live in Susannah's memory filled the room, and she found tears flowing to her temples and then into her hair. "It's a great big boy," the man at the foot of the bed announced. "You can hold him in a minute, Mama."

Susannah's tears came faster as she heard the title she'd been called. "*Mama*. I'm a real mama now, Aaron. I just can't believe it."

"You'll believe it in the middle of the night a week from now when this young'un needs to be fed." The doctor handed the baby to Hattie, who held a large square of flannel, one of a dozen that she'd hemmed carefully by hand. With gentle hands, she deposited her treasure on the mattress, snatched up a diaper from the nearby cradle and placed it strategically where it would do the most good. Then the baby was swaddled in the flannel blanket and she lifted him and offered him to Susannah's waiting arms.

A sensation of euphoria swam up from her depths, and Susannah bent her head to kiss the dark hair that was still damp. "He smells so good," she whispered.

Hattie agreed. "They all do, missy. All babies have that same smell, at least for the first little while. Now give me that little mite and let me get him washed up."

Reluctantly, Susannah gave him over and lay

back down on her pillow. Beside her, Aaron had been silent, bending close to touch the infant's cheek, kissing Susannah's and, acting for all the world like a man who'd just discovered gold, he offered her a smile that told volumes of his happiness.

"Is he sleeping, yet?" Aaron lifted on his elbow and looked over Susannah's shoulder to where his son had just nuzzled his mother's breast.

"He's full, I think," she told him and without a word, Aaron left the comfort of his mattress to walk around the bed until he reached Susannah's side.

"I'll lay him down," he murmured, holding the precious bundle against his chest. In moments, he'd placed him in the cradle, sent from Denver weeks earlier, and then bent to bestow a whispered word and a kiss against his son's face.

He crawled back beneath the sheet, turning to Susannah and holding her against himself. "I love you, sweetheart." His voice held a tinge of tears, but his next statement was guaranteed to let Susannah know that his mood was that of a happy man.

"You'll never know how much I love you. I have something I never thought would be my privilege to have. A son is every man's dream, sweet, and you've made my dream come true." He kissed her as if he could not bear to be apart from the lips that lured him. And then he dropped one hand to her back, massaging tenderly, at the same time whispering of his plans for the future of his son, and the loving care he intended to bestow on his wife just as soon as her body had healed and her time of lying-in was through.

Susannah smiled as she listened to his words and reveled in his caresses, but her eyes kept closing, a weariness such as she'd never known taking hold of her body.

"I don't think I can stay awake," she complained. "What if the baby cries, and I fail to hear him?"

"No matter, sweet. I will," Aaron promised with a new father's confidence. "I'll take care of the both of you. And in the meantime, you just think about finding a name for our son. Have you thought of anything yet? Do you think we should call him after your father?" he asked.

"His middle name, maybe, but his first name will be like yours, I think. What do you think about Aaron Bert McBain?" She smiled as she spoke her choice aloud, and then yawned widely.

"Close your eyes, love. You've had a big day," he whispered and held her close as her body became limp, sleep overtaking her as she rested in his arms.

Aaron leaned on his elbow, looking again over her shoulder to where the baby slept, a tiny mound, tightly wrapped in a blanket, cradled in his own bed. In her sleep, Susannah's hand reached to rest against the wooden frame and the cradle rocked a bit, its motion soothing the sleeping child.

Aaron's vision blurred and he found himself murmuring words of thanksgiving, thinking of all the blessings that had come his way over the past months. Since the day he'd first seen the woman he loved hovering over him as might an angel of mercy. His lips curved in a smile that spoke of his love for her, of his delight in the life he'd been granted, the happiness that was his to hold.

It was almost too much for his soul to contain, he thought, thinking of the thrill he'd felt when first he'd set eyes on his newborn son...watching as his wife counted the tiny fingers and toes. And then that ecstatic feeling when his gaze had shared with hers the joy of those first moments after the birth of their beloved child.

With a deep sigh of satisfaction, he lowered his head to his pillow once more and drifted into sleep, smiling as an image of what the future might hold entered his dream. From the depths of his mind, as if he had conjured it forth, a dark-haired lad appeared, riding on a dappled pony, his grin as wide as the great outdoors, his blue eyes gleaming with pride.

REQUEST YOUR FREE BOOKS!

2 FREE NOVELS FROM THE ROMANCE/SUSPENSE COLLECTION PLUS 2 FREE GIFTS!

YES! Please send me 2 FREE novels from the Romance/Suspense Collection and my 2 FREE gifts. After receiving them, if I don't wish to receive any more books, I can return the shipping statement marked "cancel." If I don't cancel, I will receive 4 brand-new novels every month and be billed just $5.49 per book in the U.S., or $5.99 per book in Canada, plus 25¢ shipping and handling per book plus applicable taxes, if any*. That's a savings of at least 20% off the cover price! I understand that accepting the 2 free books and gifts places me under no obligation to buy anything. I can always return a shipment and cancel at any time. Even if I never buy another book from the Reader Service, the two free books and gifts are mine to keep forever.

185 MDN EF5Y   385 MDN EF6C

Name _____ (PLEASE PRINT) _____

Address _____ Apt. # _____

City _____ State/Prov. _____ Zip/Postal Code _____

Signature (if under 18, a parent or guardian must sign) _____

Mail to **The Reader Service:**
IN U.S.A.: P.O. Box 1867, Buffalo, NY 14240-1867
IN CANADA: P.O. Box 609, Fort Erie, Ontario L2A 5X3

Not valid to current subscribers to the Romance Collection,
the Suspense Collection or the Romance/Suspense Collection.

Want to try two free books from another line?
Call 1-800-873-8635 or visit www.morefreebooks.com.

* Terms and prices subject to change without notice. NY residents add applicable sales tax. Canadian residents will be charged applicable provincial taxes and GST. This offer is limited to one order per household. All orders subject to approval. Credit or debit balances in a customer's account(s) may be offset by any other outstanding balance owed by or to the customer. Please allow 4 to 6 weeks for delivery.

Your Privacy: Harlequin is committed to protecting your privacy. Our Privacy Policy is available online at www.eHarlequin.com or upon request from the Reader Service. From time to time we make our lists of customers available to reputable firms who may have a product or service of interest to you. If you would prefer we not share your name and address, please check here. ☐

BOB07

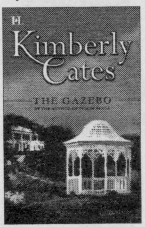

CAROLYN DAVIDSON

77149   REDEMPTION   ___ $5.99 U.S. ___ $6.99 CAN.

(limited quantities available)

TOTAL AMOUNT	$ _____
POSTAGE & HANDLING	$ _____
($1.00 FOR 1 BOOK, 50¢ for each additional)	
APPLICABLE TAXES*	$ _____
TOTAL PAYABLE	$ _____

(check or money order—please do not send cash)

To order, complete this form and send it, along with a check or money order for the total above, payable to HQN Books, to: **In the U.S.:** 3010 Walden Avenue, P.O. Box 9077, Buffalo, NY 14269-9077; **In Canada:** P.O. Box 636, Fort Erie, Ontario, L2A 5X3.

Name: _____
Address: _____ City: _____
State/Prov.: _____ Zip/Postal Code: _____
Account Number (if applicable): _____

075 CSAS

*New York residents remit applicable sales taxes.
*Canadian residents remit applicable GST and provincial taxes.

HQN™

We *are* romance™

www.HQNBooks.com

PHCD0107BL